THE CORNISH CRIME SERIES

THE POISON PROMISE

JULIE EVANS

vıncı
BOOKS

By Julie Evans

The Cornish Crime Series

Rage
A Sisterhood Of Silence
The Bitter Fruit Beneath
The Poison Promise
A Baptism Of Fire

Vinci Books

vinci-books.com

Published by Vinci Books Ltd in 2025

1

Copyright © Julie Evans 2022

The author has asserted their moral right to be identified as the author of this work in accordance with the Copyright, Designs and Patents Act 1988. This work is a work of fiction. Names, characters, places and incidents are the product of the author's imagination or are used fictitiously. Any resemblance to actual persons, living or dead, places and incidents is entirely coincidental.

All rights reserved. No part of this publication may be copied, reproduced, distributed, stored in any retrieval system, or transmitted in any form or by any means, including photocopying, recording, or other electronic or mechanical methods, nor used as a source for any form of machine learning including AI datasets, without the prior written permission of the publisher.

The publisher and the author have made every effort to obtain permissions for any third party material used in this book and to comply with copyright law. Any queries in this respect should be brought to the attention of the publisher and any omissions will be corrected in future editions.

A CIP catalogue record for this book is available from the British Library.

Paperback ISBN: 9781036702083

Printed and bound in Great Britain by Clays Ltd, Elcograf S.p.A.

For Martyn, for all your patience and encouragement.

Part I

Chapter One

PHILIPPA FLOYD, KNOWN AS 'PINKIE' to her friends, joined the St. Piran Country Club and Spa for one reason only; His Honour Judge Fenton Carlisle was a member, and she planned to kill him.

She'd made a study of the judge's routine. She'd sat outside his house, beyond the electric gates and the CCTV cameras, watching and waiting. After a couple of months, she'd decided he was possibly the dullest man on the planet. He had no vices or at least was damn good at hiding them if he did, and she wondered how someone with so little life experience felt qualified to judge others.

His lack of social life meant opportunities were limited. He attended the Combined Courts of Justice in Truro when sitting, and swam at the spa pool every day. She decided to concentrate on this element of his thoroughly uninteresting life as her access route. The spa would have to be the locus for the murder as security around the court and his house made any attempt to carry out the killing at either problematic.

Carlisle arrived at the pool as soon as it opened at seven-thirty in the morning and swam exactly fifty lengths, no more, no less. He never used the jacuzzi or the sauna or took advantage of any of the vast array of treatments available, not even a massage to ease those shoulders, tight and knotted from shrugging off other people's problems.

It was important she was inventive. She was, technically, retired, but after a lifetime in this business, she wasn't going to let the side down now. Sloppiness couldn't be tolerated.

She supposed in common parlance she would be labelled a serial killer. After all, she'd terminated many more than the three required to earn the label. But unlike many of that select club, she didn't have a *modus operandi* to pin her to her crimes, some twisted quirk or calling card. She needed to maintain a degree of originality. She didn't intend to get caught. Professional assassins like her rarely did.

Her victims were not a 'type', and nothing linked them other than they were all people who ruined others' lives without batting an eyelid. Every one of them, though totally undeserving of anything, deserved one thing: her full attention when she killed them. The judge was no exception.

She wasn't foolish enough to think she could overpower Carlisle. Once maybe it would have been an option, but she was fifty-four, and despite the rigorous fitness regime she imposed upon herself out of habit as much as anything else, arthritic spectres haunted her these days; the broken bones from her glory days in Special Ops and the years after, when she'd become self-employed and been in charge of her own rehab and skimped on the physio. Whilst the judge's pale, freckly body held no inherent athleticism, and she guessed if he stopped his regime for a day, it would revert to flabby softness, he was nevertheless sufficiently fit to fend off a physical attack from her. Also, it wasn't her style to be hands-on; to bludgeon, strangle or stab. The robbery gone wrong was an easy option but always messy. She'd worked with some who chose it. They were generally lazy types who got a kick out of gratuitous violence. She'd always liked to keep her distance from her targets; her weapons of choice back in the day, the Remington 700 with a Leopold Mark 4 Scope, or as in this case, poison. What's more, she had something very special in mind, befitting her victim's status.

Pinkie poured herself a gin and tonic with a dash of Rose's lime cordial and sat down in her favourite chair on the patio to review her file on Carlisle. The evening was warm, but the flinty Cornish sky looked as if it might be brewing for a fight. She'd become a weather watcher since moving to the county. It was difficult not to be; weather happened here. The rugged peninsula was its first stop on its journey as it rolled in from the Atlantic. It was here the brilliance flared, and pyrotechnics crackled before the beast turned tail or lumbered its way across the rest of the country. Though only eleven miles from coast to coast, one end of the county could be battered by torrential rain whilst the other sunned itself. She'd come to love the place. She accepted she could live here for the rest of her life and never be regarded as a local, but she'd made a few close Cornish friends, so she must be doing something right.

She had never really settled anywhere before. The job didn't allow for it. She'd always had a base, a bolt hole, but this cottage was the first proper home she'd had since she'd left her parents to join the Navy at eighteen. She hadn't missed having roots. She'd taken to naval life like the proverbial duck to water. The moment she finished her officer training at Dartmouth, she'd known it was exactly where she needed to be. She had no idea of the career that lay ahead of her back then or what she'd be required to do in the course of following orders, but she could hand on heart say if she had to do it all again, she would.

The only unfortunate remnant she had cause to resent was the constant state of high alert her job had ingrained in her. For many years she had lived with relentless anticipation, which meant she could rarely relax. She was always looking over her shoulder or waiting for the next mission, but since moving here, things had changed. The cottage had a well-established, though a rather unruly garden when she bought it. She knew nothing about horticulture when she moved in but had been reluctant to employ a gardener. She enjoyed her privacy too much for that. So, out of necessity, she had started working on it herself. She would go out after breakfast to potter about, and before she knew it, several hours had passed and it was lunchtime, and all she had thought about was whether the azaleas needed an extra dose of fertiliser or she ought to move the orange daylily to where it got more sun. Within a few months, what had started as a chore became an obsession. She spent her days outside and her evenings with her nose in gardening books, learning about soil acidity and how to prune clematis depending on the type. She began visiting great Cornish gardens like Trebah with its purple-hazed hydrangea valley sloping down to the sea, and Heligan reclaimed and replanted by gardening ninjas on a mission to restore it to its past glory. Slowly she'd begun to appreciate the vision of those who had passed this way before her; the plant hunters and explorers who had carted their cuttings home from far-flung places and planted their giant rhododendrons and palm trees, knowing that in their lifetime, they would never see the realisation of their vision.

She had been suddenly overcome with a need to leave something behind. Her life had been all about taking away, erasing. Nurturing a plant so it thrived, took root and grew to outlive her and those that came after her seemed almost heroic. In this way, gardening had become her passion. The more she read, the more fascinated she became. She started visiting gardens across the country, Tudor medicinal gardens, and then old monastery gardens further afield in France and Italy, full of cures, and poisons, of course.

Now Pinkie's garden was crammed with exotics; giant gunneras, like elephants' ears, tall whispering bamboos, orange cannas and amber ginger lilies, the plants she'd grown from seeds and cuttings brought back to the UK from her various trips. By day it was a tropical oasis. On summer evenings, when the starry jasmine cast its heady perfume, Pinkie would wander the pathways, running her fingers along the leaves and lifting the blooms, drinking in the scent, feeling like a child in fairyland. To her delight, many specimens were hardy enough to grow outside in the temperate Cornish climate. Others, which she considered rare or delicate, she grew in the greenhouse. Those known to be dangerous were kept under lock and key, and the prize amongst them was the one she intended to use on the judge - the rosary pea.

A couple of years before, Pinkie had brought back two seeds she'd found whilst on holiday in South America. She'd wrapped them in a pair of knickers and hidden them in the bottom of her luggage. They'd been growing wild, and she'd picked them because of their vivid colour. They were the size of a baby's fingernail, bright red with a black tip at one end. She'd scoured her gardening books for some clue of the plant's identity to give her the best possible chance of success in growing it but couldn't find a thing. In the end, she'd given up trying and planted the little beans as she would any seed in compost, repotting them as and when they outgrew their space until the plants eventually produced bright red beans of their own.

She hadn't thought much more about them until she'd visited the Eden Project and, in passing, had described the beans to a gardener working in one of the domes. To her utter surprise, without hesitation, he'd been able to tell her the plant was *Abrus precatorious*, otherwise known as the 'jequirity' or 'rosary pea'.

'Best ditch it,' he said.

'Why?' she'd asked. 'Is it invasive?'

'You could say that,' he smiled. 'The seeds you're talking about are more toxic than Ricin. You've heard of Ricin, haven't you?'

Of course she had. Although she'd never used it herself, she'd been briefed extensively on its deadly potential as a plant-based toxin derived from a species of euphorbias, the castor oil plant. It always struck her as remarkable nature provided everything required to kill or cure if you had a mind to find it and knew how to get the best out of it.

'Between you and me,' the gardener continued, 'we had a bit of trouble here a few years ago with the same seeds, but that's another story. Burn it, that's my advice, and in the meantime, don't let anyone near it.'

As soon as she got home, she searched the internet for information. Remembering what the gardener had said, she typed in, *Jequirity Eden Project*.

There it was, a headline dated 23rd of December 2011. Thousands of deadly seed bracelets recalled from sale in Eden Project's gift shop as it is revealed they are made from beans twice as toxic as RICIN.'

There had been thirty-six retailers in total who'd sold

the red and black bracelets resembling ladybirds strung together. Eden alone had sold over a thousand. The seeds contained the toxin Abrin, a controlled substance under the Prevention of Terrorism Act. The toxin inhibited protein synthesis producing severe cytotoxic effects on the body similar to those experienced when subjected to viper venom or botulism. The bracelets had come from Peru, but the plant was widespread, found in several continents, including India and West Africa, where it was made into jewellery, especially prayer beads, to ward off evil spirits, hence the term 'rosary pea'. People had been killed pricking their fingers whilst piercing the seeds to thread them as beads.

The plant had migrated to America, in particular Florida, where three children had died after swallowing the beans. This was unusual because the seed's hard shell afforded protection. However, if the inner substance was injected subcutaneously or inhaled in the dried powdered form, the results were lethal. After a latent period with no discernible symptoms, nausea, vomiting and diarrhoea befell the unfortunate victim, followed by delirium, seizures, coma and death. Three micrograms could kill a man, and there was no antidote. She could see why the gardener suggested she burn them. But despite this, she hadn't had the heart to destroy the plant, having invested so much time and effort into growing it. She was glad now she hadn't.

Distracted by an iridescent damselfly flitting between the flag irises, she paused for a second before opening her file on Carlisle. It would be her last chance to read through the dossier before destroying it. As always, she'd researched her candidate thoroughly. She had no intention of killing anyone who didn't deserve it.

When she'd worked for the powers-that-be, she followed orders. It wasn't her job to scrutinise the intel. She was part of something bigger and conditioned to trust her superiors. Once she'd gone freelance, she'd set her own criteria and could hand on heart say she had never taken a case where she felt the target was untarnished, no matter the financial incentive. Known terrorists seeking asylum, drug dealers sending kids across county lines, gang members who stole people's lives and passed young women around like bits of meat, they were all worthy candidates. Whilst the money was always welcome, it was never her primary motivation. She'd made a very good living over the years, which now, along with her MOD pension, gave her the freedom to be fussier still and do the job for free. It was her way of giving something back.

Up until a few months ago, she'd never heard of the judge, but that all changed in the space of three conversations, and now, looking at the evidence, he was more than a deserving candidate. That wasn't to say she didn't have misgivings about the mission. She was connected to one of his victims, something she'd always avoided. She could end up on the radar in an investigation. In the past, she probably wouldn't have risked it, but age gave you something you didn't have when young - nothing much to lose.

Chapter Two

Three months earlier

LIZ HOSKING WAS a member of Pinkie's gardening club. Pinkie had warmed to her as soon as they'd met but sensed a wistfulness under her veil of good humour she knew from experience was rooted in loss. Liz was a widow, and so she assumed this was the cause until the day she learnt the real reason.

She and Liz had met for a walk and lunch at Trelissick, one of the many wonderful National Trust gardens just outside Truro. Three of them from the club had started meeting on the first Wednesday of the month. This particular day, one of the trio, Sandra, had cried off. Her daughter was visiting from Gibraltar, where she lived with her husband and two children. Pinkie had never heard Liz talk about children, whereas most of the other women in the club rattled on about their kids and grandkids all the time. She hadn't pried. If the woman wanted to discuss her private life, she would. She wasn't a hypocrite. It wasn't as if she was a sharer. Whole episodes of her past remained and would always remain a secret. As far as her Cornish friends and neighbours were concerned, she was a retired freelance journalist who'd spent much of her pre-retirement abroad, latterly as part of an outreach programme delivering literacy to underprivileged women.

'It's a shame Sandra couldn't come today,' she'd commented to Liz as she tried to decide whether to push the boat out and have a starter. 'But I suppose it must be a treat for her to have her grandchildren stay.'

'Yes, I'd give anything to see mine again.'

'You don't see them?'

'No,' Liz replied, dropping the menu to reach into her bag and pull out a photograph of a pretty, blonde young woman, a little boy about four, clinging to her leg.

'Where are they now?'

'Gone.'

It was clear from her expression she didn't mean they lived away like Sandra's family.

'I'm so sorry. I didn't know,' said Pinkie, truly shocked as she reached across the table to hand the photo back.

'Richard and I didn't talk about Rachel and our Sam. We found it too painful.'

'You really don't have to tell me anything,' said Pinkie watching her friend's face crumple.

'I want to. Somehow, it's easier to speak about it now Richard's dead. He always felt responsible, you see, for what happened. He wasn't, of course, but talking about it brought the whole thing back. Our son-in-law as good as killed our daughter Rachel. Then he took our grandson.'

Pinkie was stunned. The revelation had stripped the conversation to the bone. She felt the breath she was holding escape like a slow puncture as she beckoned the waitress over and ordered a jug of tap water and two glasses.

'I didn't mean to pry. I'm so sorry.'

'No, it's fine. It's a relief to share it with someone, as long as you don't mind?'

'Of course not, as long as it helps?'

'We never warmed to Gary, our Rachel's husband. He's the son of a local councillor, Lionel Joyce. My Richard worked for the council in environmental health. He always said Joyce only became a councillor to get himself on the planning committee to influence planning decisions in favour of his developer friends, and a dodgy bunch they were too. We begged Rachel to continue with her education, and if she still felt the same way about him after university, we'd accept her choice. Gary took that as a challenge and did everything he could to convince her otherwise, including getting her pregnant at eighteen. They'd been married for three years when I first visited the solicitor's office with her.

The waitress returned with the water.

'Are you ready to order?'

Liz didn't answer, so Pinkie took it upon herself to order their favourite - tapas to share with a side order of skinny fries -as she poured Liz a glass of water and waited for her to take a sip before continuing.

'Things unravelled after I contacted our solicitor, Claire McBride, and she recommended a lawyer in her office, Marcus Annear. He dealt with domestic abuse cases, and things had got desperate. I was beside myself by then. I wouldn't have done it otherwise. I hadn't told Richard the half of it, worried he'd get worked up and make matters worse so Gary wouldn't let Rachel or Sam see us anymore. Rachel was worried too. She'd say things were getting better or make excuses, so getting her to talk to Marcus was like pulling teeth at first, but he was kind and patient, and gradually, she opened up, finally admitting Gary had been beating her for years; something I'd always suspected but she'd never admitted openly to me. I'd seen bruises and watched her wince when Sam sat on her lap or cuddled in, and once, as she pulled her top over her head, I was sure I saw a cigarette burn underneath her hair. I kept a diary, and that day, I handed the record of my daughter's misery to Marcus.

Pinkie had questions but knew better than to interrupt someone ripping open their scars. Instead, she reached across and squeezed Liz's hand. A show of solidarity in the face of tyranny was always welcome.

'Marcus asked whether Rachel had confided in anyone about Gary's violence, someone independent who could corroborate her story. She admitted she had but only once because the girl had gone straight back and told her boyfriend, who played five-a-side with Gary. Gary reacted by dragging her around to the couple's house and forcing her to say she'd made it all up as a way of getting back at him for staying out too late with the boys after a match the week before. When they'd got home, he hit her.'

'Did the solicitor report it to the police?'

'No, he explained as the incident wasn't recent, the police wouldn't give it priority, especially as it was a domestic. To be honest, I sensed he knew Rachel wouldn't let him, not then. She'd have worried about Gary finding out before the police had a chance to do anything about it. I think Marcus sensed it. He reassured her; said we needed to take control of this ourselves. He took a statement from Rachel, but I could see her getting more and more agitated as she filled in his forms, and when it came to the bit where she had to sign, she went to pieces. She ran out, leaving me there with Sam. I had to apologise and run after her. She wouldn't go back, and it was another six weeks before I saw her again.'

Pinkie listened to Liz unburden, knowing, given how this conversation had started, there would be no happy ending. She had never been a mother but could imagine how heartbreaking it would be to witness your child's systematic destruction. Liz must have despaired. Had it been her, she would have seen to it Gary Joyce never raised his hand to his wife or anyone else for that matter ever again, but Liz wasn't her. She realised North on her moral compass pointed in a different direction entirely than for most civilians.

Their food arrived, and they changed the subject as they ate their *patatas bravas*. The restaurant was filling up, mostly with ladies of a certain age, hardly a man in sight. It wasn't surprising. Statistically, women outlive men. Chances were, if your husband hadn't traded you in for a younger model by the time you were sixty, you'd be knocking on the door of widowhood one day. Pinkie was glad she'd be spared the indignity of reinventing herself as a singleton. Solitude came naturally to her. It was one of the things that made her such a successful operative; no emotional distractions. These days she wasn't so anti-social; she looked forward to her clubs and monthly lunches, but she still didn't like the idea of being tied.

Once they'd finished their rhubarb and ginger crumble topped off with a hefty dollop of clotted cream, they moved outside into the courtyard for coffee.

Liz began to talk without prompting as if she'd been desperate to finish the story she'd started in the restaurant.

'As I said, I didn't see Rachel for weeks, and then I got a

call. She was in a terrible state. She was pregnant and didn't want the baby. Gary, searching in her bag for the car keys, had found a piece of paper confirming an appointment at a clinic for a termination. He told her if she even thought about it, he'd kill her. He hadn't let her leave the house since, but she'd managed to call me when he'd gone to play five-a-side on the Sunday morning. I went round straight away. She was black and blue and scared to death. This last beating had been in front of our grandson. I think, looking back, that's why she decided enough was enough. I helped her pack, then telephoned Marcus on the out-of-office mobile number he'd given us. He tried to persuade Rachel to go to A&E, but she said Gary would find her there, so instead, I patched her up as best I could and took photographs of her injuries on my phone and sent them through to him. I knew she couldn't come back to ours, so we decided to get her and Sam away. I had a friend in Plymouth willing to put us up, and I drove us there, leaving Marcus to make an emergency application the next day for an injunction against Gary. I rang Richard to warn him Gary might turn up, which he did, with the police in tow, alleging Rachel had been acting strangely for months, and he had friends who could give evidence of her lies. He'd said his son was in danger, but Richard had the sense to keep mum. He didn't let on where we were or Marcus's plans.'

'Good for him,' said Pinkie, full of admiration for the man.

Liz's smile was bittersweet, and Pinkie guessed Richard's efforts had not saved the day.

'The next morning, Marcus called to tell us to stay put until Rachel and Sam had the court's protection. The application was due to be heard that morning. He didn't expect anyone to turn up for Gary because he hadn't served him with the papers. He said those types of hearings were made when, because of the immediate risk, there was no time to serve the respondent or to do so would compromise the safety of the applicant. We were delighted and expected the hearing to go to plan, especially with the photos and everything.'

Pinkie interrupted for the first time. 'But it didn't?'

'No, far from it. Marcus arrived expecting a quick turn-around, but Gary was there with his father and the senior partner of another local firm. Someone had tipped them off.'

'Who?'

'God knows. Gary's dad knows everyone. Maybe the judge himself. There was some talk afterwards of Judge Carlisle being a close friend of Councillor Joyce.'

'So, what happened?'

'I only found out the details later, after Rachel requested the transcript, but the upshot was Gary argued Rachel suffered from mental health problems. He said she'd thrown herself downstairs in an attempt to kill her unborn child. He produced the slip of paper from the clinic he'd found in her bag. He denied the allegations of abuse and said he feared for Sam's safety too. He said there were signs Rachel was seeing someone else, and the child she was carrying belonged to the unknown man; that she was probably with now. He said she'd threatened to leave before and had begun sleeping in his son's bedroom. That's why, according to him, he hadn't seen her naked body for months and had no knowledge of the terrible marks. His solicitor argued if they existed, they were the result of her tumble or had been inflicted by her lover, although he said they might even be fake, given she hadn't gone to the hospital and wasn't here in person to offer up proof.'

'But surely no one believed that rubbish?' said Pinkie incredulous.

'You'd think not, but you can tell from the transcript that slowly but surely the judge was choosing to believe the lies, or as Richard thought, biased from the start.'

'So, he didn't grant the injunction?'

'No, instead, he insisted the police put out an alert for Sam and ordered the local authority to take him away from Rachel and apply for a place of safety order, putting him into temporary care until the matter could be fully determined.'

'Oh God, Liz, it must have been awful for you?'

'Gary and his dad were cock-a-hoop, of course. They thought Gary would get Sam.'

'What about Rachel?'

'She lost the baby for a start. It was the stress, I think, but looking back, it was a blessing. Sam was put into temporary foster care, but at least he was safe, and it took the pressure off Rachel knowing that, and when CAFCASS delivered their report, it was clear they believed Rachel's allegations of violence even if the judge hadn't.'

'CAFCASS?'

'Children and Family Court Advisory and Support Service. Sorry. When you're in the system, you forget most people out there never cross paths with caseworkers and child welfare officers.'

'Oh, I see,' Pinkie said, thinking she could throw a few acronyms Liz's way she'd never be able to translate for her. Leastways not without breaking the OSA.

'We naively believed everything might turn out alright after all. Rachel managed to get herself a place in a refuge and, beyond Gary's influence, became more like our old Rachel. She put on weight, and it was looking more and more like she'd get custody. We got builders in to price up an extension to our house, so she and Sam could move in with us. We were determined to get our grandson back and start over. The trouble was, as time passed, it began to dawn on Gary that Rachel would probably get custody, and he's a vicious little sod, especially when he's on the back foot. He'd shown his true colours a couple of times at the foster parents' house, turning up unexpectedly the worse for wear and kicking off, and they'd reported it. Unfortunately, they couldn't stop him from seeing Sam. Whilst Rachel's contact was restricted, Gary had unsupervised access. Carlisle had seen to that by raising concerns about Rachel's stability, you see.

'One afternoon, Gary made off with Sam saying he was taking him to visit his parents and never came back. His dad got him out of the country, and we've not seen hide nor hair of him or Sam since. We had an idea where he was, of course. We heard rumours about him living in Portugal. Lionel Joyce has property there, but we've not been able to get anywhere close to tracing him because the properties are in offshore company names. Every time we got close, we hit another brick wall. The Portuguese authorities actually wrote to us threatening action if we attempted to harass any of its citizens. Gary never cared about Sam; all he cared about was losing control.'

Tears began to well in Liz's eyes as she reached into her sleeve for a hankie to blow her nose.

'That Christmas Eve, our Rachel took a handful of antidepressants and ended it all. And do you know what? I don't blame her. I guess our lovely girl had been beaten by Gary so many times, and in so many ways, she just couldn't believe she could ever win. To be honest, to this day I can't fathom why Richard and I didn't do the same when we found her, other than we held the pathetic hope we might get to see Sam again. Richard never did, and I'm beginning to think neither will I.'

This was too much for Pinkie. She'd seen terrible things in her time, but in the services, you learned to keep your feelings in check. You watched events unfold as an observer through the prism of combat. Being this close to her friend's raw, lacerating emotion was unbearable. She didn't know what she could possibly say to make her feel better.

Then it dawned on her, maybe she didn't have to say anything; maybe words in circumstances like these would inevitably sound trite. Action was what was needed. Actions always spoke louder than words. Neutralise the enemy and deliver the hostage back to his family. It was a simple enough mission statement. She wouldn't let this one go. She made a promise there and then to herself to get Liz's grandson back.

The women paid the bill and parted company in the car park as usual, but driving home along the narrow Cornish lanes, Pinkie was not thinking about watering her pot plants or what was on Netflix that evening. She was formulating a kill list. Gary Joyce was the obvious candidate, and his father who enabled him, but there was another who had to take his fair share of the blame, Carlisle. He was the one whose job it was to protect the innocent from monsters like Gary Joyce. Whether his abject failure was down to an error of judgement or cronyism, she wasn't sure, but she'd get to the bottom of it one way or another. First, she needed to know more about the judge and what's more, she had an idea who to ask.

Chapter Three

THE FOLLOWING EVENING, Pinkie shouted over the privet hedge to her neighbour, Agnes Chenoweth, as she walked up the garden path, 'Fancy a glass of sauvignon blanc and some spaghetti? I've made way too much for one.'

Agnes hadn't needed second bidding. Two minutes later, having dropped her bag off, she was sitting on Pinkie's patio sipping wine.

Agnes worked for local solicitor Eden Gray and regarded herself as the oracle on all things legal or crime-related in the area. She could be cantankerous but had a good heart under the spiky veneer. Pinkie suspected her asperity was down to basic shyness. As one of those babies referred to as a 'late surprise', her adult siblings took it for granted their little sister would be the one to stay at home to look after their elderly parents when the time came. As it turned out, their geriatric decline lasted longer than anyone expected, and by the time Agnes's mother finally gave up her vice-like grip on life, Agnes was in her late fifties and too set in her ways to risk her heart. At least her siblings had the decency to recognise the house should be hers.

Despite being one of the incomers or 'blow-ins' Agnes moaned about, and the fact the woman still berated Pinkie for calling her evening meal 'supper', which Agnes insisted was cheese and biscuits or a bowl of cornflakes before bed, they rubbed along well enough to regard themselves as friends.

Pinkie knew to get the best out of her interviewee. She had to tread carefully. She started with something suitably innocuous.

'How is work these days?' she asked. 'How's that new trainee of yours getting on?'

'Molly's settled in fine. I wasn't sure it was such a good idea at first. I thought we needed an older solicitor. Someone with a bit more gravitas.'

Agnes lobbed the word gravitas into conversation regularly, particularly when reminiscing about her old boss Douglas Basset. Pinkie had an inkling Agnes had held a torch for the lawyer, although she was certain she would never admit it. She'd worked for Douglas for over twenty years and had done everything for the man, including ironing his shirts occasionally, which seemed beyond the remit of a secretarial role in anyone's book. When he'd announced at the ripe old age of fifty-one that he was getting married for the first time, having rekindled a university romance, Agnes handed in her notice the same day, only returning when he begged her to come back with the promise of a free run of the office and a substantial pay rise. Reading between the lines, Agnes spent the next few years making Douglas pay for what Pinkie suspected was a broken heart.

When Mrs Basset died of breast cancer five years later,

Agnes was forced to witness her boss's devastation daily, and she confided she was relieved when he decided to retire and sell out to Eden Gray. Nevertheless, Pinkie had listened to her constant complaints for six months after her new boss took over. She thought Eden was impetuous and a bit of a lefty, always in the press talking about women's rights. She took on clients Agnes at best disapproved of and at worst thought guilty as sin. Yet as the months passed, Pinkie noticed Agnes developing a grudging respect for the lawyer.

The only thing she moaned about these days was her tendency to go AWOL when the forecast predicted a clean swell. Agnes didn't approve of Eden's obsession with surfing. *"How could anyone expect to be taken seriously in a wet suit. Douglas never sat on a surfboard in his life, and look how well respected he was."*

'So you like the new girl?'

'I wouldn't go that far. Like's a strong word.'

Not really, thought Pinkie, although she said nothing.

'She's hard-working and not full of herself like some because they've got a law degree and think it makes them better than the rest of us. All in all, it's worked out very well. Eden's pleased too.'

Ah, so it's Eden now, is it, thought Pinkie? *First name terms, that's progress.*

'Talking about lawyers, I went to lunch today with a friend who mentioned one of the local judges in conversation.'

'Really?' asked Agnes, eyes widening at the prospect of a bit of insider gossip. 'Which one?'

'Oh, something beginning with C … Carter, Chanter … Carlisle … that's it, Carlisle.'

'Oh, *him*,' Agnes grunted. 'Most of the judges are alright, but the girls in the court office haven't got much time for him. He's a right snob; mean too. Never goes to any of the socials or gives cards at Christmas.'

She went on to say whenever a new judge arrived, the staff made it their business to get the heads-up on what to expect from their colleagues in the courts outside the county. The information bounced back on him had been neutral, so it came as a surprise when he turned out to be such a stickler, spiteful and unforgiving towards those he considered intellectually wanting.

'He's a bad-tempered old beggar. He snipes at the ushers and terrifies the wet-behind-the-ears solicitors. He likes to make them squirm in front of their clients.'

She revealed Douglas had complained more than once about the ruthless dissection of his case by Carlisle. He said the judge had taken on the role of cross-examiner, doing the other side's job for them, and through his inappropriate intermeddling, his sure-fire case became a lost cause.

'Of course, Douglas was an experienced trial lawyer,' said Agnes puffing out her chest in a show of pride. 'He was a match for anyone, but he said if the judge decided to take against you, you rarely won. He's been reported loads of times, but it never seems to do any good. Look at what happened to Marcus Annear. All the solicitors were up in arms about it. The local law society even got involved. You remember, don't you? It was in the papers, the young solicitor who died. That was down to Carlisle.'

Pinkie's ears pricked up at the mention of the name. She vaguely remembered reading about a young lawyer who had died of a seizure in the court building, but it hadn't crossed her mind it was Marcus when talking with her friend yesterday, and Liz hadn't said anything. But as Agnes rattled on, things began to gel.

'Why do you think Carlisle was responsible?'

'Because it was Carlisle who made him spend a night in the cells. The judge ordered him to give up his client's whereabouts. It was a domestic violence case involving the son of one of Carlisle's golfing pals. Marcus refused, worried for the young woman's safety if her husband found out. The judge held him in contempt and made the usher take him down to the cells to be brought up the next day. He told him if he didn't purge his contempt by giving the client up, then he'd go back down again until he changed his mind.'

Pinkie knew there and then Agnes was talking about Liz's daughter Rachel.

'Could he do that; legally I mean?' asked Pinkie.

'Technically, yes, but no one had ever heard of it being done to a solicitor before, certainly not overnight. Joyce was a big wig on the planning committee and chairman of the golf club. We all thought Carlisle did it to impress Joyce. Of course, the cells weren't built for it. They're only meant to house the accused for short periods during the trial. Prisoners don't generally stay there overnight. Marcus had a panic attack and died. He was in his twenties, his whole life ahead of him.'

'That's terrible.'

'It's worse than terrible; it's criminal if you ask me. Carlisle knew about Marcus's claustrophobia and what happened to him when he was a boy. Marcus's boss, Claire McBride, made sure of it as soon as she heard what the judge had done from the court staff. She even delivered a doctor's report. The judge ignored it all.'

'What happened to Marcus when he was a boy?'

Pinkie knew she was in for one of her friend's meanderings. She'd been trained to be concise in debriefings, and this tendency to waffle drove her to distraction, but she'd have to bite her tongue.

'His mother was tried for manslaughter. Douglas defended her.'

Agnes began her blow-by-blow account as Pinkie regularly refreshed her empty glass.

'Marcus, his mother and his two-year-old sister were waiting at the front of the queue to take the ferry across the river to Truro after visiting the children's grandparents in St. Mawes. You know what it's like in summer, always teeming with visitors.'

Pinkie had taken the King Harry Ferry often. The approach was via a precariously steep tree-canopied lane which opened up at the bottom to the ferry slipway and the river. The cars were often lined up behind each other halfway up the hill when busy. It was a relief when you arrived to find you were nearer the front of the queue than the back and wouldn't have to wait the fifteen-minute turnaround for the next crossing.

'Back then, there was always a van selling ice creams at the bottom of the hill. The ferry had just left for the other side. They were at the front of the queue, but the kids were fussing and Marcus's mum, knowing they had a bit of a wait, got out of the car to buy the children lollies. She was paying when she heard screaming, and people began running down the road past her. She'd forgotten to put the handbrake on. Her Vauxhall Astra had rolled down the slipway and into the water. I typed the witness statements. They were terrible things to read. Within seconds the water was lapping around the door handles, steam rising from the engine. A chap swam out and tried to open the doors, but the weight of the water made it impossible. Another man, a fireman on holiday with his family as it happened, armed with a jack from his car, swam out, shouting to Marcus to undo his seatbelt and move away from the back window. By now, the water was up to the children's necks, and he was trying to free his sister from her car seat. She was crying and clinging to him. The man whacked the rear window with the jack, and on the second thump, it shattered, sending water into the back like a waterfall over the heads of the children. He reached in to grab the little girl, but she fought him, so he couldn't get a grip on her. He told Marcus to swim through the window, but the boy wouldn't leave his sister. In his evidence, the chap said he could hear him telling her it would be okay, that Mummy would be there soon. I can tell you I could barely type that bit.'

Pinkie's throat tightened at the thought of the boy.

'In the end, the man caught hold of Marcus and pulled him through the window, kicking and screaming. Someone swam in and took the boy off him while he tried again for the little girl, but the car lilted, and it sunk to the bottom.'

Agnes glugged down her glass of wine in one.

'Marcus's mum was acquitted, and Douglas admitted it was because the jury couldn't imagine she should be punished anymore, rather than because of his defence. You see, strictly speaking, on the evidence, she was guilty. She was, understandably, shot to bits after, but the dad was still around, and Marcus grew up to be a remarkably well-adjusted young man, all things considered.'

Until the judge brought his life to an abrupt end, Pinkie thought.

The deaths of Marcus Annear and Liz's daughter seemed to be twisting to form the noose to hang Carlisle, but Pinkie had to be sure everything happened just as Agnes said. A man's life was at stake. She had to be certain of Carlisle's guilt before she tied the final knot.

Agnes had said there had been an enquiry into Marcus's death, and Liz had mentioned a transcript of the trial.

Later that evening, she rang Liz.

'Hi Liz, I'm just ringing to check you're okay after yesterday?'

'Do you know what? Our little chat really helped,' Liz replied. 'I think I'd like to talk some more. You're a very good listener. I slept through last night. Perhaps for the first time since Richard died. Why don't you come around this Saturday for something to eat? Nothing fancy, a bit of salmon and salad. It'll be nice to have some company. I always find weekends the most difficult.'

Pinkie was moved. No one had called her a good listener before. She'd moved around so much over the years that it had been difficult to establish the kind of friendships that lead to confidences being exchanged. It was a nice feeling knowing she had helped her friend.

Chapter Four

PINKIE ARRIVED the following Saturday evening as arranged. They talked about everything other than Rachel and Liz's grandson. Eventually, Pinkie realised she'd have to make the first move. She reached into her bag and brought out a notepad.

Liz looked bewildered.

Pinkie took a deep breath.

'Liz, I have to admit I had an ulterior motive when calling you the other evening ... of course, I was concerned about you, but I wanted to talk some more about your daughter and her case. You see, I've been asked to write a piece on domestic abuse by the charity I used to work for. It's part of a feature about how our courts deal with it in comparison to other jurisdictions around the world. I gave up being a freelance journalist years ago, as you know, but I said I'd do this as a bit of a favour to raise awareness that we in the West are not as enlightened as we may like to think. I refused at first, but when you told me about Rachel, I began to have second thoughts. No names will be used, and even the location will be secret, save it's in the UK. Please feel free to say no but if it could help someone else and raise money for the charity, then—'

Liz jumped in; 'No, I'm happy to help, and while I know you can't mention names, I bloody well hope someone reading it realises who it's about.' There was fight in Liz's voice as she spoke. 'Right, this calls for more coffee,' she said, wiping a tear from the corner of her eye as she rose from her chair.

Pinkie scanned the magnolia walls decked with photographs of Rachel and Liz's chubby-faced grandson and heaved a sigh. They must be a constant reminder to her friend of her loss, but what was she supposed to do, lock them away, pretend they'd never existed? People talked about wallowing in pain as if it were a bad thing, but when it was all you had, it was precious, something to be cherished. Sometimes it was the only thing that made life bearable. Without those memories, painful as they may be, your loved ones' short existence might seem a pointless, cruel waste of time. Pain had its own terrible beauty. Pinkie had learnt that lesson long ago.

Liz returned with the coffee and two brandy glasses. 'I thought I might need one, but I can get you something else if you prefer. Richard and I always enjoyed a brandy after a nice meal out, but I know it's not to everyone's taste.'

'No, it's fine,' said Pinkie lifting the glass to warm the honey-coloured liquor between her palms. On the tray resting beside the coffee pot was a thin file of papers Pinkie guessed was the transcript of the hearing.

Liz lifted it from the tray, flicked through the earmarked pages and began to read out loud. '"Your Honour, my client is not having an affair. There is no other man in her life, violent or otherwise, and she certainly didn't leave with such a man. He is a fabrication, a phantom conjured up by the respondent to disguise his own violent behaviour towards his wife. Mrs Joyce has merely taken herself and her son to a place of safety. I know where she is, and I can assure you there's no man with her." You can tell from that bit Marcus is furious, and that's where it all began to go wrong. Here, read it for yourself.' Liz handed Pinkie the well-thumbed court transcript of the hearing, then leant back in her chair, sipping her brandy. Pinkie began to read.

'Is Mr Weller Gary's solicitor?' she asked, trying to make sense of the document.

Liz nodded.

'And the HHJ?'

'His Honour Judge Carlisle.'

Pinkie continued reading in silence.

Mr Weller: 'Is Mr Annear telling this court he knows the whereabouts of my client's wife and child, bearing in mind a warrant has been issued this morning for her immediate return?'

HHJ: 'Mr Annear, if you know the whereabouts of your client, you must divulge it now or I will hold you in contempt of court.'

Mr Annear: 'I'm afraid I cannot divulge the information at this time, Your Honour, as it may compromise my client's safety.'

HHJ: 'Then I have no alternative. You will be taken down to the cells until you are willing to purge your contempt and give up your client's whereabouts. Do you understand me?'

Mr Annear: 'Yes, Your Honour.'

HHJ: 'You will be kept overnight and appear before me tomorrow morning when I hope you will be prepared to purge your contempt. Take him down. Case adjourned.'

Pinkie doubted if the dry words of the transcript could ever express the frustration and anger of the young lawyer or the tension in that courtroom when the usher escorted him out. Carlisle must have revelled in it, the odious man. Power in the wrong hands was every bit as poisonous as anything she could dish up. It could inflict wounds as deep as any weapon.

'There, you can see for yourself how it went, and things only got worse after that.'

'How so?'

'Marcus's boss, Claire McBride, called Richard to tell him what had happened. She said she'd been called by the usher and had rushed up to the court and spoken to Marcus, who had told her the whole saga. She said he looked terrible and was concerned the confined space was already affecting him. She'd tried to see the judge to advise him Marcus suffered from chronic claustrophobia, something to do with an incident that happened in his childhood. She said she'd been sure Carlisle would see reason and that even if he wouldn't let Marcus leave, he'd allow him to be held within the confines of the main building for the rest of the day and then release him upon her undertaking as his principal to return him the next morning. But the judge had refused to see her. He wouldn't even look at a letter from Marcus's GP she'd handed in for his attention. The message came back via the usher that he had a full list and did not intend to make any more time for this matter, which had already disrupted his day. He'd said he'd deal with it in the morning, and that was that. She'd rung us to ask if we were prepared for Marcus to tell the judge where we were. We immediately said yes, of course. We knew by then the police were already involved in tracing Rachel and Sam. I couldn't expect my friend to put us up in those circumstances, and to tell you the truth, Rachel was almost relieved, and Claire had already arranged for her to go into a refuge outside Bodmin. We thought that would be the end of it, and we'd get a call back saying the judge had let Marcus out once he'd told him we were on our way back, but the next morning we heard Marcus was dead. He'd had some kind of fit during the night.'

'So why hadn't the judge let him go?'

'Nobody knows. There was an enquiry, and Claire McBride gave evidence to say she was convinced the judge had acted in response to a previous encounter he'd had with Marcus.'

'In court?'

'No in the judge's chambers.'

'Go on.' Pinkie was insistent now.

'He'd only been in front of that judge once before, three months earlier. He'd won the case easily, not understanding why the judge had such bad press from his colleagues. It was only later he got an inkling of why. After the hearing, one of the ushers tapped him on the shoulder and asked if he'd join the judge in his chambers. He said the judge wanted to congratulate him on his first win in court as a newly qualified solicitor and that he was always keen to help bright young lawyers with potential in any way he could. Once in the room, the judge poured them drinks, and everything seemed fine, but as he was leaving, Carlisle patted him on the back, then ran his hand down and squeezed Marcus's buttock.'

'Disgusting man, abusing his position like that. What did Marcus do?'

'He was shocked and left mortified. It was common knowledge Marcus was gay. He was an activist in the local law society campaign against discrimination within the profession. According to Claire, he confided he'd heard rumours about the judge but had always defended his position, finding the homophobic asides deeply offensive. Although he was sure he was reading the signs correctly and was cringingly embarrassed, he thought he needed to make it clear he wasn't interested in case this happened again. Claire wanted to report the slimy bastard, and she offered to ring the bar council and the Lord Chancellor's office, but Marcus thought it would only serve to attract the wrong type of media attention to a cause he'd campaigned long and hard for. It would be another excuse for a pop at gay men, another opportunity for the stereotypes to be wheeled out. In any case, he thought Carlisle was hardly going to admit it. It would be his word against the judge's, so Marcus decided to put it behind him. Of course, he didn't know about the others then.'

'Others?'

'Claire told us later that other young gay lawyers had confided in her after Marcus's death, but none wanted to give evidence. They feared causing embarrassment to their families and worried any allegation might jeopardise their careers. Of course, this was before me too. Things might have been different if this had happened nowadays.'

'So this creep, this judge, is still out there, probably still doing the same thing.'

Liz nodded.

At the door, Pinkie turned.

'Liz, by way of background for the article, I need you to write down everything you know or think you know about Gary and his father; family history, relatives, business and social connections, club memberships like the golf club, for example, and of course details of the houses you think he might own in Portugal and elsewhere, through these offshore companies. Don't worry if it seems irrelevant or you're not sure if it's fact or hearsay; just let rip. When you're sure you have absolutely everything, that you've squeezed the last pip from the lemon, send it to me at this address. Don't email. Post it here.'

Pinkie scribbled an address in her notebook, ripped out the page and handed it to Liz.

Liz first scanned the note, then Pinkie's face for an explanation.

'It's the postal address I always use for my stories. People can send things to me here anonymously; whistle-blowers and the like who are afraid of losing their jobs or other repercussions if someone finds out they've been talking to me. There is no paper trail this way like there would be if they telephoned or e-mailed me; nothing to link the story back to them.'

Pinkie didn't like lying to her friend, but it was imperative Liz wasn't implicated in anything that was to come.

'Can you do that?'

'Of course,' said Liz. 'When will this article come out?'

'Oh, soon, everything will be dealt with soon.'

Liz hugged her as she left.

Pinkie drove away even more determined to punish the people responsible for this tragedy. She decided to first concentrate on the candidate closest to mind and to hand, Carlisle.

Chapter Five

EXACTLY HOW SHE would use the rosary pea on Carlisle without endangering others had eluded her at first. But just like all her other victims, the judge had unwittingly revealed a weakness.

Pinkie had been attending the spa for a month or so before she noticed something odd about Carlisle. He was excessively demanding, more so than the other members, and that was saying something. It cost an arm and a leg to join, and it was the spa's policy to push the luxury and exclusivity of the venue. That inevitably drew certain types with high-end expectations. Everything was provided; warm, fluffy robes, towelling slippers, and expensive toiletries in the shower rooms, but still, the judge shouted for the pool staff to fetch him his towel or his robe, even when they were right under his nose.

It wasn't until she'd watched him very carefully she realised this behaviour didn't extend beyond the pool complex. In the plush dark lounge, where he took his mint tea after his swim, his attitude was completely different.

There, his voice was measured, and he was civil if a little terse. She hadn't understood the difference until one morning, standing in front of him at the entrance to the pool, she picked up a towel from the pristine stack and, without thinking, handed him one too.

He took it but looked straight through her with no indication he knew her at all despite the fact she'd swum in the lane next to him every morning for weeks.

At first, she thought he was being unconscionably rude. She stared into his vacant grey eyes for some hint of recognition, but there was none. He'd turned to walk away without a thank you. She was about to call after him, forcing him to engage in conversation, when she thought of a funny story Sandra from her gardening club had told her about a friend of hers who was so appallingly short-sighted that, without her glasses, she was blind as a bat. She'd forgotten her glasses on a trip to Tesco, got lost and had to put an announcement out on the tannoy for her husband to collect her from the tills like an errant toddler.

That was it, she thought; *he couldn't see*. She'd never seen the judge wearing spectacles, so assumed he wore contacts and took them out to swim. That's why he hadn't recognised her, and that's why he was constantly asking the pool attendants to wait on him hand and foot. At that moment, she formed a plan as to how she'd poison him. She just had to get access to his locker.

Chapter Six

THE SPA'S changing rooms housed lockers for guests to stash their clothes and valuables. On joining, each member was given a four-digit code to punch into a keypad to release the door, just like a safe in a hotel room. Before she went any further with her plan, she decided she needed to experiment, and so one morning after her swim, she padded her way to the front desk.

'I'm sorry to bother you, but I've been a complete idiot and lost my fob with my code attached and can't get my clothes,' she smiled helplessly.

'Another one,' the attendant said, rolling her eyes at her colleague before flinging an exasperated smile at Pinkie. 'It happens all the time. If you wait there a moment, I'll be with you soon.'

Pinkie stood dripping onto the terrazzo floor whilst the woman finished writing.

'There,' she said, slamming the leather-bound book shut for all the world as if she'd just completed the last line of a great novel. 'Follow me.'

Pinkie waddled after her to the changing rooms.

'Which one?' the girl asked, scanning the lockers, annoyance rising off her like sauna steam.

'That one there.'

The girl walked forward and tapped in a code to override the system. Pinkie stood behind, watching carefully. The month and the year; *not very secure*, she thought.

'Thank you for your help.'

'It's a good idea to hand your fob into the desk when you use the facilities if you're forgetful. That's what we recommend to our elderly guests.'

'I will ... thanks again,' Pinkie smiled, thinking, *well you can shove your fob where the sun don't shine, you patronising little witch*, as the girl walked away, no doubt to deal with some other earth-shattering crisis like a broken nail or an Instagram post of her lunch.

As soon as she was gone, Pinkie tried out the woefully inadequate security system herself. She shut the locker door, tapped in the wrong code and when 'err' flashed up, typed in the same code as the attendant used. Just like before, it opened. She now needed to try the same trick in the men's locker room just in case they had a different system. She'd decided it was too busy then, but the next morning she waited until the judge was in the pool and headed for the men's changing rooms. It was generally quiet that early in the morning, but if she met anyone, she'd decided to look suitably confused and say she was searching for the ladies' loo.

As luck had it, there was only one closed locker, and when she typed in the override code, it opened straight away. Inside was a wallet and a small wash bag. She flipped open the wallet to reveal the owner's driving licence; sure enough, the judge stared out at her from the plastic insert.

She carefully unzipped the washbag and looked inside: brush, deodorant, aftershave and hair putty. She guessed the last of these was an impulse buy based on wishful thinking, given the little hair he retained sat in downy blonde tufts across his back.

She rooted around but couldn't see any contact lens case. Disappointed she'd misread the signs, she was just about to give the plan up as a lost cause when she noticed a side pouch with a second zip; inside a case, contact lenses swimming in their individual puddles of solution.

Pinkie punched the air. She had a plan, and she liked it. She liked it a lot. It was ambitious and imaginative, requiring meticulous execution. To pull it off she'd need focus and dedication both of which had been sorely missing lately but she'd never been one to shy away from a challenge. In fact, a challenge was just what she needed.

Chapter Seven

SHE HAD COLLECTED the jequirity seeds and left them to dry out on kitchen paper in the greenhouse for a couple of days. She liked it in there on those early spring afternoons when it was still a little chilly to work outside. It was cosy, basking in the watery sunlight. She loved the yearly ritual of ordering from the seed catalogues, then preparing the plastic trays in the greenhouse once they arrived. She'd write the labels while she listened to the radio. It was an activity full of hope. It signalled the lengthening of the days and the end of winter, the beginning of another year, new possibilities and fresh starts. This was different; her work today was about endings, not beginnings.

She laid out her chosen tools on the bench and opened the box of one hundred white latex gloves she'd bought from the chemist. She imagined the medical horrors requiring that many as she slipped on a wafer-thin pair and flexed her fingers. Next, her army-grade tactical respirator mask with goggles to cover her face. She hated the sweaty, rubbery smell it gave off, but needs must. Her plan didn't include her own death by poisoning in the greenhouse; that would be very *Midsomer Murders*.

She placed a small white plastic chopping board on top of the foil-lined kitchen tray she'd prepared earlier to contain everything in one defined space. She then carefully positioned the two red seeds on the board. Picking up the razor-sharp penknife she used for taking cuttings, she pinned the first bright red rosary bean to the board with the index finger of her left hand and split the outer case carefully peeling it back to reveal the pale flesh inside. She began to scratch away at the first seed until she was left with a pile of tiny shavings. She then repeated the process with the other. When she felt she had enough, she spread the shavings out to dry for about thirty minutes while she sat immobilised in her lab assistant's fancy dress, not wanting to touch anything or move until the task was completed. As her goggles steamed up, every itch, every urge to scratch her nose or shake loose the little tickle in her throat had to be resisted.

After about twenty minutes, the shavings had shrunk and curled in the heat of the greenhouse and, eager to finish, Pinkie scraped them off the board into the spice grinder she'd bought from a New Age shop in town. It was very clear from the drawing of a hemp plant on the outside of the pocket-sized device its main purpose was not to grind spice, well, not the sort you put in curry anyway. She slowly ground down the contents, repeating the process until she'd been left with a fine off-white powder which she tapped out onto the back of a small square of greaseproof paper cut from the roll she used for baking. Once she was satisfied she had contained all the powder in a single pile in the centre, she folded the paper around the powder to form a cone and poured the contents as carefully as possible, so as not to spill any, into an empty vitamin capsule, pushing the lid of the capsule home to seal the deadly contents inside. She held the capsule up to the light. The amount of powder she'd managed to produce was minuscule, less than a tenth of the capsule's 5mg capacity, but if the statistics were to be believed, the tiniest amount would suffice.

She'd only need a few micrograins to kill the judge.

Chapter Eight

THE NEXT MORNING, she drove to the pool as usual. She spotted the judge's car in the car park as she arrived. She knew, the creature of habit he was, he'd be in the water doing his laps.

The ladies' changing room was empty. She kicked off her shoes and discarded her jeans before grabbing a robe and wrapping it around herself over her t-shirt. Reaching into her bag, she retrieved a pair of latex gloves along with a small, sealed sandwich bag holding the capsule and a toothpick. She slipped the bag into her robe pocket and headed for the steps leading to the men's changing room.

She was relieved it, too, was empty. It stank of bleach and lemon-scented cleaning fluid. A tap drip, drip dripped, echoing in the empty space. It was a good sign; it meant the cleaner had already been and gone. She walked over and turned it off. *No need to waste water,* she thought.

The shiny aluminium lockers gaped open-mouthed. Only two were closed. She wriggled her fingers into the gloves before opening the judge's locker, punching in the digits of the month and the year. There, just as before, was the washbag with the lens case inside. She lifted it out, set it down on the polished granite sink surround and held her breath.

She'd practised the manoeuvre over and over again at home with an identical lens case she'd bought at Boots and a capsule filled with a few grains of vitamin C and hoped the hours of tedious finger-cramping manoeuvres would pay off. Unscrewing first the right, then the left cap, she stared down at the contacts floating in their saline puddles. She lifted the bag from the robe pocket and carefully rolled the capsule out into the palm of her gloved hand. *Now for the difficult bit*, she thought.

Taking care to hold the capsule vertically, with the powder in the bottom section, she twisted the top away. Holding it steady in her left hand, she used her right to dip the toothpick in the shallow pool of solution, making sure she didn't damage the lens. Coating the toothpick with a few grains of the deadly powder from the capsule, she then reintroduced it into the solution around the lens, mixing it until no discernible trace remained, then repeated the exercise on the other side.

She dropped the empty capsule and the toothpick back into the plastic bag, which she then slid into her robe pocket. After sealing the lens case, she placed it in the washbag before returning it to the judge's locker.

The clenched fist in the pit of her stomach released its grip. Looking at her watch, she noted the whole process had taken seven minutes. She placed the washbag back in the locker and pushed the door shut.

She headed back to the ladies' changing room, pulling off the gloves as she walked. Turning them inside out and rolling them into a ball, she slipped them back into her handbag along with the small plastic bag. She was sweating profusely under the heavy towelling robe and couldn't wait to get back into her jeans and get out of there. After that, it would simply be a matter of waiting for the rosary pea to work the magic it had worked for centuries in the capable hands of poisoners just like her.

She sensed her body sinking back into its natural rhythm and the feeling of exultation she always felt after a kill. It was strange how killing made you feel so alive.

As she walked past reception, she heard someone shout after her.

'Miss Floyd ... can I have a word?'

Pinkie froze for a second before turning to face the poker-faced receptionist.

'Yes, what is it?'

'Can you spare a moment? The manager would like a quick word.'

'I'm in a bit of a hurry.'

'It won't take long.'

Pinkie's mind raced; the calm she'd felt only seconds before was beginning to melt away. Had she been spotted? Maybe there was some device she didn't know about attached to the lockers monitoring their use? Worse still, what if someone had come in when she was fiddling with the judge's locker or depositing the poison into the lens case, and she hadn't noticed? She'd been concentrating so hard on what she was doing it was conceivable they'd opened the door but hadn't entered.

She wanted to run but knew it would look suspicious and may be remembered later if the police questioned anyone.

'What is it? Is there a problem?' she asked as calmly as she could.

'If you would come with me please,' the girl said, marshalling her into a side room where at a large mahogany desk sat the hotel manager.

Pinkie had seen the man before, busying himself around the place, barking orders at the staff in a way hardly in keeping with the tranquil vibe the place promoted.

'Ah, Miss Floyd,' he said, looking down at a card in front of him, obviously reading her name. 'Philippa, if I may call you Philippa?'

'Yes, fine,' she said impatiently. 'What's this about? Why do you want to talk to me?'

'It's rather a delicate matter,' he said, beckoning her to take a seat.

Her stomach hollowed as another thought scudded through her mind. Maybe they weren't going to rap her over the knuckles for being in the wrong changing room or even fiddling with the lockers. Maybe they thought she'd been stealing from them and were keeping her there like a kid caught shoplifting while they waited for the police to arrive? God almighty. All these years, all the successful missions she'd carried out across the globe against drug cartels in fucking war zones, and she was going to get banged up because of this?

'Can you please tell me what you're talking about?' she said. Despite her attempt to keep her cool, she could hear the hysterical pitch of her voice.

The man shuffled the papers in front of him, looking embarrassed.

'I've noticed, despite numerous reminders, you have not renewed your membership.'

Pinkie stared at him blankly, unable in the shadow of her previous conjecture to fully process what he was on about.

'Technically, for the last two weeks, you have been using the spa's facilities without paying. Obviously, if this is just an oversight on your part and you propose to renew, that's fine, but if not, then I'm afraid I will have to ask you to refrain from attending the private spa facilities from today.'

Pinkie felt her carotid artery pulsing.

'What?!' she screamed. 'You dragged me in here like a naughty bloody school child to tell me this. Why didn't you just speak to me in reception?'

She reached down into her bag, hand shaking, to pull out her chequebook.

'Okay, how much do I owe you? Just for the times I've been here since my membership ran out, I can assure you I won't be renewing,' she snapped.

'Well, there's really no need to take that attitude. You must understand it's not fair to our other members to allow—'

She cut him off. 'Two hundred, will that do? Two-fifty then, that should cover it.' She scribbled out the cheque, signed her name with a flourish, then ripped it from the book, tearing it slightly as she did so, before slamming it on the desk in front of the dumbfounded man. She got up, picked up her bag and pushed past the open-mouthed girl, exiting into the foyer.

'We prefer card payments. This will need someone to run to the bank.'

'Just as well your sidekick's a fit little gym bunny then,' she whispered under her breath.

As she crossed to the revolving doors to the car park, she spotted Carlisle out of the corner of her eye, reading his newspaper and sipping his green tea. He didn't look up.

'Let's get the hell out of here,' she whispered to herself.

As she settled in her car seat and started the engine, she

longed for the return of the sensation she'd come to crave, like the embrace of an old friend after a mission, but it wouldn't come. She turned on her iPhone – perhaps some music would calm her down. She started the engine and sped away along the narrow gravel driveway to the sound of REM, singing about losing their religion. She'd nearly lost a lot more than that. Two minutes before, she was thinking how, with the limited items in her handbag, she could immobilise the snotty hotel manager and his leggy sidekick and make her getaway. She was getting too old for this lark.

She glanced in her rear-view mirror by way of a final goodbye just as a Range Rover rounded the corner, running her off the road and onto the verge. She slammed on the brakes, swerving to avoid the hedge. Her car ground to a halt, mud and gravel skirting around her wheel arch as she was thrown forward in her seat. Her hands gripped the steering wheel, knuckles white. She tried to straighten up, pain biting at her shoulder blade and across her chest where her seatbelt had done its job. It hurt to breathe, and she felt a little faint. She was jolted back from the brink by a tap on the car window.

'I'm so sorry,' the blonde pony-tailed woman was saying. 'I didn't see you in time to slow down.'

'I'm okay,' Pinkie shouted through the glass, wincing as she raised her hand.

'Are you sure? You look a bit peaky.'

The woman obviously wasn't going to leave until she spoke to her without the barrier, so Pinkie reluctantly pressed the button to wind down the window. 'Yes, really, I'm fine. No harm done, honestly.' She hoped it would be enough to assuage the woman's concerns, but she jabbered on.

'Only, I'm a member here, and they have a medic on

tap, so he can give you the once-over if you like; I'm sure he wouldn't mind.'

Pinkie needed to get away from there. She'd already wasted too much time. If the judge was taken ill as the toxin raced through his system she could be in trouble. He must have put the lenses in to read his paper. It should take time for him to die, but he might have an immediate adverse reaction before she could get away.

'No,' she said emphatically, raising her voice in the hope the woman would get the hint. 'As I just said, I'm perfectly fine. Now, if you don't mind, I really must go.'

She put the car in reverse, hoping it wasn't stuck in the trench she'd made in the perfectly tended lawn. Slipping it into first, she sped away, leaving the woman wide-eyed, mouth open.

AMY REYNOLDS HURRIED to the spa's reception desk to ask for some goggles and to complain.

'I've just had such a shock. I was nearly run off the road by the rudest of women in an Audi.'

The receptionist looked up. 'Miss Floyd,' she said, eyes narrowing. 'She's no longer a member here. The manager just had words with her. I know exactly where you're coming from; she's very aggressive and rude. I think she's probably menopausal,' she whispered the word as if it might be catching. 'Not the sort of person we encourage here at the St. Piran.'

'Well, she seemed completely unhinged to me; she didn't want to stop. I wasn't going to report it, but if you say you think her behaviour is irrational, I really think I must. Who knows what damage she might do driving like that … but I didn't take her registration number?'

'It's okay. I have all her details on file, including her registration. We keep them so we can check only members are using the car park.' The girl pulled up Pinkie's details on the computer and handed her the phone from behind the desk. 'Please use our phone. Reception is not great for mobiles here.'

'Hello, police, I'd like to report an accident … No one was hurt, and no damage, but the woman driving the other car was driving like a mad thing, and I'm afraid she might cause another collision … Yes, my name is Mrs Amy Reynolds, and you'll want the woman's name. Her name is Floyd. Philippa Floyd.'

The women smiled conspiratorially, satisfied they'd done their civic duty.

Chapter Nine

PINKIE WENT about her normal business, nervously waiting for the rosary pea to do its job.

Once diluted, the amount used would have been undetectable to the judge when he placed the lenses in his eyes. However, once introduced, the poison would have passed through the membrane and then the blood vessels of his eyes, quickly working its way into the judge's nervous system.

She'd got the idea from an anecdote in one of her horticultural books about Victorian ladies using belladonna extract to dilate their pupils and give the impression of sexual arousal. Then there was the highly-publicised trend amongst British students in the nineties known as 'eyeballing' where vodka shots were taken through the eye to induce drunkenness at breakneck speed. The effect on the judge wouldn't be breakneck, not unless he fell down the stairs once it kicked in. The Bulgarian dissident Georgi Markov had taken four days to die after being assassinated with Ricin from a tiny platinum pellet into the back of his leg from an umbrella. She remembered being lectured on it in the eighties. The 1.7millimetre pellet had two 0.35-millimetre holes drilled through it to form an x-shaped cavity to hold the poison. The holes were then sealed with a substance that would melt at blood temperature. Ingenious by anyone's standard.

The toxin she'd used was more powerful, but her method less direct. There was no template for this one. All she could do was bide her time.

She didn't have to wait long. The following Monday evening, Agnes came knocking. She'd had to file some pleadings at court that afternoon and had been met with the hushed tones of the staff discussing the judge's unexpected and sudden demise at his house on Saturday night. There were whispers that the circumstances were suspicious. He'd been found by his gardener in the kitchen on Sunday morning and had been dead for several hours

Over the following weeks, snippets of information were relayed by Agnes via the less-than-discreet staff who had apparently been questioned by the police.

Two weeks later, she arrived with a bottle of Merlot and the news the pathologist found kidney failure as well as other things but was stumped as to the cause. He'd ordered blood tests to check for toxic substances. The police had found some rather extreme political material on the judge's computer, along with compromising pornographic content. The judge was a frequent visitor to various dubious sites and a fan of Skyping young men who then performed sexual activities whilst he watched. *No wonder he never went out much*, thought Pinkie. Word was, he'd become involved with the wrong crowd and got in too deep. The rumour mill was in full spin, and it all served to protect Pinkie from detection.

When it was finally announced to the public, the speculations died away largely because the truth was even more shocking. His Honour Judge Fenton Carlisle had, the authorities believed, been poisoned with a very rare deadly agent with no known antidote. They also hinted they thought this could be a professional assassination carried out by terrorists or activists in response to the judge's right-wing politics. Other members of the judiciary were warned to be vigilant, and the court buildings were placed on high alert.

Chapter Ten

DI ROSS TRENEAR hadn't had a day off since Judge Carlisle had been found dead in suspicious circumstances.

All hell had broken loose once the autopsy revealed he'd been poisoned with a substance resembling Ricin. Given the state of high alert the country was experiencing, there was a very real possibility his murder could be part of a larger terrorist plot to target individuals working within the criminal justice system, those perceived as instruments of the state. Cornwall was under the spotlight, having last year hosted the G7 in St. Ives. What a nightmare that had been in the middle of COVID.

He and his colleagues in the Devon and Cornwall force had been relegated to interviewing everyone who had connections, no matter how tenuous, with Carlisle. The investigation proper had been taken over by a counter-terrorism team sent down from the command centre in London, one of whom - a condescending git called Dyson - now occupied Ross's office and, by the look of him, was quite at home there. The arrogant little sod was even using his mug.

Like the rest of his team, he'd trawled through dozens of names connected with the judge but had been unable to find anyone prepared to call themselves his friend. He'd been a member of several committees and organisations, the usual candidates, including the golf club (though not the Masons), but the man's life was generally a closed book. Other than a minor incident when he was young involving a rent boy and some dodgy porn on his laptop, there was nothing to suggest he was an obvious target for terrorists or anyone else.

He'd not tried any cases involving members of organised crime, being the only other candidates likely to be able to get hold of the stuff that had killed him. They'd scrutinised his financial affairs, and there were no large deposits or withdrawals to suggest he was being bribed or blackmailed.

They needed to get some kind of grip on why terrorists picked him, a relatively unknown circuit judge. Once they established the why they'd have a better chance of identifying the who.

It was accepted he might have been an easy target. Generally speaking, other than when hosting international conferences attended by the leaders of the free world, security in the county was patchy, to say the least. But then again, it was hardly a hotbed of racial tension or radical ideas. The local news was limited to 'dog rides surfboard' stories and the winners at the County Show.

It all seemed extremely unlikely to Ross, and he wasn't convinced by the tenuous conclusions drawn. In his experience, poison (and he'd be first to admit his experience was limited to Agatha Christie), no matter how rare or exotic, was personal.

The information that had come back on Carlisle had been mostly routine. Oxbridge, Inns of Court in London, high-flyer on an upward projectile with the promise of a higher judicial office like that of his father and grandfather before him who'd taken silk and later both become senior high court judges. But there was a rumour Carlisle's meteoric rise to QC had been abruptly halted because of an unfortunate incident in a gents' toilet off the King's Road. He'd been arrested for importuning. Strings had been pulled by his late father's chambers to ensure that matters went no further, and the incident had been shrugged off as hijinks following the consumption of too much champagne at an impromptu party after winning a case where he'd been junior counsel. There were no obvious repercussions in respect of his day-to-day career, but he'd never made QC and eventually, when he'd decided on a career within the judiciary, it was clear that although bright and ambitious, he'd hit a glass ceiling not to be cracked.

The irony was that his homosexuality had not been the issue. Had he admitted his preferences and openly lived the life of a gay man, it may well have proved an advantage at a time when the political emphasis was on appointing with an eye to diversity. It was the fact he'd revealed himself as someone with something to hide, someone who might be vulnerable to extortion or pressure from others that could compromise his ability to make sound judgements. As a direct consequence, he'd had to witness many young gay barristers less able than him climb the career ladder whilst he remained stuck in a professional and personal limbo where he couldn't marry and have children without being tagged a hypocrite and where he was not welcome amongst the openly gay fraternity because of his continued and objectionable denial of his sexuality. It was all very interesting but old news. It was very unlikely any of it was relevant to his murder. There was nothing for it but to keep banging on doors hoping to get an answer before that smug lot from out of county beat the Devon and Cornwall boys to it.

Chapter Eleven

ROSS HAD PRE-BOOKED the interview with the receptionist at the swanky St. Piran Spa the judge had attended daily when alive. He didn't mind going for a look at the place. He was thinking of booking a treatment for his daughter Livvy's sixteenth birthday present, a manicure or facial with a friend because, according to her mum Karenza, girls of her age didn't like doing things like that on their own. *Whatever happened to a trip to the cinema and a McDonald's after*, he wondered?

The young woman emerged from the room behind the reception desk wearing an expression that would have qualified as serene were it not for the knit of her caterpillar eyebrows. She padded across the tiles in her bamboo flip-flops, her black mandarin collared tunic and wide-legged trousers lending her the appearance of a jujitsu master. Close up, he could see although young, she was hardly fresh-faced. She was what Karenza called 'high maintenance'. There was a cushiony over-plumped look to her cheeks he assumed was down to fillers and a whiff of caramel he associated with fake tan. He was having second thoughts about sending Livvy there. Perhaps he'd get her surfing lessons instead. They sat opposite each other in the deep tan leather seats, a black marble table-top littered with price lists between them. The girl sporting a badge with the virtually unpronounceable name of Tialiahsa pinned to her left breast spoke first.

'So have you lot worked out what happened to that judge then?'

He assumed by 'you lot' she meant Her Majesty's Constabulary. 'Well, that's why I'm here,' he said, 'as part of the ongoing investigation.'

'So that's a no then.'

Ross smiled benignly. 'As I said, the investigation is ongoing.' It was going to be a long morning.

'Well, I can tell you I'm not surprised someone got him. He was a really difficult man, always wanting us to dance to his tune. He said it was because he had poor eyesight, but I didn't believe that for one instant. I'd seen him reading his paper in the foyer after his swim, and it's one of the small print ones, and how could anybody do all the paperwork you'd have to do as a judge if you had dodgy eyes? I reckon he just used it as an excuse to throw his weight around.'

Ross attempted to rewind her. 'Poor eyesight, you say?'

'Yeah, he wore contacts but not in the water. He said he had to wear special ones because of his condition, *asphyxia* he said it was.'

'You mean astigmatism.'

'Yeah, that was it, asthma thingy, what you said. I told the rest of the girls, "my sister's got contact lenses, and she wears them in the pool all the time". I never got what made him any different.'

'Where did he keep his lenses while he swam?'

'In his locker, I suppose. All our guests have a locker with a special PIN they keep all their personal stuff in. I know he didn't wear them in the pool, so that's where they must have been. I showed the locker to the policeman who came the other day. There was nothing in the locker when he looked, but why would there be? He left here right as rain.'

'Had the room been cleaned before the other policeman saw it?'

The girl looked incredulous.

'Of course. We clean up three or four times a day. It's the sweat, you see,' she said, crinkling her nose. 'It lingers.'

'Okay, can you just run through what you remember about that day, the last time you saw the judge?'

The girl puffed her cheeks out even further, reminding Ross of one of those chubby-faced cherubs you see on Christmas cards.

'Well, it had been a really hectic morning. He came early for a swim just like every other day, demanding this and that, then sat reading his paper over there in his usual seat drinking his three-mint green tea; Twinings.'

She pointed to a corner seat by the revolving doors to the car park.

'And then we had all that kerfuffle with that awful woman.'

'Awful woman?'

'Miss Floyd. The manager had to speak to her because she hadn't paid her membership fee. She must have thought she could swim here for free, like at the council pool in town. She'd had the discount introduction for the first month as well. Flipping cheek.'

'So the manager was distracted dealing with her while the judge was here?'

'Not really. It didn't take long, and the judge was out by then. That pair usually swam at the same time, but I didn't see her go through to the pool that morning.'

'What was she doing here then? Did she have a treatment booked?'

The girl gave out a particularly piggish snort. 'Miss Floyd? You must be joking. She doesn't even tint her hair, just lets it hang there, grey. Even my gran bothers to get her hair tinted, and she's sixty-three.'

She said the number as if her gran was right up there with Methuselah. Sixty-three didn't seem that old to Ross, but he supposed it might have done when he was in his twenties. The girl continued.

'So, we lost two nightmare members in one day; result I say.'

Ross didn't bother reminding the girl one of those 'nightmares' was now dead.

'Miss Floyd was difficult?'

'Oh yes. I'm glad she won't be around anymore. The manager gave her her marching orders. All I did was ask her to come into the back office to have a word, you know, a quiet reminder about the fees, and she kicked off big time. Then she nearly crashed into another one of our guests on her way out. Practically ran Mrs Reynolds off the road.'

'Really?' Ross's interest was piqued.

'Yes, poor Mrs Reynolds was quite shaken up by the whole thing. I insisted she report it, and we rang you lot, but I don't expect you did anything about it.'

'And you're absolutely sure this was the same day as the judge swam here for the last time?'

'Yes,' the girl huffed. 'I know it was that day because I'd had a few days off, and she'd been a nuisance the last time

I'd been in too. I remember thinking I could do without coming back to this.'

'In what way had she been a nuisance before?'

'She'd lost her fob with her passcode on it, and I'd had to show her how to override the system to unlock the lockers. I told her "if you're elderly and can't manage, you should hand your fob in".'

Ross felt a quiver of excitement tickle his neck.

'Could you give me this lady's details?'

'Like I said, Mrs Reynolds already rang them in.'

'Nevertheless, if I could have them too.'

The girl preened herself before getting up to walk back behind reception to retrieve Philippa Floyd's address. Ross flipped over his notepad.

'Well, thank you very much, Tia …' he attempted to pronounce her name before giving up, '… Miss. You've been very helpful.'

The girl flashed a self-satisfied smile. 'You're welcome.'

Ross headed for the exit. Just as he was about to push the revolving door, she shouted after him:

'By the way, if you'd like a voucher, there are some there on the table. We've got a special offer on for gentlemen at the moment; the full back, sack and crack wax for fifty pounds.'

Ross kept walking.

Chapter Twelve

PINKIE WATCHED the car pull up and the policeman get out. It was clear what he was, even in plain clothes. The measured way he cast his eye over the building as he closed the car door, assessing everything, exactly the way she would have in his position. He was alone, so was he there to interview rather than arrest her? The question was, why? Was it because she was one of the last people to see Carlisle alive, or was she a suspect?

There was only one way to find out; let him in but not quite yet. She knew how to play this game. If she answered the door before he reached it, he'd assume she'd been expecting him. It would beg the question why would she be expecting a visit from the police unless she saw herself as a person of interest, and if she did, surely he should too. No, she'd make him wait, her face painted with surprise when she finally opened the door. Whoever got the upper hand in the first few minutes of an interrogation often won the day, and it wasn't always the one being questioned. She'd heard tales from colleagues of suspects falling asleep amid brutal interrogations. She'd even heard of one terrorist at Guantanamo who slept through waterboarding. Now wouldn't that be disheartening?

Misdirection was always the primary weapon where mind games were concerned. All you had to do to gain the upper hand was shift the balance.

She felt fairly confident she'd disposed of all the evidence. She'd had the unhappy task of clearing the greenhouse and burning the plants, including the rosary pea, in a steel oil drum at the end of the garden. It had been rather sad watching all those years of careful nurturing wilt and crackle to ash. She'd be lying if she said she hadn't been tempted to keep one seed, but she'd resisted. She couldn't be ruled by sentiment at a time like this. In hindsight, the rosary pea had been a tad flashy for the job at hand. It had attracted way too much attention. There were other plants less showy and equally good for purpose. It wasn't the end of the world. After all, plants didn't have the limitations people did. So long as you could find a seed or cutting, you could start afresh.

She had a feeling she, too, would have to start afresh if this interview didn't go to plan. She could see via her porch camera the policeman was almost at the door. Of course, everyone has one installed these days, linked to their phone. It was hard to walk through a supermarket without hearing the familiar alert pinging through the aisles as people checked their Amazon parcels had arrived.

It was a blessing for the likes of her, who'd always required security but had previously needed to justify why. Nervousness after a burglary or intimidating cold-callers, you name it, she'd used it in the past. She answered the door with a dishcloth in her hand.

'Hello, can I help you?'

The man was sporting a couple of days' stubble, and she deduced he was, therefore, a senior detective. Lesser ranks wouldn't get away with it. He flashed his warrant card confirming it.

'Good afternoon, Miss Floyd. Detective Inspector Trenear. I'm conducting routine interviews with members of the St. Piran Spa concerning Fenton Carlisle. You may have heard about the investigation in the news?'

'Yes, of course; a terrible business and here in Cornwall where you just don't expect something like this to happen.'

'Do you mind if I come in? I would normally have rung to make an appointment, but I was interviewing another member not far from here and thought I'd drop by on the off-chance. If it's not convenient, I can come back another time.'

Clever, thought Pinkie, *but a bit too much detail for it to be the truth*. She could teach the police a few things about interview tactics, given half a chance. Keep it simple would be at the top of the list, along with debunking the myth your detainee was lying if they looked to the left when you asked a question.

'No, not at all. I was just washing up the breakfast dishes. Come through.'

Pinkie could feel the detective's eyes burning into the back of her head. If he was worth his salt, he'd be taking it all in – her height, weight, approximate age and what she was wearing; cut-off M&S trousers, Crocs and a red hoodie that had seen better days.

She decided to take him through to the kitchen. Kitchens were anonymous rooms provided you avoided posting your calendar on the fridge.

'I'm afraid I won't be much help to you. The man was a

very private person. I don't think I spoke more than a dozen words to him the entire time I was a member.'

'You're not a member anymore?'

Pinkie guessed he already knew that. He'd done his homework.

'No, no, I'm not. Let's just say I decided the benefits didn't warrant the expense. I joined to swim, but they were constantly pushing the treatments, trying to get me to invest, offering a free facial once a month if I paid an extra hundred pounds a year. You know the kind of scam, I'm sure. I wasn't interested and got the feeling my reticence meant I was not ideal membership material as far as they were concerned.'

'I see. But whilst you were a member, you swam at the same time as the judge every day?'

'Yes, but as I said, we didn't speak.'

'Can I ask, did you notice his poor eyesight?'

Pinkie felt a hot rush of adrenalin as she weighed up her response. She knew the pause was a fraction too long. Trenear's stare, like a surgeon's knife, dissected her face, and she knew if she faltered, he'd construe she had something to hide. A lie detector test would have recorded a change in temperature and increased pulse rate. Whether a test had been invented to detect her roiling stomach, she wasn't sure, but it was real nonetheless.

'Yes, I did, as it happened, only because he seemed to need a lot of assistance to enter and exit the pool, especially when negotiating the steps in the shallow end, which I noticed had ridiculously faint markings. I missed my footing a couple of times. Why, do you think he took the poison the papers are talking about by accident because of his poor eyesight?'

'It's just background information, but it's useful to get a

fuller picture of the man and any disability which might have made him vulnerable, say, at night when he didn't have the benefit of the contact lenses I understand he wore.'

Pinkie didn't believe a word of it.

'I understand from the reception staff at the spa you had a run-in with another car on the last day you swam with the judge at the club?'

Pinkie spotted the attempt to trip her up. 'I didn't swim that day. I realised when I got to the changing rooms I'd foolishly left my costume at home drying on the line. Then as I was about to leave, I was called into the office by the manager to discuss the renewal of my membership. As I said before, I declined.'

'As it happens, it was the last day at the spa for the judge too.'

'Gosh, there's a coincidence,' Pinkie said, trying to keep the sarcasm out of her voice.

'Can you tell me about the accident?'

'Oh, it wasn't an accident; there was no collision. I was leaving and a Range Rover coming the other way ran me off the road and onto the verge. It was something of nothing.'

'It was enough for the other party to report it to us.'

Pinkie didn't have to feign shock this time.

'What? She reported me when she was the one at fault? She was driving like a mad thing in that monster of a car. I had to slam the brakes on.'

'She said you were rather brusque when she stopped to check how you were.'

'Nonsense,' Pinkie said, annoyed now. 'I was perfectly fine but the persistent young woman seemed hell-bent on taking care of me as if I were an invalid. I had just argued with the manager and cancelled my membership. I had no intention of being dragged back in there to ask for anything from that lot. I wouldn't have gone back in if my leg was hanging off.'

Trenear cracked a smile that lit up a rather handsome face. Had she won him over a little, at least? She could work with that if she had. If not, she might have to put another plan into play.

'Would you like some coffee?' she asked.

'Yes, that would be lovely.'

'Why don't you go outside on the patio while I make it? It's such a lovely day.'

Chapter Thirteen

ROSS WANDERED AROUND THE GARDEN, enjoying the sweet fresh smell of morning grass rising in steamy whispers. A pathway bordered by flowering shrubs led to a wooden greenhouse in the far corner, its windows running with condensation.

His grandad had been obsessed with growing veg. Ross remembered the smell of tomatoes ripening when you slid back the greenhouse door and the taste of their warm red flesh on his tongue.

He peered in through the windows. It was completely empty of any greenery. His mother's greenhouse was already filled to brimming point with trays of pot marigolds and petunias ready to be put out once the last of the frosts had passed. Miss Floyd was clearly a gardener, and he wondered why hers was a wasteland.

Sliding the door open, he stepped inside, taking in the tangy smell of dank soil. The layout was familiar to him, scrubbed slatted benches above shallow earth beds; a pile of terracotta pots neatly piled in a corner along with a stack of black plastic seed trays still in their cellophane wrappers. On the shelves above his head sat the usual gardener's weaponry. Slug pellets, sprays to combat greenfly and tomato feed, all designed to tame nature and, in this particular case, all organic. Nothing unusual, other than at the end of the shelves, sat a large box of latex gloves. His mother wore gardening gloves but never latex, after all, what protection would they give against rose thorns and brambles? They were more his cup of tea; the blue variety a familiar part of his uniform. He knocked himself back, his father's words in his ear; *steady boy, don't get ahead of yourself.* Looking down at his feet, he noticed the concrete pavers running through the centre of the greenhouse were textured to resemble the sawn sections of fallen tree trunks.

Why not use the real thing? he thought, then remembered his grandad telling him the importance of meticulous cleanliness in a greenhouse to stop cross-contamination - just like a crime scene. It was then something wedged between two of the pavers caught his eye. Though small, it stood out because of its bright red colour. At first, he thought it might be a dead bug that had managed to get itself trapped in the stifling heat of the empty greenhouse, but when he bent down to get a closer look, he could see exactly what it was. He'd spent night after night looking at photographs of it. *Abrus precatorius*, the rosary pea. The scarlet seed thought to have been used to kill Judge Carlisle.

He froze, stunned by the ridiculous proposition that the substance being investigated by the counter-terrorist team had been found in this woman's garden. Granted, Philippa Floyd knew the victim and admitted to having seen him on the last day he'd been reported alive but even if she had opportunity and means, what on earth was her motive? She'd said she'd hardly even spoken to the judge. Plus, there must be hundreds of seeds out there the same colour. He'd seen his mother labelling seed trays so she could tell one variety from the other. That had to be it, and the rest was a coincidence, surely?

He felt a rush of nausea, but then suddenly, despite his objections, the inner policeman kicked in. Reaching into his top pocket, he retrieved his biro. He lay it on the floor and stamped on it, shattering the plastic casing. Taking one of the plastic shards, he manoeuvred it to lift the seed from its hiding place. Then, balancing the seed carefully, he reached for one of the latex gloves from the shelf.

His hands were sweaty, and he knew he didn't have time to put it on. He held the glove flat on his palm and tipped the bright red seed onto it. Wrapping the glove around it, he slipped the seed into his pocket along with the remnants of the broken pen retrieved from the ground. He left the greenhouse just as Philippa Floyd came out of the kitchen with the tray of coffee.

Ross took a deep breath. He wasn't sure what to do, or rather, he knew exactly what he should do. He should ask her to accompany him to the station to answer some questions before she had the chance to engage her brain and line up her defensive ducks in a row. Two things were holding him back - disbelief and fear of being wrong. He'd look a complete idiot. He could just imagine the look on the faces of the anti-terrorist team that had taken up residence in his office. Oh yes, they'd love a laugh at the expense of the Cornish plods. They'd live off it for weeks. Not to mention what it might do to the genuinely nice lady he was accusing if the press got hold of the story she'd been taken in for questioning. It didn't bear thinking about. He couldn't risk it. The seed in his pocket was more likely than not, some harmless variety, and there would be no going back. No, he'd pop the seed into the lab for analysis before he jumped the gun and confronted the woman.

'I've just had a call from the station. I'll have to give that coffee a miss, I'm afraid.'

'I'm sorry I couldn't be more helpful, but as I said, the judge was a very private man.'

The woman walked him back through the kitchen and out the front door.

On the step, he turned to face her. 'Your garden is lovely, but I couldn't help noticing there was nothing in your greenhouse. My mother's is full to brimming point this time of year.'

'As is mine usually, but I had a biblical plague of whitefly a couple of weeks ago. I had to burn everything in it and fumigate the place.'

'Ah, that explains it,' he smiled, turning to walk away, 'and thanks again.'

Back in the car, he checked the woman had gone back inside before opening his glove compartment and pulling out an envelope. Discarding the contents, he gently retrieved the latex glove from his pocket. Making sure it stayed tightly wrapped around the seed, he placed it in the empty envelope, resealing it as best he could before depositing the paperwork into the compartment and closing the door.

AS HE DROVE AWAY, Ross rang his friend, Rob Devlin, a senior forensics analyst at the lab in Plymouth.

'Rob, can you do me a favour? There's a drink in it for you. I think I might have found one of the seeds the judge was poisoned with. To be honest, mate, I'm not a hundred per cent sure, and you know what it's like around here at the moment. It's becoming a bit competitive. I don't want to let the side down.'

Rob Devlin's response was suitably droll. 'Sorry, friend. I think you've got the wrong number. Try Porton Down. They'll give you the heads-up on your seed. Or if they can't help, try Monty Don.'

'Ah, come on, mate? I can have it with you in an hour.'

'Where exactly did you find this seed you think might be deadly?'

'Trust me, you wouldn't believe me if I told you.'

Chapter Fourteen

SOMETHING about that final question sent Pinkie heading for the greenhouse the minute the detective's car pulled away. As she slid back the doors, she knew he'd been inside. A latex glove hung from the box on the shelf the way they did when you pulled one free. She had used three of the one hundred pairs but knew if she emptied the box, at least one additional glove would be missing. There could be only one reason for Detective Inspector Trenear to feel the need to slip on a latex glove; to preserve evidence or search for something he thought might be dangerous. Neither scenario boded well for her.

She slid the greenhouse door shut behind her, walked back to the house and headed upstairs.

The suitcase on top of the wardrobe was, as always, packed. She lifted it down onto the bed before slipping off her clothes and heading for the bathroom.

Reaching into the cupboard under the sink, she retrieved a box of natural brown permanent hair dye, perfect for covering grey, or so the blurb on the back promised. She opened the box and mixed the contents in the bottle supplied before applying it carefully so as not to miss a single strand. Forty minutes later, having washed it out, she was drying a glossy mane of chestnut hair, which she tied back into a sleek chignon. She looked fifteen years younger, which of course, was the plan.

Although she longed for a decent haircut, she'd had fun going au natural for the last few years and didn't relish the root touch-ups from here on in, but she was used to it. She'd be hard-pressed to think of a hair tone she hadn't tried before, though brown had been her natural colour and suited her best. More importantly, it was a match for the photograph in the passport she'd chosen to use for the second part of her mission; the part that would reunite Liz with her grandson.

She pulled on a pair of jeans, designer trainers, a white blouse and a fine-knit cashmere sweater. Layers were always best for travelling. She walked around the bed and unscrewed the finial on the left-hand side of the wrought iron headboard. Reaching inside the hollow rail, she retrieved the keys to her lockup outside Truro, where her second car and the rest of her things were stored, including her travel bag, passports, credit cards and a little cash in various denominations. Lifting her laptop from the bedside table, she made a reservation for that evening; business class, one-way to Lisbon.

Part II

Chapter Fifteen

PINKIE SAT at her usual table in the lounge bar of The Hotel Britannia off the Avenida da Liberdade. Biting into her *pastéis de nata*, she savoured the sweetness of the custard tart, licking the buttery crumbs from her lips. Washing it down with the last of her syrupy expresso, she was ready to face the day.

The hotel had always been her favourite place to stay in Lisbon since her grandmother had taken her there for a weekend break in her teens. The art deco interior oozed old-world glamour. The honey-coloured cork flooring laid in a geometric pattern, the mirrored walls and brass fittings. It was like a scene from *The Great Gatsby*. Omar Sharif was rumoured to have played bridge in this hotel. In its time, it had entertained poets and intellectuals, free-thinking politicians and those who liked to watch the roulette wheel spin until dawn. Henry Miller had met friends in this very lounge long before he married Marilyn and looked despair in the eye. In its day, it had been a hotspot for scandal, radicalism and conspiracy. She felt she was keeping good company.

She'd booked a suite with a ridiculously decadent turquoise tiled bathroom complete with roll topped tub. Up to her neck in bubbles the evening she arrived a week ago, she'd felt like an old-school film star herself. The hotel was select, with only a handful of rooms; no children or large groups. There was no pool or restaurant. She liked it that way. The foodie in her preferred the goodies the local eateries had to offer, and in her experience, fellow guests tended to sidle up to you in hotel restaurants if they noticed you were eating alone, and the last thing she needed was company. She was here on a job after all.

The staff knew as much about her as she'd chosen to feed them over the years. As far as they were concerned, she was Stephanie Nixon, an American widow with a love of all things European. She co-ran her late husband's business with his two brothers, Abe and Larry. They specialised in importing antiques and decorative fine art for sale in their store on the West Coast. On the side, she indulged her flare for textiles, operating a niche interior design showroom.

Absorbed with swathes of fabric and mood boards, putting looks together to wow her clients on her return, her fellow guests noticed but never bothered her. It wouldn't matter if they did. She could bluff her way through interior design. If asked, she'd tell them she had a home in LA and an apartment in New York, near her imaginary son Rory, his French wife Fabienne and her grandchildren Arthur and Amélie. Her imaginary daughter Mindy still lived at home with her. They were close but not without their problems. Rory was a recovering addict, and Mindy had an eating disorder and a tendency to whine. She didn't worry unduly; unlike real parents, she could get rid of her offspring easily.

She could invent a terrible tragedy. A car crash for Rory; perhaps a cult for Mindy. The possibilities were endless if you had imagination, and she had it in spades.

Imagination had been the key to her success as an operator. It was why she'd outlived adversaries and colleagues alike, many of whom had lost their lives through lack of imagination. They, unlike her, never bothered to conceive their ends.

She, on the other hand, was prepared for the worst. There wasn't a death in the catalogue of terrible deaths she hadn't conjured for herself. She liked to think if she was ever on the receiving end of a fatal attack, she'd see it unfold seconds before, in slow motion like a shootout in a Spaghetti Western.

'More coffee, madam?'

'No, thank you, I'm fine, dear.' Pinkie smiled up at the doe-eyed waitress.

She pondered why she only used 'dear' when in the guise of an American and concluded it sounded patronising and dated with a British accent. She'd had a boss in the services who called her 'dear girl'. It smacked of privilege and upper-class superiority and had always riled her.

She checked her watch. It would take about forty minutes to weave her way along the promenade to the hairdressers. She'd dyed her hair in a rush when she'd had to leave Cornwall, and whilst it wasn't a bad job given the circumstances, it wouldn't cut the mustard with the people she needed to impress over the next few days. A trim and some highlights would do the trick, along with a manicure and salt brush Turkish massage to make her tired skin glow.

Her imaginary husband had been dead for five years and had left her financially independent. It had to look that way. She could thank her lucky stars her father's genes kept her lean and athletic. Her body had not surrendered to matronly softness yet. Once, she would have changed her look as easily as slipping on a new pair of shoes. It had been fun, but nowadays, it was a drag.

She'd got too comfy in Cornwall. The suitcase she'd packed had seen her through the first few days, but the clothes were not quite up to par for an interior designer working on a luxury villa. A couple of outfits in the windows of the upmarket boutiques near the hotel had caught her eye, and she reconciled herself to her bank balance taking a battering. Usually, she would have put the purchases down as expenses, but this one was on her. Then again, it was only money. It wasn't like she had anyone else to spend it on, and if things went well and she delivered Liz's grandson back to her, it would be worth every penny to see the expression on her friend's face.

Chapter Sixteen

THAT EVENING PINKIE stepped into the hotel lobby scrubbed, primped and pedicured. Hermès scarf tied loosely around her neck, white palazzo pants and a midnight blue silk shirt. She looked the part. She handed her keys to the porter behind the desk, who moved swift as an arrow to open the heavy glass door for her.

'*Obligado*,' she smiled, pushing a crisp new note into his hand.

Although the evenings here were not bathed in the late light she enjoyed so much in Cornwall, the air held on to the day's warmth, and she didn't need a jacket or wrap.

She'd arranged to meet her contact in a quirky bar called The Yellow Gecko. The place had become a widely-known secret since the likes of TripAdvisor had homed in on it. Once pointed out, it was hard to ignore with its giant yellow lizard above the solid door firmly closed to casual passers-by. Tourists soon learnt you had to book ahead and press a buzzer when you arrived. If they liked the look of you, they let you in. If not, they didn't. The place had a mysterious, illicit vibe, nineteen-twenties speakeasy style. She'd been there many times before but not since lockdown and was pleased it had survived and, what's more, had not felt compelled to change.

'Welcome back, madam. So good to see you again.'

'You too, Dana,' replied Pinkie smiling at the elegant hostess who led her down the dimly lit staircase to the even darker basement.

'Would you like a table?'

'Maybe later. I'm expecting someone. I'll wait at the bar.'

'Of course, please let me know if you change your mind.'

'Thank you,' Pinkie smiled, surveying the mesmerising array of concoctions reflected in the mirror.

'What would you recommend to a gin drinker?' she asked as the whiskered mixologist slipped a small white napkin in front of her. He was a new face.

'You could try one of our signature cocktails, maybe an Aviator,' he replied in an accent she recognised as Eastern European.

'What's in it, other than the gin, I mean? I'm a bit of a traditionalist as far as alcohol is concerned and the name makes me nervous. I'd like to walk rather than fly home to my hotel.'

He got the joke and was bright enough to counter.

'Not to worry, it's low octane. London Gin, cherry and rhubarb liqueur and a hint of lavender.'

The first two sounded fine to her. She preferred things on the sour side, but the lavender smacked of old ladies' knicker drawers, so she thought she'd give the Aviator a miss.

'I'm afraid I'm not that adventurous. How about a Gimlet instead?'

'Perfect choice,' he smiled.

As he worked his magic, she swivelled on her stool, checking out the clientele, mostly couples or groups of four. Chunky candles flickered on the tables, casting long shadows in a room otherwise so dimly lit it was impossible to get a proper look at those wedged in the far corners. She noticed several people in the room were smoking.

'You can still smoke here?' she asked, reaching to take a tentative sip of her green-tinged cocktail, sharp, just as she liked it, with plenty of lime and a hint of saltiness from the sea fennel floating in the mix. Delicious.

'Yes, madam. This place is treated like a private members club. Different rules.'

She inhaled the air.

The smell of booze and tobacco brought back memories of her parents and their parties, of fish bowls full of cocktail Sobranie. Of slim-hipped women balancing gold-tipped cigarettes. She inhaled deeply, remembering the sexual tension lacing the smoke as men circled other men's wives, leaning in to light them up, whispering in their ears, licking their lips with desire.

It all seemed so tame now. She imagined today's equivalent would be less romantic; a bag of coke procured by the hostess from the dealer she kept on speed dial along with her therapist and children's music teacher. A sweaty fumble in the stairwell and a vomit in the loo before bedtime.

There was nothing sensual about the tension she felt this evening. It was fixed like a knot in her stomach which by now was beginning to rumble.

To her left, a foursome tucked into a platter of lean Iberian black pork and São Jorge cheese. She was about to ask for a dish of olives when she felt a tap on her shoulder. She turned to face Ewan.

'You're late,' she said, the reprimand part jest, part not. Tardiness annoyed her and he knew it. She'd worked with him for enough years to know if he was late it was no accident.

'You're lucky I'm here at all,' he replied, sliding onto the stool next to her. 'Why couldn't we meet somewhere I could get a decent pint? Plus, you can hardly see your hand in front of your face in here,' he coughed.

Ewan Davies was the best marksman she had ever had the pleasure to work with. He was also the messiest drunk she'd ever known. He was never nasty in drink, quite the contrary. He was the sort who asked a girl to dance, not noticing the boyfriend glaring from the bar; who, if he spilt someone's drink, bought a round for the whole pub; the sort who woke up in the early hours on a train he had no recollection of boarding. She had picked the place precisely because it didn't serve beer, and she'd never known him to touch anything else.

'You used to smoke when I first knew you,' she teased.

'None so zealous as the converted,' he said.

'You're right there.'

He leaned back on his stool to get a good look at her. 'You're looking alright for an old bird. How long has it been?'

The comment from someone else may have been met with a swift knee in the groin, but from him, she took it as a compliment of sorts. They'd always had one of those relationships where insults were lobbed but never meant to sting. She played the bossy sister to his annoying kid brother.

'Not long enough,' she rallied.

He, too, had weathered well. He had never carried a spare inch of flesh, although how he managed that given his diet had always baffled her. His dark hair was still thick, and his blue eyes still smiled even when his mouth didn't.

'So what's this all about?' he asked, twiddling a toothpick he'd pulled from a tortoise shell holder on the bar.

'True friends shouldn't ask questions or be quick to judge.'

'What a load of horseshit. Where did you get that from, a cracker? True friends have a duty to ask questions, especially when they're worried and are by far the best people to judge.'

'It's personal. That's all I'm prepared to say.'

'I bloody knew it. Is it the father? Did you do a job and not get paid? Or is he an old flame? Mind you, he's not your usual type; he's a dumpy fucker; face like a slapped ass.'

Pinkie laughed. 'Give me some credit … no, it's a favour for a friend, a very deserving friend who's run out of options.'

Pinkie thought of Liz, her daughter, husband and grandson and wondered why she was risking everything on this mission; why it was so important to return what remained of Liz's family to her. If she was honest, she knew why. She'd reached that time of life when having no family of her own had begun to gather importance. She had no one to care for and none to care about her, not in the way Liz cared about her grandson. She was utterly, utterly alone and running out of time to do anything about it. She'd always assumed she had years to make those life-changing connections, to fall for someone and retire, to build a proper life, but time had played a spiteful trick on her. The older she got, the more intransigent and wary she'd become. Even if she could get over her scepticism, how could she find the kind of relationship she craved when there could be no honesty? Whole chapters of her life would need to be redacted. The truth could only compromise and endanger.

'That's something, I suppose.' Ewan continued. 'I was worried for a second you'd let your standards slip living in the back of beyond, as far from the hub as you can get without falling off the edge into the sea. What the hell do you do with yourself all day?'

'Hey, city boy, Swansea's hardly a metropolis. Anyway, there are plenty of good-looking men in the sticks, and I thought you Celts stuck together.'

'We do, especially on match days when we're playing the English, but the Cornish are English, aren't they?'

'Don't you let them hear you say that. I can tell you I learnt that lesson the hard way, but I've settled in now, and I keep myself active. I walk and garden a bit,' Pinkie said, thinking of the rosary pea.

'Jesus. I told Matt I'd thought you'd lost it, and I was right.'

The mention of his name was a blade between the ribs. Even in the dim light, she could see Ewan's face redden as he realised the slip.

'You've talked to Matt about me?'

She drained her glass, spilling the last trickle on her new blouse as she rose to leave, anger roaring in her ears.

'I only mentioned you were here in Lisbon, that's all.'

She was furious. 'You had no right …'

'Look, I'm sorry okay? Please just sit down and let me explain.'

Reluctantly, she sat back down.

'I didn't think you'd mind. It's been such a long time, I thought you'd come to terms with it. He was pleased to hear you were here. He's on his own now, you know.'

She didn't know. She'd made it her business never to think about Matthew Eastley, let alone keep up with his news.

'He and his second wife, the Portuguese one, divorced. She went back to college to retrain as a ... psychologist, I think. She ran off with the tutor. There were no kids so ...' he floundered, clocking her glowering face. 'I'll shut up, shall I?'

'I should if I were you,' Pinkie snapped, heart thumping.

She had first met Ewan and Matt when she was in her final year at Cambridge studying modern languages, living out of term time with her parents in Hereford. They were both in the army and friends of her brother. Rob had gone to Sandhurst as an officer cadet straight out of sixth form before going on to join the paras. It had always been on the cards. Their dad, who had been a warrant officer and served in Northern Ireland and the Falklands before retiring, had made it his mission.

The three of them were stationed together at Credenhill when they panned up for lunch one Sunday. Rob and Matt were roughly the same age but Ewan was a couple of years younger and slightly in awe of them both. It wasn't unusual for her brother to bring home waifs and strays. Rob had always collected friends like most kids collected Pokémon cards. He picked them up in the pub or on the train or when he was younger in the playground or at rugby practice. He was always at the centre of the group holding forth, mates hanging on his every word. His easy charm might have led to jealousy or even the kind of sibling rancour that lasts a lifetime if not for two things. Firstly, she adored her big brother as much as, if not more than, all the rest of his admirers put together. Secondly, Rob's life was cut short by a sniper's bullet the day after his thirty-second birthday whilst he was on undercover operations as a liaison officer for the UN in Sarajevo. The loss had been unbearable and she'd needed someone to blame. That someone was Matt. He was meant to be with Rob on the day he was ambushed but was hungover from the celebrations the night before. Rob had covered for him. She'd only learnt the truth when Ewan let it slip at the funeral. As Matt and Rob's comrades sang 'Lili Marlene' at the wake she'd been filled with fury. Fury at their bravado in the face of tragedy, fury at her father's pride at losing a son in service, but most of all, fury at Matt for letting her brother down. It had been so much worse because before his last tour of duty she and Matt had got engaged. They had made a commitment, and for the first and only time in her life, she'd fallen head over heels. She'd left him at the wake and when he rang the next day and every day after that for a month, she didn't take the call. After she sent back the ring he didn't call again and they hadn't spoken since.

'Go on then, what's he up to?' she asked partly out of curiosity and partly in a concerted effort not to show Ewan she was overly affected.

'He's with Europol, part of a cross-border task force working with the MAOC here in Lisbon.'

'MAOC?'

'The Maritime Analysis and Operations Centre.'

'Drugs?'

'No, not this time, he's sharing intelligence with them on something else.'

Pinkie knew a little about Portugal's decriminalisation of drug taking. Heroin addiction had been at record levels and HIV rife prior to this The average tourist holidaying in the Algarve had been oblivious to the sobering truth they were venturing into one of the drug capitals of Europe. Nevertheless, whilst it never appeared in the brochures, it was easy to find if you had a mind to look.

'What then if not narcotics?'

Pinkie was well aware joint task forces were difficult set-ups at the best of times, let alone when they required cross-border co-operation.

'People traffickers.'

'Ah.'

'The cynical bastards taking advantage of those desperate enough to risk their lives in an inflatable dinghy.'

'So Matt's developed a social conscience. Better late than never, I suppose.'

'Beats dodging landmines, and he gets to keep his army pension. You know he still talks about you, about those days round at your parents' house.'

'Yeah, well, like you said, it was a long time ago.'

The uncomfortable silence told them both it was time to move the conversation on. Ewan passed her a note, a phone number and one word written on it. BARFLY.

'If you need me ring that number and say the word. Whoever answers will know how to reach me.'

'Okay, but only if I'm desperate.'

'Fair enough, let's hope it doesn't come to that. Do what you need to do and get the hell out of there, but this ... this posh look is all wrong, totally wrong.'

'What are you on about?' Pinkie asked. She could usually read him, but she was bemused.

'For what I've set up.'

'What do you mean? As far as I recall all I asked you to do was root around for local info on the Joyces?'

'Here,' he said, lifting a folded brown envelope from his

inside pocket and slapping it down on the table. 'God, I need a drink.'

'Can I get you something, sir?' asked the bartender, one ear cocked.

Ewan eye-balled the man as if he were mad to ask.

Pinkie slipped open the envelope. Reaching inside, she pulled out a dozen or so photographs. Ewan watched her with amusement as she strained to see.

'Hope you wear your specs when you're on the job,' he snorted.

'On the job, I'm usually looking through the sights of a rifle.'

She could make out Gary Joyce lounging by a swimming pool, a stubby bottle of Portuguese beer in one hand, and a little boy she recognised as Liz's grandson Sam splashing about in the water with a dark-haired young woman.

'Where did you get these?'

Ewan hesitated, and for a moment, Pinkie thought he'd had a change of heart about the drink.

'Matt.'

'I thought you only told him the basics, that I was here?'

'I did, but Joyce's name slipped out, and then he got really interested. You know what he's like when that happens, like a dog with a bone.'

'Or a rat in your case.'

'Now hang on a minute—'

'How exactly does he know Joyce?'

'I don't know, but it's not a good sign. Not for Joyce and not for you either.'

'Who's the girl?'

'The nanny, or should I say ex-nanny.'

'She's not the nanny anymore?'

'No, that's where you come in.'

'Me?' Pinkie said, her voice rising an octave. 'What's it got to do with me?'

'The last one was given her marching orders from the grandfather after skiving off for a little afternoon delight with Gary and losing the kid. I'm thinking, in the circumstances, you should look a bit more Mrs Doubtfire, a little less Sharon Stone.'

Pinkie choked on her cocktail. 'You're joking. You're telling me you've got me a job as nanny to Lionel Joyce's grandson?'

'Don't be ridiculous,' Ewan replied, an impish grin splattered across his face.

Pinkie relaxed.

'I've managed to get you an interview tomorrow afternoon. Whether you get the job is down to you, Mary Poppins.'

Chapter Seventeen

EWAN PICKED his way through the crowds of alfresco drinkers spilling from the bars onto the lamplit piazza. He could murder a beer but not here. This crowd were too young and beautiful, and he had no intention of setting himself up as a middle-aged saddo to be poked fun at. He had plenty in the fridge back at his apartment where he could don his headphones and listen to Metallica without feeling like a dinosaur.

He began the long walk down the hill towards the harbour.

They'd said their goodbyes at the door. He'd leaned in to kiss her on the cheek only for her to turn at the last minute, forcing him to stamp a kiss on her forehead as if she were a child.

Yet another embarrassing moment to add to the catalogue.

She looked amazing. When she'd swivelled to face him, it was as if she'd reached up and plucked his heart from his chest.

He could never tell her, of course.

As usual, he'd smothered his feelings with a smart-ass quip, calling her an old bird. He winced at the thought of it. The whole sorry situation was embarrassing. Only a complete loser would go all these years without saying anything about how he felt.

It wasn't as if he was shy. His family back home in Wales called him 'Chopsy' because he talked too much. He'd been chatting up women since he was fourteen, for Christ's sake, but in her case, he'd given himself every excuse in the book not to ask her out over the years. He'd thought twice originally because firstly, he had been petrified of her old man and secondly, she was Rob's sister, and if things didn't work out it might mar their friendship. He'd prevaricated and been pipped at the post by Matt. After Rob was killed and she broke off her engagement, she'd made it clear she wanted nothing to do with men, especially the uniformed variety. Later, when they became colleagues in Special Ops, it had seemed inappropriate, and the tone set then had carried through to their freelance work. He'd shelved his feelings so many times the thing was hanging off the wall like a DIY disaster with the sheer weight of his frustration.

It wasn't as if he hadn't had plenty of opportunities. They'd worked together often and were a great team but there had never been any hint from her this could be anything more than friendship. He'd stood by when she'd flirted with other men when they were working away, dreading they might get a foot in the door he was too much of a pussy to knock on. He lay awake in the next room on those occasions imagining all sorts and letting his aggravation spill over into the next day. When she asked what was wrong, he'd made excuses; he'd been up all night with some girl he'd met in a club or had eaten a dodgy takeaway.

He'd let down his guard, let her see him warts and all so often he'd convinced himself she wouldn't be interested in a moody sod like him. Other times he'd played the joker only to find he'd become the joke but couldn't seem to help himself. Even now, on the wrong side of fifty and old enough to know better, he was still acting the fool. Why had he raised the subject of Matt when he couldn't stand the thought of him being back on the scene? To gauge her reaction, of course. To once again convince himself there was no point trying because he didn't have a chance. What kind of masochistic saddo did that make him? It wasn't as if Matt was good for her. He was a selfish bastard. He also hated to lose. He might as well forget about her if Matt had plans to rekindle something. He'd best keep out of it; leave the pair of them to do what the hell they wanted.

There was music coming from the open windows of the bar up ahead. He'd been there before. They served beer and tapas. He was tempted but decided he'd stick to his original plan if it was too crowded. He poked his head around the door. It was busy but not rammed. An older crowd was listening to a guitar trio and a striking grey-haired woman singing Fodo. He decided to brave it. He was Welsh, after all; he knew all there was to know about sad songs. He made his way to the bar and ordered two pints, the first of which he downed in one. He carried the second to a corner close to the guitar players and the sultry singer warbling heartache.

And so began a long evening that turned into a long night ending with him buying the band drinks and standing on a table to sing Delilah. His powerful tenor voice hewn on many a rugby tour, hushed the crowd as he bellowed his damaged heart out.

'I felt the knife in my hand and she laughed no more;

Why, why, why Delilah? ... Forgive me, Delilah, I just couldn't take anymore.'

He brought the house down.

Chapter Eighteen

PINKIE SET off early the next morning in her rental car to the Algarve. It was a three-and-a-half-hour uninspiring drive along the A2, so instead, she opted to turn south off the motorway towards Sines, taking the scenic route along the coast. It was a longer drive, but she had time and hoped the Atlantic breakers would be a steady distraction, a welcome reminder of Cornwall and home.

She wished she'd had more time to think the whole thing through. Ewan had certainly pulled out all the stops. Never in her wildest dreams had she imagined she'd be a cuckoo in the Joyce family nest this soon. She'd envisaged renting a property and routine surveillance at first. She'd talk to the locals on the periphery who might know them before she made her move. She had invented a design job close by. It would enable her to become a regular visitor to the neighbourhood. Most of the properties were second homes, and no one would be keeping track of comings and goings. A few rolls of fabric, a back seat littered with samples and a tape measure would do the trick. She'd thought she'd tail one or other of the Joyce's, maybe even play a round of golf as a guest at the golf club, build rapport. Joyce was a wealthy widower, and she was a glamorous widow of means. Why wouldn't they hit it off? She'd wrangle an invitation to visit, and sooner or later, he'd ask for help picking the wallpaper or the paint for the guest bedroom. She'd done it before with more difficult subjects than Joyce. She'd reckoned weeks, maybe even months of inveigling, but here she was heading for an interview with Gary and his father at their villa in Othos D'agua on the outskirts of Albufeira this very afternoon.

She was happy enough with the persona she'd cobbled together at short notice and was grateful she hadn't chucked all her Cornish clothes. The relaxed look would come in handy now. The face on the passport and driving licence was about right, and the identity had not been used before. She had told the hotel manager in Lisbon that she was off on a design job and to hold her room for a couple of weeks, so had been able to travel light.

Ewan had admitted it had been pure coincidence he'd heard about the nanny's post. He'd been exploiting his usual sources, registers as to residency and property records, to check if Gary Joyce's move to Portugal was permanent. He'd come across a planning application concerning Joyce's property and had clicked a link to a notice advertising a meeting in the town hall to discuss plans to build a substantial annexe in the grounds. There had been a separate link featuring the same address in the employment ads advertising for a nanny. He'd rung the paper on the off chance the position hadn't been filled, pretending to represent an agency specialising in qualified help for ex-pats. When told the job was still available, he'd fished for info on whether the family had employed a nanny before and why the previous candidate left in case there was anything about the child requiring specialist care. The advertising executive, cagey at first but after some silver-tongued persuasion, divulged there was nothing wrong with the little boy, but the previous nanny had been let go. The child had been left unattended and wandered out of the garden and down the cliff path to the beach. Luckily one of the builders working on the property had spotted him. He was a friend of her father's, and that's how she knew about it. For good measure, she'd added she was not surprised. The nanny had gone to work for the Joyce's as a cleaner and been promoted to the position. She had only been employed because she had good English, having worked in one of the local bars on The Strip in Albufeira. She was a party girl and certainly not qualified to look after a young child. Bingo.

Ewan followed up and got her the interview.

Pinkie had some sympathy for the girl. She felt equally out of her depth. Here she was heading off to become a nanny when she had never looked after a child in her life. To be honest, she didn't even like children much. From the little contact she'd had, they seemed as unpredictable as Labrador puppies and less easy to train. She wasn't even sure if she knew what she was expected to do. She'd had a friend who'd been an au pair in her youth but all she seemed to do was drive the kids to school and do the shopping. She was sure a nanny was required to do more but was she meant to teach or just make sure the child didn't choke or get run over by a passing bus? Would she be expected to have some sort of itinerary in mind for this interview? She couldn't think about it now. It would only make her more nervous and she needed to concentrate on the road.

She wondered what Albufeira was like these days. She'd visited in the eighties with a couple of friends. Which year exactly, she couldn't remember, but it was before uni. Back then, it had been little more than a fishing village, whitewashed houses with red-tiled roofs; only a handful of hotels freckling the undulating hillside. The travel guide she'd bought in the tobacconists on her way back to the hotel the evening before said the town was now the biggest resort in the Algarve, with the population swelling to three million at the height of the summer season. The photographs in the guide showed a long avenue of bars and nightclubs known as 'The Strip' where her predecessor had worked. There were numerous high-rise apartments and swanky hotels amidst boxy modernist villas built by those priced out of the Costa del Sol now the Russians had moved in.

Lionel Joyce's place looked restrained by modern standards in Ewan's photos, even a little dated. It sat wedged like an ugly sister between two sleek glass-fronted beauties doing their level best to grab the limelight.

Despite the lack of bling, it was on a huge plot, and it was a mystery how a Cornish councillor like Joyce could have ever afforded the place. According to Ewan, the photos were a few months old, and the villa was undergoing massive renovations. Apparently, Lionel Joyce now spent at least eighty per cent of his time there, possibly more since Gary had arrived with Sam.

The road hugged the cliffs widening only occasionally when she approached one of the many small fishing villages along the route. It was set to be another scorcher. Even here on the coast where she would have expected the sea breeze to sway the Monterey pines, there was a stagnant quality to the air that back in Cornwall would have heralded a storm but which here burned itself out by mid-morning. Even the silvery sea seemed to have given in to the heat. It lay flat and exhausted under the white-hot sun. She was glad she'd brought a bottle of water with her. She had thought she might stop along the way for a bite of lunch at one of the tavernas recommended in the guide, but as she lifted herself away from her seat, her blouse stuck to her back, and she decided against it. She was better off staying within the confines of the air-conditioned car. At least that way, she'd avoid turning up to her interview with embarrassing sweat patches under her arms.

By the time she was on the final approach to Albufeira, she'd wished she'd taken the fast route. The land was barren and dusty, completely unlike the verdant approach she'd remembered with its vineyards and picturesque smallholdings. Driving past Lidl and an enormous water park, her nose twitched as the unmistakable whiff of drains seeped through the air vents. Town planners like Lionel Joyce the world over had a lot to answer for.

As she took the left-hand turn to Othos D'agua, her stomach roiled. She wasn't used to interviews. Generally, her reputation went before her. It wasn't as if you could demonstrate the skills she offered; there wasn't much opportunity for a dry run in her line of business. Her satnav eventually led her past the mini-mercado and medical centre into a cul-de-sac lined with pine trees shading a mélange of old and modern detached properties. A few were the kind of places you would come across on any relatively affluent suburban housing estate in the UK, their huge gardens and long curved drives lined with hibiscus bushes belying their modest proportions. The newer properties, though flashier, occupied smaller plots nearer the road. Their angular roofs and two-storey glass extensions borrowed from *Grand Designs* had clearly been slotted in. Minimalist water features and architectural yuccas graced their handkerchief-sized lawns.

The Joyce residence – 'Casa Margarita' - which Pinkie

assumed was named unsentimentally after the cocktail rather than Lionel Joyce's dead wife who, if she remembered correctly from her notes, had been called Diane, occupied the largest plot at the end of the cul-de-sac. Hunkered down behind oleander hedges ablaze with cerise blooms, the house was invisible from the road.

Pinkie could see workmen in the distance fiddling with the gates to the property. As she drew closer from the signwriting on their van, she deduced they were electricians. They were installing a new security system, an expensive one.

In her experience, people only needed that level of security if they had something to protect or something to hide, and often the two went hand in hand. Either way, it meant her comings and goings would be closely monitored. She pulled in at the entrance, stopped by a spidery-limbed man in his early twenties, wearing tracksuit bottoms and a vest. As he leaned in the window, Pinkie sensed brutality behind the pale grey eyes that made her flesh crawl. She spotted the tattoo on his neck, a rose wrapped around a dagger encased in barbed wire. She recognised it immediately as gang-affiliated, telling those in the know he'd served time for violence before he'd reached eighteen. Whatever Matt thought Lionel Joyce was up to, it wasn't anything to do with the hospitality trade.

The man's blond, shorn head jolted upward with the unspoken question she answered without prompting.

'I'm here for an interview for the nanny's position. I'm expected.'

'Name?'

'Smith, Patricia Smith, Patti.'

The man, still leaning through the open window, tobacco breath hot on her cheek, turned his head to shout to his friend a few feet away. The second man, a carbon copy of the first save for his tatty scribble of a goatee, shouted back in Albanian, the gist of which Pinkie understood to be along the lines, 'the father will be pleased, no chance the son will be fucking this one. She's old enough to be his mother.'

She smiled as if oblivious as the man waved her through.

The drive skirted the garden boundary before snaking back towards the property, which from the angle of approach, appeared single-storey. She knew from Ewan's photos the building was split level, and the other side faced the sea. She charted her escape route the minute she arrived at any new location. Most people only looked for the entrance, but for Pinkie, exits were key. She rarely left a building the same way she entered. To the left of the bougainvillea-covered portico was a wide flight of concrete steps down to the gardens. It would be an alternative route back to her car without going through the house if she needed it.

Noticing out of the corner of her eye the pulsing light of yet another security camera, she rang the bell. She thought of the home camera system she'd installed that had given her five minutes grace to compose herself as DI Trenear walked up the garden path.

She was jolted back to the here and now by the creak of the heavy wooden door.

The woman who answered was short and round as a Christmas pudding, greying dark hair scraped back from a nut-brown forehead shiny with perspiration. The apron suggested a cook or a housekeeper, again grandiose given Joyce's background. According to Liz, he lived in an early seventies detached bungalow on the outskirts of Truro, nothing fancy. Here he had staff. Then again, anybody could afford help if they could get away with paying a pittance in exchange for free board.

Pinkie got in first before the woman had time to speak.

'Good afternoon. I'm Patricia Smith. I'm here for the interview for the nanny's position.'

Suspicious eyes raked her over from head to toe.

'Come in please. Mr Joyce will see you straight away.'

'You're very kind,' Pinkie said and noticed the smallest smile pull at the corners of the woman's mouth before she turned, beckoning her to follow.

'I'm Margarita.'

'Like the villa?'

'Yes, like the villa.'

Pinkie was relieved the woman spoke perfect English. Though her language skills were one of her primary assets and the reason she'd been recruited to the service in the first place, she'd decided not to divulge she could speak Portuguese. Ewan hadn't noted it on her CV, and she knew those around her would be less guarded if they thought she didn't understand the lingo.

The woman walked her down a short staircase to a massive reception room filled with dancing light. Glass doors led out to a level patio and one of the longest private pools Pinkie had ever seen. The doors were concertinaed open, and a warm breeze fluttered the voile curtains. Outside, a radio blared with an advert for plastic guttering over the buzz of an electric saw, and Pinkie guessed builders were working around the corner just out of sight.

Archways at either end of the room led to other open-plan spaces. To her left, Pinkie spotted a large American-style fridge and guessed the kitchen lay that way. Margarita led her through the right-hand archway into a lounge dominated by a massive plasma TV screen that took up the majority of the far wall. Sitting in a leather armchair with his back to it was Lionel Joyce.

'Thank you, Margarita,' he said, dismissing the woman before carefully folding the newspaper he was reading and slipping it down beside him.

The photograph Ewan had of Joyce in a dinner suit at some function or other was clearly years out of date. He'd appeared overstuffed and self-important, a man with his fat sausage fingers in every pie. Instead, she was faced with a frail-looking pensioner dressed in khaki shorts and a polo shirt at least two sizes too big. The combover she'd imagined stuck to his sweaty pate in this heat had gone. He was completely bald.

He gestured to one of the three enormous cushiony sofas in the room.

'Miss Smith, pardon me for not getting up. Take a seat.'

His voice was refined with the tinge of an Irish accent. She didn't know why but she'd expected him to have a West Country burr, but now she thought of it, the name should have given her a clue. He was so soft-spoken Pinkie found herself straining to hear him as she perched on the edge of the cream linen seat, which for all its plumpness, felt uncomfortable. She crossed and uncrossed her ankles, trying to pitch herself forward, hands clasped together in her lap for ballast. She would have preferred a more formal setting for the interview. She would have felt less exposed with the man on the other side of a desk. Here they had to sit close, their knees practically touching.

Joyce leaned forward to pick up a sheet of paper from the table she recognised as a copy of the CV Ewan had put together for her, and she'd spent the evening committing to memory. It contained a long list of her previous positions, and she expected to be quizzed on them.

'Impressive,' he said, scanning the sheet. 'I see from here your last post was in Dublin.'

'Yes.'

Damn it, Pinkie thought. Of all the places in the world, why the hell had Ewan picked Dublin? Knowing him, it was probably random. Maybe he'd been drinking Guinness that night. It was likely that given the man's accent, he had friends or family there and might decide to scrutinise her story. Ewan had at least the sense to attach her references to the CV, and the contact numbers given would go through to someone who had been briefed to say how marvellous she had been and how sorry the family were to lose her, but it was risky.

'You were with the family for several years there in Malahide. Why did you leave? I'm from Cork originally, although I left as a child, but I've heard it's a nice place to live. Doesn't Ronan Keating live there?'

Pinkie didn't have a clue.

He looked up now, removing his glasses and, for the first time, met her eye.

She took a deep breath.

'I'm a bit old for boy bands,' she smiled. 'It was the usual, my charges grew up and I became superfluous to requirements.'

'How do you feel about that?' Joyce asked, his stare uncomfortably intense.

She'd anticipated and formulated stock replies for all the typical interview questions she could think of and had even ventured off Ewan's CV and prepared a list of courses she had taken over the years to enhance her child-caring skills but had not thought Joyce would delve into her feelings.

She coughed, desperately trying to gather her thoughts.

'You get used to moving on. I specialise in younger children, and inevitably, they grow up. I try to take pleasure in seeing them progress. It's a reward in itself. Sometimes when the family is large, I get to stay longer, but there have been other times where there's one child, and I'm only there for a couple of years until they go off to boarding school. You come to accept these things.'

'And what made you decide to come to Portugal?'

'I'd been here on family holidays in my teens and loved it, and I was tired of all that Irish rain.'

'I'm with you there. I live in Cornwall when I'm in the UK, and it's not much better, but you won't see much rain here,' Joyce said, looking out to the garden where two sprinklers rotated a steady fine rainbowed spray across the pristine lawn sloping down to the cliff edge.

'We're going through an extended period of drought. You can blame global warming, but at least we can make use of the beautiful weather being so close to the sea. I suppose you've already been told your charge will be my grandson. Sam is seven and a half.'

'Yes.'

'He attends a local private school, so there will be no teaching as such, but you'd be in charge of seeing to him when he's here before and after school. The holidays are long like everywhere else these days. I want you to keep him occupied, not sitting watching TV.' He gestured to the massive screen behind him. 'That monstrosity is down to my son. I've avoided television in this house for nearly thirty years. He's here two minutes and this arrives. Sam is bright. He has a mechanical mind that needs to be engaged in activities.'

The conversation was suddenly interrupted by a

commotion outside, arguing followed by a large splash, then the sound of shouting and thrashing about in the water.

Lionel Joyce dropped the sheet of paper and rose with considerable effort from his seat. Pinkie did the same, following him as he moved gingerly on arthritic legs out onto the patio.

'You're a bloody bastard, and I don't want you to be my dad anymore. I hate you and never want to see you again. You're not a proper dad. Proper dads aren't mean like you ... go away, go away, I hate you. I hate you!'

Tear-choked curses stuttered from Sam Joyce's mouth as he flayed about in the water, fully clothed. The anger was visceral and uncontrolled. Raging as he was, he sounded like he meant every word, as if he instinctively knew he could survive the loss and would be better off without a man who thought it was funny to throw a child in the pool in a fit of anger. Despite the language, the words filled Pinkie with admiration for the boy with the firecracker temper.

Pinkie knew what bullies looked like; she'd been raised by one. She'd seen misery inflicted daily by her father, not violence but the sneering psychological kind or if the mood took him the silent treatment when he'd ignore her and her mother for days on end as if they were invisible. She'd spent the first fifteen years of her life wondering what on earth they could have done to make him behave that way. After all, he was hail fellow well met with everyone else. When, after he died, she plucked up the courage to ask her mother why he had been so cruel towards them, she'd told her it was because she was a girl. He hadn't even bothered to visit her in the maternity hospital.

She had been shocked to the core, thinking her mother

must be wrong or hiding something, but on quizzing her further, she'd been surprisingly frank.

'Your father wasn't an ignorant man. He never considered it your fault.'

She'd said this as if his actions were logical; as if it was right she should take the blame for being the wrong sex.

'That's because it wasn't my fault, and it's ridiculous in any event because you already had a boy. You had Rob.'

'He always thought he'd got it wrong with Rob.'

'What do you mean, got it wrong?'

'Rob was so … contrary, especially when he was little.'

It wasn't the Rob she remembered growing up. He was never what you could call rebellious. She had certainly enjoyed more freedom than him. Her father wanted his son to follow him into the army, to make a man of him. He monopolised Rob's every waking hour when he wasn't away with the army, mostly berating him for spending too much time in the kitchen with his mother and not enough outside in the fresh air. These things were partly remedied when Rob was packed off to boarding school in Monmouth, but her father still kicked off if he caught him chatting with her in her bedroom during the vacations and on one occasion when Rob had blue-tacked a poster of Bowie to his wall, she remembered her father ripping it down in a rage.

In the final analysis, she had come to believe she had got off lightly, and it was not such a bad thing being a girl in her family. Her father never ripped down any of her posters. He had, however, hit the roof when she'd crossed to the other side and joined the navy. She could remember his face to this day. Spittle-lipped, effervescent with rage as he ranted for a good twenty minutes. It was the only true reaction she'd got out of him in her entire life.

'Shut up, you little shit and give me your hand,' shouted

Gary Joyce through a false laugh designed to mask his embarrassment now the builders had stopped working to watch with grim-faced disgust, not for the child but the man.

'I don't need your help,' Sam shouted back.

'Give me your fucking hand,' cursed Gary, 'before I come in there and drag you out.'

'No.'

Pinkie rushed forward.

'Now, Sam,' she said. 'I want you to swim to the steps and get out. There's a good boy.'

Everyone looked, wondering who this woman giving orders was.

Lionel Joyce chipped in now.

'Do as Miss Smith says, Sam, there's a good lad.'

Gary stared at them both, face like thunder.

Sam did as they asked, and as he walked towards them, Pinkie reached for a towel to wrap around him.

Gary turned to face the workmen.

'What are you lot looking at? Get back to fucking work before I sack the lot of you.'

The men walked away, muttering amongst themselves.

Gary turned his attention to Pinkie and his father.

'Sam, why don't you go dry off in your room.' Pinkie said, dipping down to the boy's level and looking him in the eye to reassure him she had his back.

Sam looked nervously between her and Gary, who by now was striding purposefully their way.

'Who the hell are you?' he spat.

'This is Miss Smith, Sam's new nanny,' said his father, chin jutted forward as if daring his son to defy him.

'Is it fuck. I'll pick who looks after my kid, and it isn't gonna be this interfering old bitch.'

Lionel Joyce, who had managed to stay calm and collected up until this point, reddened, his blue eyes steely. 'And why's that, Gary? Is it because you did such a good job picking the last one? Out of interest, are you intending to pay for your excellent choices, or will that fall to me, just like it falls to me to pay for every cockup you make? Now for Christ's sake, take a shower and sober up before you make an even bigger show of yourself.'

Gary looked for an instant as if he might thump his father but thought better of it. Fists clenched by his sides, he followed Sam indoors.

Lionel Joyce turned to her.

'The job's yours if you want it, although I wouldn't blame you if you didn't after that spectacle.'

'I've seen worse.'

She could tell by his raised eyebrows he didn't believe her for one minute.

'If you are prepared to take us on, and may I say, on that performance alone, I'm delighted you are. When can you start?'

'Whenever you want me. I drove straight here, so I have all I need with me. I've reserved a room in town, but I can cancel if you wish me to start right away?'

'Excellent, why waste any more time? Margarita will show you your room. Take the rest of the day off to sort yourself out. You can start tomorrow.'

'Fine by me,' she replied, noticing Margarita was already standing by the patio doors waiting for her.

'I hope you won't think too badly of Gary. He and Sam have had a lot to deal with. Sam's mother took her own life, and neither of them has got over it. Such a tragedy.'

Any sympathy she had momentarily felt for this man evaporated like the rain-bowed spray from the sprinklers.

Chapter Nineteen

PINKIE SAT cross-legged on her bed. She needed to find a decent hiding place within the grounds to stash her gear. Whilst there was a bolt on the inside there was no way of locking the room when she was out. At the very least, Margarita or the cleaners would need access, plus she couldn't guarantee her room wouldn't be searched. It was too risky to carry this stuff with her all the time. It wouldn't do for the nanny to be caught with multiple passports and the spare burner phones shoved in her handbag. Ewan had been right about the security around the villa being ramped up.

She'd decided to wait until the household was taking its siesta before she unpacked. The area around the pool was quiet now everyone had retreated to the cool of the villa. Very sensible too. Only tourists hell-bent on taking home a tan were masochistic enough to barbecue their bodies in this blistering heat.

Pinkie had always admired the bravado of the average holidaymaker, the never wavering misconception tricking them into believing a fortnight of sunshine and the excitement of being rescued from a sinking pedalo could compensate for the other fifty weeks a year of rainy-day drudgery. She could do with a bit of their die-hard optimism right now.

Although she desperately needed a shower, she felt too hot for the steamy thrash of water, so decided instead to change out of her sweaty interview clothes and go for a swim. She packed her beach bag, placing a rolled towel on top to hide the plastic bag containing her passports and phones in case the whole scam went tits up before she'd had time to hide them. Her next move remained a mystery. Any ideas she'd initially considered had fallen by the wayside. Without a plan, she could hardly bring anyone else in despite knowing that without proper backup, she was vulnerable. She appreciated she hadn't had backup when she killed the judge but at least she had an end game in sight, whereas now she had none. She'd contemplated blackmail, but all she had was innuendo and hearsay from her friends in Cornwall and veiled hints from Ewan. Having met Joyce, she knew that wouldn't be enough. The man was astute. He would have covered his tracks over the years. What's more, he cared about Sam. Thinking about it now, she wondered why she'd ever assumed he wouldn't. Gary was the weak link here, but she'd already managed to seriously piss him off. This was going to be harder than she thought.

She could always neutralise Gary and his father and run. She hadn't brought any firearms, something she'd regretted the minute she'd seen the two goons at the gate, but Lionel Joyce was a frail old man, and his son was, from what she gathered, generally drunk or high. How hard could it be? She'd lay bets both were snoring in their beds right now and wouldn't put up a fight, but there was a fundamental flaw with this. She couldn't take the boy with her. He didn't know her yet, and she had no intention of forcing him to leave. Having him in the car would arouse suspicion. If he wasn't with her, she could tell the guys on the gate she wouldn't be taking the job after all and was leaving. She concluded the Joyces' deaths might only serve to complicate things further. The only certain mission statement she'd given herself on the plane to Lisbon was to get Liz's grandson home to her in one piece. The death of the boy's father and grandfather in their Portuguese holiday home would, at the very least, spark an investigation. The finger of suspicion may not point her way, but it could result in Sam being placed into care in Portugal. It might take months for Liz to get a suitable lawyer to wade through the red Euro tape that would follow, and even then, she might not succeed in winning custody. No, a very much alive Gary Joyce had to be made to voluntarily give up his son to his mother-in-law, and what's more, his overbearing father had to agree to go along with it.

She stepped as quietly as she could along the cool marble corridor back downstairs and out onto the veranda. The mirrored dance of the sun on the pool dazzled her for a second, and she retreated under an umbrella. She shook off her flip-flops, the pavers scorching the balls of her feet as she propped her bag against the leg of a lounger before shedding her robe to reveal the polka dot bathing suit she'd bought in Lisbon on her last shopping spree. It was too glamorous by far for her current persona, but it was that or nothing, and nothing would have raised a few eyebrows. She didn't intend to swim all afternoon, just long enough to freshen up. She resisted the urge to dive in, not wanting to make a splash. Slowly lowering herself into the deliciously refreshing water, she stood, eyes closed, letting it take the heat out of her body before beginning her laps.

She'd only taken up swimming as a hobby after moving to Cornwall. She'd passed all the compulsory training at Dartmouth naval college, of course. She could save a drowning man, tread water for two hours and make a pretty convincing life raft using her inflated uniform trousers and her belt, but she hadn't swum for fun until then. She'd joined a group of ladies who, every Saturday morning, no matter the weather, took to the water to indulge in wild swimming. They were called 'The Water Babes', and the first time Pinkie saw them in action one freezing October morning, she came away thinking they were out of their tiny water-logged minds. Nevertheless, not one to be beaten, she'd gone back the next week. The week after that, she had eventually taken the plunge and come to find pleasure in submerging her goose-pimply flesh in cold water. She'd certainly enjoyed it more than the chlorinated heat of the spa, but the sedate velvety warmth of Lionel Joyce's pool topped both. It felt decadent to float on her back with the sun on her face.

Eventually, she dragged herself away to dry off. Once dressed, she slipped her bag over her shoulder and headed for the long single-storey wooden building, which she guessed from the slow hum of machinery coming from within, housed the pump and filter system. Attached to it was a small summerhouse pitched above ground level on wooden legs, possibly once used as changing rooms before the house was extended to include a ground floor gym and wet room. Glancing behind to check no one was watching, she took the steps up to the narrow veranda and tried the door. It was unlocked.

Inside, the blue and white tiles lining the walls were

intact, but the paintwork was peeling. She noticed the putty around the window frames had shrunk and was crumbling away in places, and a couple of panes cracked. It had obviously been a pretty feature in the garden once.

She remembered her greenhouse at home in Cornwall, the proliferation of colourful flowers and vegetables before she'd had to burn the lot along with the rosary pea.

She wondered whether Detective Trenear had returned to search the house yet. That name bothered her; she knew it from somewhere. It hadn't struck her when he'd called, but afterwards, when she'd been rushing to get away, it had niggled. She couldn't think where she'd heard it. She shook it from her head, consoling herself with the thought whoever he was, he wouldn't find much. He'd discover from the paperwork on her desk the house was owned by a trust, and she'd been the tenant for six years. Trusts were perfect for masking the identity of the true owner. Switzerland had based a whole economy on doing just that. If he spoke to Agnes, he might learn about her career as a journalist and her charitable work but not much else, and if he'd taken the trouble to look for her, the trail would have gone cold at the Cornish border.

Thinking about it, she should at least have left a message on Agnes's answer phone saying she was going away for a couple of months. She could have told her an old friend recovering from a hip operation had called and asked if she could move in for a while during her recovery. She could have been purposefully scant on detail, trusting Agnes to embellish the story sufficiently as to cause the maximum confusion for anyone with the will to listen. She could kick herself for being so spooked by the visit and panicking.

She shook Trenear and Cornwall from her head. A post-mortem of her shortcomings wouldn't put them right.

She had to concentrate on the here and now, on this room's potential as a hiding place for her gear.

Despite her initial assumption, the building had never housed changing rooms. There was a large dresser at one end and a dusty table in the middle. She traced her finger through the dust and sauntered towards a tiny pot-bellied stove rusting in one corner. She couldn't imagine it had ever been used other than on the coldest of winter evenings or perhaps to boil a pot of coffee. The floorboards around it were blackened and brittle. She leaned all her weight against it, shoving it a few inches to the left. Utilising her damp towel as a mat, she lay on her stomach and felt beneath the stumpy iron feet. There was a hole underneath. The tray below had rusted straight through, allowing the cinders to fall onto the floorboard, which over time, had burnt away. It was lucky the whole place hadn't gone up in flames the first time it happened, but she guessed subsequently the ashes had fallen below the building and extinguished in the damp earth.

She decided to ask Lionel Joyce if she could use the building as an outside classroom for Sam, a place where he could make a mess outside the main house. If she could manage to take control of the building, make it her domain without arousing suspicion or the prying eyes of cleaners, it would be a safe place to hide her gear. Pleased she found a solution to at least one problem, she left.

Now the workmen had down tools for the day, she could hear the sea she had glimpsed at the bottom of the garden earlier and decided to go and take a closer look.

The grass felt plump and springy beneath her feet, quite unlike her lawn at home thatched with clover and dotted with brown patches where the local cats had paid a visit. The green path serpentined through rockeries and raised beds full of spikey agave, thickets of lavender and silvery leaved rock roses. It had all been carefully planned to withstand the drought conditions Joyce had talked about and to survive the daily assault of salt spray. The slope steepened nearing the end of the lawn, and she caught sight of the low picket fence marking the boundary. A table and chairs perched very near the cliff edge under the shade of a large palm tree acted as a full stop beyond which the cliff sloped away sharply.

To the left was a gate which she could see led onto steep steps down to the narrow beach below. She could understand why Joyce had sacked the nanny. No child should be left unsupervised here. But for an adult, someone wanting to make a quick getaway, now that was a different matter altogether.

Chapter Twenty

ROSS TRENEAR SWIVELLED in the unfamiliar chair to get a better look at the man who had hijacked his office just as Special Officer John Dyson looked up, arrogance slithering behind his benevolent smile like a snake that had just swallowed your children.

Ross had spent the afternoon weighing up his options and come to the conclusion they were far and few between. His mistake had been to sit on the test results for over a week despite knowing he'd been right about the seed he'd found in Philippa Floyd's greenhouse. It was *Abrus precatorius*, the rosary pea, and full of the same toxin responsible for Carlisle's untimely death.

He'd been cock-a-hoop the morning he received the confirmation from Rob Devlin. Heart pounding, the sheen of anticipation flushing his cheeks, he'd planned how he'd make the arrest and deliver the good news to those smug London bastards he'd caught their assassin.

But by lunchtime, doubt had begun to chisel at his resolve. After all, when it came down to it, what proof did he have the seed he'd found in Floyd's greenhouse came from the same plant as the one used to murder Carlisle? Hadn't he read the plant was commonplace in some parts of the world? It grew wild by the roadside in some countries where it was regarded as a weed. He'd read about one woman who had bought a hand-built wooden train back from her holidays for her five-year-old grandson only to have it seized at customs when it was discovered the headlamps were tiny red *Abrus* seeds. She wasn't the only one. Dozens of similar items were seized at airports every year.

His mother took cuttings from friends and neighbours and helped herself to seeds from plants when she visited gardens listed in her little yellow book. For all he knew, she had one of these things growing in her garden. She had foxgloves, and weren't they meant to be poisonous? Would he be reeling her in too for questioning if he found a rosary pea in her potting shed? Then again, his mother hadn't swum with the judge at the Saint Piran Spa every morning. She, like all those other people around the world who handled the seeds to make bracelets and souvenirs, didn't have a profile embracing the second of the cardinal stepping stones to criminal intent, opportunity. Philippa Floyd, on the other hand, did. She had the means and opportunity. All that was missing was motive. He needed to know more about her, but how on earth was he going to be able to investigate her without drawing unwanted attention? He couldn't crank up the police database without an explanation. Officially, she was neither a victim nor suspect of any crime. She wasn't even a witness to one, and delving into her background, couldn't be justified. Data protection saw to that. He'd held off interviewing her again, hoping he'd get more information from the counter-terrorism team, but yesterday they'd announced they were off, and he'd finally be getting his office back.

They had concluded the judge was likely to have been killed as part of a campaign launched by one of several Ecoterrorist organisations on their radar following the G7 summit in Cornwall. It was to be viewed as an isolated incident probably planned as a direct result of the international publicity the county had attracted during that period. Neither Cornwall nor its population was considered to be the object of any ongoing terrorist plan, so they were off back to the smoke. There had been no attempt to explain why the judge had been the target and not one of the dignitaries who had attended, someone who had been actually involved in one way or another with the summit.

So, the burning question was, should he tell Dyer what he knew and let him decide what to do with it? Or should he pay the woman another visit first, give her a chance to provide an alibi and clear her name?

As luck would have it, that very afternoon the decision was made for him. An unexpected phone call from a woman called Agnes Chenoweth who rang to report a missing person - her neighbour Philippa Floyd. Part of him was delighted. Her disappearance lent credibility to his theory that she had something to do with the judge's death, but as he pulled his jacket from the back of his chair, he was suddenly struck with the terrible realisation his prevarication may have allowed a murderer to slip through his fingers.

Chapter Twenty-One

ROSS WAITED PATIENTLY in his car outside Philippa Floyd's house. He'd missed lunch, and breakfast seemed a long time ago as he pulled a packet of cheese and onion crisps from the glove compartment. He'd been tempted to stop in Truro and buy himself a pasty to eat while he waited but tonight was date night. Karenza had been released from bar duties in the pub and was cooking a curry from scratch, and if he couldn't do it justice, date night would pretty soon become, *don't bother to follow me up. I'll be reading my book night.*

He still couldn't believe he and his ex-wife were back together. He woke some mornings expecting to see the damp walls of the depressing flat he'd rented during his forced bachelorhood. Then he'd feel her breath on his neck and reach out for her. He'd lie perfectly still, listening to the slap of waves against the harbour wall as he watched her sleep.

It had taken him longer than most to appreciate small wonders, to realise the stuff he'd sweated over for so much of his adult life was foam on the sand compared to family or one of his families anyway. He saw practically nothing of his two younger children these days. His second wife Trudy's new bloke, was bringing them up for all intent and purpose as his own. The visits had got shorter, and when they happened at all, the kids regarded him as an interference to their routine. They spoke about all the things they did with their stepdad Mike and their mum, making him feel more and more redundant. He had become a kindly uncle who paid for special trips and never missed a birthday. They tolerated him, even hugged him if he was lucky, but he knew the gap would widen as they got older. If he was truthful, it was a relief they were managing without him. He was glad Trudy had found a sound bloke who loved his kids and, more importantly, who his kids loved back.

He had lost his way for a while, focusing on the job, chasing respect and recognition in all the wrong places. He'd thought promotion to DI and the money that came with it, the better car, and the extension to the kitchen would set his marriages straight. He'd learnt the hard way all either of his ex-wives had ever wanted was his time. The revelation came too late to save his marriage with Trudy. There were other issues at the heart of it outside his control, not least her near-pathological distaste for Cornwall and all things Cornish, including, by the time they split, him. She'd gone back to Bristol, hoping he'd never follow. You could take the boy out of Cornwall, but you could never take Cornwall out of the boy. Luckily, he and Karenza were older and wiser. They'd both been around the block a few times since their divorce, and neither was interested in looking back. The scabs healed quickly because of it, and of course, it was taken as read that neither would ever live anywhere else. Cornwall was God's country as far as they were concerned, and the little part of it they called home was just about as close to paradise as anyone could hope for. Heaven for him was the morning sun licking the curl of the perfect wave.

He could see now why the marriage had failed in the first place. He'd been addicted to the job. Police work was mind-numbingly boring in the main other than when by some miracle of chance, a case came your way where the outcome mattered, and you had a part to play in it. Those few cases were worth every monotonous hour of paperwork. He'd chased that rush for twenty years before realising he needed to get a grip. His last case had cured him. Holding his teenage son in his arms, knowing he had been instrumental in the trail of events leading to him taking a bullet, had changed everything for him. Yes, Piran had been in the wrong place at the wrong time, but the trigger-happy idiot holding the gun fired because he'd foolishly cornered him without thinking of the probable outcome.

An inch either way and Piran wouldn't have survived, and it would have been his fault. Despite this, and to his utter surprise, he'd been commended for his part in bringing several members of an organised crime gang to justice, not to mention his nemesis, local gangster Jem Fielding. He hadn't received the elusive promotion to DCI, the move to more admin and regular hours Karenza craved and dreaded. It would have been a bridge too far, having endangered the public whilst committing the cardinal sin of keeping his superiors out of the loop. Hindsight was both wonderful and elusive as far as he was concerned, and here he was out on a limb again, following a hunch.

The green double-decker drew up in the lane opposite and he watched Agnes Chenoweth step down onto the pavement. Tilting back his head, he poured the last of the crisps into his mouth before screwing up the packet and pushing it into an empty Costa coffee cup.

When he spoke to her to make the appointment, she'd told him she'd be available after four o'clock when she got home from work, adding she left early on Tuesdays. He waited until she'd had time to settle in before walking up the path.

The theme from *The X-Files* chimed as he pressed the doorbell.

The woman was certainly a queer fish. He'd come across her name before through his dealings with her boss, local solicitor, Eden Gray. He'd known Eden a long time, though strangely enough not through work. She'd practised up country before coming back to Cornwall, and their paths hadn't crossed yet. He largely dealt with cases in the far west of the county and was only here now because of Carlisle's murder and the fact his boss, Luke Parish, was on secondment to the Met until the end of the month. He had no idea why.

He and Eden were connected through a shared passion for surfing. They'd both done the rounds of the local surfing competitions when young, although she was much better than him these days. She, unlike him, still had plenty of time to practice. She was divorced and lived alone, only a stone's throw from the beach. His location in St. Ives was just as good, but she had the benefit of working sociable hours. When he did get a weekend off, he felt duty bound to help Karenza in the pub to save on the wage bill now her dad had signed over the business. When he wasn't pulling pints for the tourists, he was running his teenage daughter here, there and everywhere. Whilst part of him couldn't wait for her to get her licence, he'd had too many harrowing chats with the traffic boys about novice drivers coming to grief on lethal Cornish bends to buy her a car of her own. At fifteen pounds a pop, she'd had twice as many lessons as he remembered to be the norm back in the day and still hadn't been put forward for her test. Either she was rubbish or the instructor was on to a good thing. Perhaps he should jack in the force and give driving lessons instead.

The door opened.

'Before you say a word, show me your ID.'

Ross pulled his warrant card from his pocket. The woman glanced at it, then turned her attention downwards.

'Can you take those off, please?' Agnes Chenoweth said, looking disapprovingly at his feet.

Ross bent to unzip his Chelsea boots, hoping the socks he'd grabbed from the overflowing laundry basket were matching, which wasn't always the case.

The woman didn't linger to inspect him. She'd strode on ahead. Leaving his boots outside, he followed her in, wincing as he stepped on a hook protruding from the clear rigid protective matting he hadn't seen around for years, covering the first three feet of oat-coloured carpet.

A shout echoed from the kitchen.

'Tea? Before you ask, I don't do skinny lattes and flat whites or cappuccinos. Tea was good enough for my mother, and it's good enough for me.'

She slammed a mug of tea and a plate of custard creams down on the table.

Ross took a sip. 'Lovely,' he smiled.

'Biscuit?' she said, pushing the plate towards him. 'Take more than one. There's another pack in the cupboard.'

Something told him she had at least another pack, same biscuits, same brand. This was a woman you could safely say was set in her ways. He took two.

'Thank you,' she said, staring.

For a moment, he was thrown before realising she was prompting him like a mother would a child to mind his manners.

'Oh yes, sorry, thank you,' he coughed, the dry biscuit catching the back of his throat.

This woman ought to join the force, he thought. He didn't rate anyone's chances of not breaking under her interrogation.

He swallowed hard.

'As I said on the phone, I'm here to ask you a few questions about your neighbour Miss Floyd. When was the last time you saw her?'

Agnes leaned back in her chair, mug hovering.

'It was the morning of the 5th on my way to work. She waved from her front window.'

Ross felt the bite of adrenaline. He had called that afternoon.

'And you haven't seen or heard from her since?'

'No.'

'Do you know her well?'

'Oh my, yes, we're very good friends,' she replied, leaning forward. 'Hardly a day goes by when we don't talk or have a glass of wine together in the garden after work, weather permitting.' She paused. 'Aren't you going to write this down in your notebook?'

Ross lifted a finger in compliance before reaching inside his jacket pocket for his dictating machine.

Satisfied her words weren't going to waste, Agnes continued. 'As I said, we were more than neighbours. Pinkie sought my advice on all sorts when she first moved in. Blowins always take time to settle in; the least we locals can do is lend a hand.'

Ross sensed the warm welcome Philippa Floyd received from her neighbour was the exception rather than the rule.

'Miss Floyd ... Pinkie wasn't local then?' It was an apt nickname for a woman who might as well be on the dark side of the moon, for all the luck he was likely to have in tracing her if he didn't fess up his suspicions.

'Wasn't? Why do you say wasn't? Has something happened? Oh God, she hasn't been kidnapped, has she?'

'Kidnapped. Why on earth would you think she's been kidnapped?'

'Because it happens there all the time, doesn't it? It's where all the pirates live?'

'Where?' asked Ross wondering if the woman was talking about Penzance.

'Somalia.'

'Somalia, what would she be doing in Somalia?' Ross asked, bemused.

'Charity work, of course, helping refugees. She's often asked to go at short notice if other volunteers drop out. She's quite the globetrotter. She's lived all over the world covering her stories.'

'Stories?'

'She was a journalist before she retired to Cornwall.'

This was news to Ross. He tried to process the information. Somalia and with a charity. It might explain why he'd not been able to trace any record of her leaving the country on any passenger list despite ringing all the major airports. A charity may well have booked a special charter, and she might operate under a pen name.

'This has happened before?'

'No, of course not. She usually tells me where she's off to and leaves a key with me, so I can make sure the mail doesn't pile up. Why do you think I rang you lot to report her missing?'

'So let me get this straight you have no idea where Pinkie is now?'

'No, all I know is something's not right.'

He wasn't about to argue with her there.

'So has something happened to her or not?'

'Not as far as we know.'

'You don't think she's in the house, do you, been knocked unconscious and bundled into a wardrobe? I know most of the local ne'er-do-wells through work, but I've not seen any of them hanging around. Then again, I'm at work during the day, and you hear stories, don't you, about people being found bludgeoned to death in broad daylight.'

Ross decided to run with the woman's paranoia. He could hardly say he had a hunch Agnes's friend had done a flit the day he found a tiny red seed in her greenhouse because she was guilty of killing a high court judge. It still sounded ridiculous even to him. In any case, it gave him an excuse to gain access to snoop around without a warrant.

'Has anyone else got a key?'

'I don't think so.'

'Then we might have to break in.'

'I don't know about that.'

'What choice do we have if Miss Floyd is in danger?'

He was playing to the woman's penchant for drama now.

'Well, if you think it's absolutely necessary.'

'I do,' said Ross solemnly, adding, 'I'll make sure the house is secured afterwards and be careful to do as little damage as possible. It would be helpful if you could come with me to let me know if there's anything out of the ordinary or missing.'

The woman pulled her cardigan around her readying herself for battle.

'Of course, anything I can do to help,' she said, barely able to hide her excitement.

ROSS KNEW from his previous visit to Philippa Floyd's place; the front door was solid, and there was no way he could force it open on his own.

'We'll try the back first,' he said.

'The patio might be best,' said Agnes, eyes like hubcaps.

'I see she's got cameras installed,' noted Ross, looking up to the small lens pointing in their direction as they walked up the path.

'She has an alarm too,' offered Agnes with authority.

'I assume you know the number.'

'Naturally,' replied the neighbour, clearly warmed by the mantle of trustworthiness. 'I don't know she'd like me to give it to anyone, though.'

Ross glanced at her over his shoulder. 'I'm a police officer.'

She didn't look convinced.

'Okay, assuming I manage to gain entry and there's nothing untoward, you can follow me in and head for the alarm to disable it.'

'Roger that.'

Line of Duty had a lot to answer for, thought Ross.

The vertical blinds were closed, never a good sign. Ross noticed the patio doors were the old-fashioned kind that slid back rather than concertinaed. He knew there was a knack to opening them when you locked yourself out but had completely forgotten what it was. It was something to do with them having latches rather than locks. He was contemplating whether he should lift one half of the door from its tracks when a large rock flew past his ear, shattering the glass.

'What the hell?' he shrieked, ducking.

'You said we were breaking in. Pinkie was going to build a rockery this summer but never got around to it. There's a pile of stones round the back of the shed.'

Ross was dumbstruck. How would he explain this lot if one of the other neighbours heard the commotion and came to investigate? He might have to call it in.

Pulling the blinds back, he gestured for Agnes to step over the frame ahead of him. The woman was a menace. He needed to know where she was at all times.

She read his exasperation. 'You said the police would pay for the damage. You shouldn't have said it if you didn't mean it.'

Ross didn't comment. He needed to get on.

'Sit there and don't move,' he said in a tone he might use to one of his kids.

'But …'

'Sit.'

The woman, arms folded, plonked herself down onto the sofa opposite.

Other than the damage they had done, the room was tidy and undisturbed. He sniffed the air, and to his relief, there was no whiff of decomposition. He had no desire to find Philippa Floyd's decaying body, the victim of a burglary or a stroke or piracy, come to that. The alarm was beeping loudly.

'Can you go and turn that off?'

'If I'm allowed to move, I can.'

Ross raised his eyebrows. 'Yes, you can move to do that. Just don't touch anything else.'

The woman flounced off down the hall, the same one he'd walked down with Miss Floyd the day he called. On the left of the door sat an alarm box. Agnes tapped in a four-digit code, and the home fell silent as she turned to rejoin him in the sitting room.

Ross gestured for her to sit again. 'I'm going to have a look round. I'll call if I need you.'

The woman did as he asked without argument.

'I'll check down here first,' he said, walking through to the adjoining kitchen.

It was tidy, the worktops clear of the detritus a family would accumulate. He would have known this place belonged to someone single, although if he'd been asked to hazard a guess at the sex of the owner, he would have struggled.

Though the layout was the same as the house next door, the decor was the antithesis of the knick-knacky busyness of Agnes Chenoweth's bungalow.

Ross pulled his gloves from his pocket and opened the fridge, lifting the milk to check the date. It had gone over, as had the ready meals on the shelves and the salad in the drawer.

'Shall I go and pick up the post from the mat?' Agnes shouted from the sitting room.

'No, don't touch it yet, not till I've checked everywhere.'

He reckoned Agnes's prints were all over the house anyway, but there was no need to make the job any more difficult than it was, and if he was right about Philippa Floyd, God only knew what the woman might find if he allowed her to go poking around. If there was any evidence to be had here, whether to convict or help decipher where his suspect was, he wanted to be the one to find it. He hadn't stayed quiet about his suspicions this long so the likes of Miss Marple here could pull off a coup de grâs.

He opened the cupboards and drawers, sifting through them, trying not to disturb the contents too much. A couple of newsletters from her gardening club, along with a new membership card. Scanning the page, he noticed she was treasurer this year. No paraphernalia hinting at the membership of any pseudo-political organisations. That would have required the kind of luck he seldom saw. He slipped the piece of paper into his pocket, thinking the names might prove useful. It didn't help he had no idea what he was looking for. Even if Philippa Floyd was the judge's killer because he lacked a motive, he had no clue as to whether she was part of something bigger or just a mad old bat with a personal grievance. If the latter was the case, he could hardly hope to find a poster of the judge. KILL HIM written across his forehead.

He made his way upstairs. The bedroom, like downstairs, was uncluttered and comfortable, everything neutral and in good taste. The bed was made. He lifted the duvet cover, nothing untoward. He noticed two long grey hairs resting on the pillowcase. Pulling an evidence bag from his pocket, he lifted them one by one before sealing the bag and returning it to his pocket. Moving to the wardrobe, he tentatively opened the door, despite all logic, half expecting a body to tumble out onto the carpet. To his relief, there was nothing unusual here either other than clothes hung from every hanger. She had not taken much with her. He moved to the dressing table and slid open a drawer. Underwear neatly organised, walking socks in a ball, several bathing costumes; a rash vest the same make he used himself under his wetsuit when surfing. She liked her water sports then.

That hardly singled her out in Cornwall. He dug deeper and lifted a pink leather passport wallet. Inside was a passport in the name of Philippa Floyd; the face staring from the page was the same as he remembered from his visit. So, she was still in the UK. He took his phone from his back pocket and snapped and saved the number and the photograph before putting it back.

Next stop the bathroom. Again, it lacked the feminine touch. He couldn't move at home for scented candles and bath bombs, but there was none of that here. He opened the medicine cabinet; plasters, a box of ibuprofen gel, spare brush heads for an Oral B and a jar of Verbena Gardener's Hand Balm with a National Trust label.

He slammed the door shut, depressed by the look of frustration clouding his mirrored face. He looked tired, hardly date night material. He was ready to turn and leave when out of the corner of his eye, he clocked a small silver aluminium waste paper bin, the lid lifted slightly by its overflowing contents partly hidden behind the towel strung over the radiator. He walked over to it and pressed the pedal to flip the top revealing a squashed box of brown hair colourant. He pulled it free, two empty bottles and a pair of used latex gloves, the smell of ammonia lingering. He hadn't noticed any makeup on the dressing table, and he remembered when he met her, Miss Floyd was grey-haired and barefaced, with not a hint of vanity about her. The girl at the spa had specifically said she didn't bother to dye her hair.

He carried the box downstairs. Agnes was where he'd left her hands folded in her lap.

'Did your friend dye her hair?'

'Pinkie?' Agnes shrieked, incredulous, 'Never ... never.'

'Well, I found this in the bathroom bin.'

Ross rarely used the word flabbergasted, but it was the word to perfectly describe Agnes Chenoweth's reaction. He pondered whether she could appear any more astonished if he'd discovered something really gruesome, like a shrunken head. It was as if her friend Pinkie had committed the ultimate spinster sin. He thought it might be a good time to take her off guard.

'Did Pinkie ever mention Judge Carlisle?'

The woman looked at him blankly.

'The one killed by terrorists, you mean?'

'Yes, I understand she swam with him at the spa pool most mornings.'

'She did, although she also did that mad wild water swimming. She was lucky she didn't end up with pneumonia; ridiculous.'

'Back to the judge,' Ross said, reeling her back on point. 'Did she ever talk about him?'

'Well, as a matter of fact, she did. Only the once. She asked me what I knew about him.'

Ross felt a tingle at the back of his neck.

'She said she had been talking about him with a friend and asked me what I knew, you know,' she preened, 'because I work in the justice system.'

'A friend, do you know the name of this friend?'

'She never said. I suppose it might have been one of those wild-water women.'

An image of bikini-clad Amazonians surfed through Ross's mind.

'Or one of her gardening clubs, maybe. She was a great one for joining things. I suppose she got used to it because of her charity work. I'm happy with my own company. I was never one for female bonding.'

No, Ross thought, *I didn't have you down as a team player.*

Then again, he shouldn't be too quick to criticise her for that. After all, neither was he. If he was, he wouldn't be going out on a limb in this case.

'What exactly did she ask you about the judge?'

'Nothing specific that I remember. She just said she swam with him. It was me who told her all about him, you know, about him not being liked by the court staff and all the fuss there had been about the death of that young lawyer Marcus Annear.'

The name rang a bell.

'Remind me.'

'The judge locked him in the cells for contempt, and he fitted and died. He had a medical condition, poor man. It should never have happened.'

He remembered. He'd got a call from Claire McBride. She'd been Marcus Annear's boss back then. He and Claire had known each other for years and were still friends despite the fact she was at present serving time in jail for fraud and had been struck off the solicitor's roll. She'd been pushed to her limits and made wrong decisions. As far as he was concerned, whatever she'd done, she'd paid for. When she got out, he'd help her all he could to get back on her feet. Good people like Claire McBride deserved a second chance.

He had totally forgotten about the incident Agnes referred to until now. He remembered how she'd been in a real panic about Marcus and asked for his help. There had been nothing he could do. The judge had acted within the letter of the law in finding the young lawyer to be in contempt for failing to give up his client. It didn't mean it was the right thing to do.

'When you told her the story, how did she react?'

'What do you mean?'

'Was she shocked, angry ... did she make any comment at all?'

'Not that I remember. She opened another bottle of wine.' Suddenly her eyes widened. 'You don't think the same people who killed that judge have taken her out, too, do you?' She put the back of her hand to her mouth in a dramatic gesture that summed her up, Ross thought.

'No, nothing like that. I just need to know as much as possible about Miss Floyd's life if we're going to find her.' He decided not to press the point further, not at this stage. He needed facts, not histrionics. 'One more thing,' he said. 'Has Miss Floyd got friends or family out of county? I found her passport in the drawer upstairs, so she's not left the UK.'

'Unless she's been smuggled out.'

This woman should write penny dreadfuls, Ross thought. *She's wasted in a solicitor's office.*

'Family or friends?'

'If she has, she never said so. Come to think of it, I have no idea if she has family or not. I know she's never been married. We had that in common, you see, but whereas I had a mother to look after, she was able to travel with her job and her charity work.' The comment was laced with martyrdom.

'Okay, I think that's enough for now. You go home; make yourself a cup of coff ... tea. It must have been stressful for you, but at least now you know nothing has happened here in the house. You did right to report it, and you've been very helpful. You can leave it with me now, but if Miss Floyd makes contact, please let me know straight away.'

'Yes, of course. I would never want to waste police resources.'

'In the meantime, we will begin to put out alerts, but we do need to rule out that she's not just gone away for a few days.' Ross knew in his water she hadn't, and there was more to this than met the eye.

'What about the window?' she asked as he walked her to the front door to let her out.

'Don't you worry. I'll see to it,' Ross reassured.

Once he closed the door behind her, he rang his friend Pete who ran a double-glazing business in Penzance.

'Hi mate, I've got an emergency job for you.'

'No problem, text the address and the details, and I'll send someone around as soon as I can. Invoice to Devon and Cornwall as usual?'

'No ... no, not this one. This one's on me.'

Chapter Twenty-Two

ROSS PULLED up at the station car park just as the counter-terrorism team was loading the last of their gear. He wasn't sorry to see the back of them. Muttering 'good riddance,' through a clenched-toothed grin, he waved them off.

A good day just got better as far as he was concerned. Not only did he have a glimmer of motive for his suspect in the Carlisle murder, but he also had his desk, his chair and his favourite mug back. Result. Normal service was resumed, and he could continue with his investigation without interference. From the torrent of good-humoured banter rising from the corridors, he could tell he wasn't the only one glad to see the back of the supplanters.

He held the door open for a plump, red-faced young man struggling with his arms full.

'Cheerio, Gringo,' he heard the desk sergeant shout after him.

Ross closed the door behind him and then turned to Jack Fairchild for an explanation.

'What's with the Gringo tag?'

'He asked me last week where he could get a decent vegan burrito. I told him El Paso.'

Ross thought this a little harsh from a man who regularly tucked into an M&S sushi platter for lunch. As if reading his thoughts, Fairchild, shuffling his papers, said;

'It doesn't do to make the likes of them too comfortable. They might decide to stay. You know what they say about fish after four days? Well, that bucket of eels has been stinking the place out for weeks.'

Ross walked through to join his team. The atmosphere reminded him of the last day of term exams finishing and the beach beckoning. Foot off your neck at last. They had felt under permanent scrutiny from people who treated them like a bunch of inept country bumpkins.

He, unlike his London counterparts, had no doubts about the diligence and commitment of the officers he worked with and intended to prove their worth by nailing the killer in this case.

He began unpacking his belongings from the box he'd transported to his old room.

At six o'clock, DS Denise Charlton put her head around the door.

'There's no place like home, is there?' she said, her grin reflecting her amusement at the pleasure he was getting from carefully positioning his belongings back in their original place. 'We're off down the pub to celebrate having the place to ourselves. You fancy it?'

'No, not this evening. Got all this stuff to move, and Karenza's cooking dinner.'

'Lucky you. Takeaway for me on the way home.'

'Any news when Luke will be back?'

She blushed.

Rumour had it she and DCI Parish had had a bit of a fling back along. None of his business, but it would be nice to know when things would be back to normal and perhaps, she was more in the loop than he was. He could do with a long leash for a week or two.

'He's back next month.'

'Right … good. See you tomorrow then.'

Generally, he would have been the first to join the team at the bar but not today. He had the bit between his teeth and had always enjoyed this part of the job. Raking together all the snippets of information to make your case. It didn't happen often, but when you got to slot the last piece of the jigsaw into the gap, it was the best feeling in the world.

He logged into the system and began typing Philippa Floyd's details to create a new missing person's file. He wasn't a hundred per cent sure she was missing, but she fulfilled the criteria, given her whereabouts couldn't be determined at present. He wasn't prepared to ratchet this up a notch to a person of interest in respect of a crime just yet, especially a crime as high profile as the killing of Judge Carlisle. Grabbing his phone, he e-mailed the photo he'd taken of her passport to himself and searched the database for verification. She had one of those faces which would be difficult to age or describe if he had to for a photo fit. Smooth-skinned and trim, she could be aged anything from forty to a sprightly sixty; nothing prominent or unusual. Green eyes, grey hair, regular features neither plain nor pretty; no distinguishing marks. Other than her height, which he noted when he'd called on her was around five feet ten, tall for a woman, average in every conceivable way. Forces around the country would now share her image and data as part of the 2009 Code of Practice. Now this was official, he could look at CCTV footage around her property on the days after he'd first called. He knew it was unlikely to yield much, if anything. There were no cameras in the street, he'd checked, and not much after that. Miles of country lanes meant the county largely escaped the surveillance commonplace in most towns. Some villages still didn't even have broadband. Nevertheless, he could have a look and check her mobile records and obtain her dental files to add to the missing person database. Best of all, he'd be able to submit her DNA. The box of hair dye contained a bottle with a comb attached, presumably to assist the home dyer, but the DNA would be corrupted by the chemicals. There had been no toothbrush in the bathroom, only the replacement heads in the cabinet, but the couple of fine grey hairs from the pillow would hopefully be enough. He'd keep the DNA test under wraps for now. It would take a couple of weeks to come back anyway. It always made him smile how, on the television, DNA came back the same day. What a joke.

The main objective in the meantime was to ensure he was appointed duty officer on the inquiry, so he had complete control over the information passing to his superiors. Whoever had killed the judge had been careful, that was certain. They had left nothing at the scene, but he was pretty sure whoever did this, and he believed he knew her identity, was no novice. You don't start at the top. Killers generally worked their way up to murder. No one need know what he was really up to until he'd built his case. Until then, this would stay a missing person enquiry. That in itself would not be an easy ride.

Whilst the public often branded the force as disinterested in missing person cases, in reality, they were never taken lightly. They cost too much for that. They'd had it hammered home to them in the regular budget briefings they were forced to attend that the cost of the average missing person investigation was higher than for theft or assault. They were often a fruitless drain on valuable resources, especially where there was no evidence that there was any crime involved and the person was making every effort to stay missing. He guessed Luke would have more than enough on his plate playing catch up when he got back to worry about what he was up to, but he knew he had to keep costs low to stay under the radar. That meant doing the grunt, perhaps even when he was off duty. He didn't care. He had a feeling about this, and it wouldn't go away.

Every night when he closed his eyes, he remembered the tiny red seed and thought of Philippa Floyd. He knew he was right about her, that somehow, she was involved. He'd lay money on it, and he didn't have a lot of money to bet. The discussions she'd had with her elusive friend may or may not have some relevance to the judge's untimely demise. That, in turn, may or may not have had something to do with Marcus Annear's death, but for now, he couldn't see how the accidental death of a young lawyer could be the sole motive so many years after the event.

His stomach rumbled, and for a split second, he wished he was sipping a pint of rattler and tucking into a plate of fish and chips with his team in the pub. Feeling his reserve begin to slip, he pulled himself up. Life was too good at the moment to risk it.

He looked at his watch; nearly seven. He needed to get a move on, but before he could head home, he had one more thing to do. He reached for the plastic bag in his pocket containing the few hairs he'd managed to retrieve from the woman's pillow and placed them in a padded envelope.

Once labelled, he put it with the others waiting to be collected for testing.

At least the after-work traffic would have eased by now. He'd do Truro to St. Ives in twenty-five minutes. Rush hour in Cornwall was a non-event after the summer season ended; a nightmare during it. On the drive home, he called Karenza.

'Are you on the road?' she asked.

'Yep, I'll be home in ten.'

'Good day?'

He thought of his reclaimed office and Agnes Chenoweth throwing a rock through her friend's patio window and laughed out loud. 'Bloody brilliant.'

Chapter Twenty-Three

IT HAD BEEN a fortnight since Pinkie arrived at Joyce's villa, and nothing she had seen so far had changed her mind about Sam. She needed to get him away from the place and the toxic no-mark who called himself his father. There had been no repeat of the episode by the pool. Gary Joyce seemed to do his level best to avoid both her and his son. He was mostly absent from the villa. She had no idea where he went and knew better than to arouse suspicion by asking. He spent days away, the roar of his car engine heralding his unwelcome return.

When he was there, he was usually accompanied by a young woman - rarely the same one - and for the entire visit would be drunk or high, more often than not both. On these sojourns, the unmistakable musky aroma of marijuana pervaded the landing outside his room, but Pinkie guessed from his nocturnal shenanigans he was taking a lot more than that. She had no interest in his downward spiral into addiction other than to make sure Sam stayed away. From what little she'd seen of him, he'd revealed himself to be a selfish, careless prick, and she didn't trust him to be responsible enough to keep his gear out of Sam's reach.

Lionel spent increasing amounts of time in his bedroom at the far end of the villa. She guessed it doubled up as his office as she'd seen Margarita showing the building foreman upstairs on more than one occasion, plans rolled under his arm presumably to discuss the work. His room had a double door out onto a balcony overlooking the pool, and he was often there in his chair watching her and Sam in the afternoons.

She was beginning to wonder if the man wasn't mobile and maybe the enormous annexe being constructed in the grounds was for him. She'd noticed he wasn't too steady on his pins and the open tread staircase was a challenge. Perhaps he needed somewhere level with better access. The thought filled her with dread. Whilst it was crystal clear Lionel Joyce had supported his son to the hilt over the years, it was equally clear there was no love lost between the two, and her fear was if Lionel moved out, Gary and one or more of his hareem of leggy Lolitas would move in and with his father ensconced in the garden who knew what Gary would get up to.

The only proper conversation she'd had with Lionel since her interview had taken place the morning after when she had gone to see him about Sam's itinerary. He'd given her the school pickup times and told her she would not be driving herself but would be driven to the school twice a day there and back by his driver Miguel.

She'd told him she had hired a car and was more than happy to drive Sam herself, arguing it would make things easier if she wanted to take a detour after school, say for ice cream or one of the cave tours she'd read about in her tourist guide.

Joyce had been polite but firm. There would be no impromptu activities. He needed to know where his grandson was at any given time. If she wanted to take the child anywhere, she must liaise with him first, and if he thought it was a viable suggestion, he'd arrange for Miguel to take them, wait for them and drive them home.

None of it made any sense. The security level, the paranoia about his grandson's whereabouts. She knew for sure he didn't worry about Sam's mother turning up to snatch him back. He and his son had made sure that was never going to happen. No, this only made sense if Ewan and Matt were right about Joyce and he was involved in something, but if he was, she'd certainly seen no evidence of it. Other than the two louts at the gate, who she hadn't clapped eyes on since, she'd seen no one remotely suspicious at the villa. The team of builders from the village arrived in their battered Jeep every morning at about eight, just before Sam and her set off for school. They worked until midday, when they retreated to the shade of the loggia to eat a lunch prepared by Margarita, who fussed over them like a mother hen. The delicious smell of fish stew and warm cornbread or grilled sardines reminded Pinkie of Cornwall. Occasionally, she and Sam would venture round to see the workmen before they knocked off. One of them had taken a shine to Sam and was helping him build a wooden toolbox for all his bits and pieces.

She had learnt from Margarita that the row she'd witnessed her first day had escalated because Sam had been with the builders. Gary had turned up drunk, as usual, demanding he come with him and swim laps in the pool. He'd been bragging to his latest conquest what a good swimmer he was. Pinkie remembered the blonde by the pool that day, young and painfully thin, Bambi legs teetering on stilettoed heels. Sam had refused, saying he'd already been in the pool that day and was helping the men. The rest she remembered only too well.

She was amazed at how well-adjusted Sam was, all things considered. He was a warm, friendly little boy, and she enjoyed his company. Bright as a button, he liked to know how things worked and was always taking things apart and putting them back together. The workman's radio had been dismantled and reconstructed more than once, as had Margarita's food mixer, to the housekeeper's dismay. He liked books but wasn't interested in stories. He read magazines about cars and could tell you the in and out of any luxury vehicle you threw at him. It was a game the builders played with the boy. They shouted the make and model, and he shouted back the stats. They never checked them, of course. He recited the information on nought to sixty, torque and bhp with such authority no one thought to challenge him. Lately, he'd turned his attention to boats. Not sailing dinghies or ribs. He seemed to have no interest in learning to sail, and when she'd asked if he might like lessons when he was a little older, the response had been a definite 'no'. She supposed she'd got used to children learning to sail at an early age in Cornwall, where having a dinghy to muck about in was no big deal. Then again, he was young when he'd left, and she'd never got the impression from Liz that Lionel Joyce had any interest in sporting activities other than golf. Golfers rarely had time for much else in her experience, especially when they were into the social side of it, and according to Liz, Lionel Joyce certainly was. He'd met Carlisle at the golf club, for one thing.

Sam had recently swapped his car magazine subscription for *Motor Boater*, which he pored over, committing every detail to memory. One morning on the car journey to school, the reason became apparent.

'Grandad's bought a Princess.'

For a moment, she'd had to think what he was talking about before it clicked. He meant a boat.

'It's a Princess X80. It's amazing.'

'Are you sure?' asked Pinkie, worried he might be making it up and get into trouble for doing so if he repeated it at school.

'Of course, I am,' Sam replied, indignant she should question him. 'He showed me the photo of it and the brochure. It's not new, but it's in excellent condition. It cost over a million.'

Pinkie almost fell off her seat. The boy looked at her quizzically.

'That's a bargain,' he said, fiddling with his school bag. 'They're lots more millions new.'

Pinkie said nothing.

She hadn't discussed days off with Joyce and decided as soon as she dropped Sam off, she'd go and see him. She needed to get away from the place, if only for a few hours to get some perspective on what the hell was going on here.

AS SOON AS she returned from dropping Sam off at school, she headed for the kitchen to ask Margarita if she could see Mr Joyce that morning.

'It will have to wait till later on. He has a visit from his doctor at ten.'

Pinkie had watched the comings and goings from Joyce's bedroom since she arrived but had not seen the doctor there before.

'Is Mr Joyce unwell?' Pinkie asked, already guessing the answer but adding a dusting of surprise to her expression for Margarita's benefit.

'I need to tell you something, but you must not say a word.'

The woman's eyes were glassy, her face drawn with worry.

'Of course not.'

'Mr Joyce is a very sick man.'

The woman lifted her apron to wipe away a tear. She was clearly close to her employer. She spent a great deal of time with him. Pinkie had noticed she usually went to Joyce's room after she'd cleared away the breakfast things and stayed there for an hour or more whilst the two cleaning ladies from the village whisked through the villa. They never entered Joyce's room. Margarita always dealt with that herself. Pinkie had assumed it was because Joyce didn't like to be bothered by the women's incessant chatter while he worked. On reflection, it was probably because he was too ill to be disturbed.

Margarita came to fetch her at midday.

'Mr Joyce will see you now. When you have finished, come down and join me for lunch. I have made us something special, Bacalhau and for afterwards, apple cake.'

She reached out and touched Pinkie's arm as they walked along the corridor. 'Please don't keep him talking too long. He tires easily but likes company, so tries to hide it.'

They paused outside the bedroom door, Pinkie behind Margarita as she knocked.

'Come in.'

The voice, thin and rasping, was barely audible.

Margarita gently opened the door to reveal a space more hospital than bedroom.

The curtains were half-pulled. Joyce's single bed was raised, with space on either side for easy access, and next to him was a stainless steel trolley stacked with pill bottles too numerous to count. Hanging from the corner of the bed were a mask and a canister of oxygen.

'Open the curtains, Margarita. Let's get some light in here.'

The sunlight gilded the walls pink and gold as Margarita pulled back the drapes, but the illuminations did nothing to cheer the room or its occupants.

'Help me to sit up,' Joyce grimaced, his frail arms lacking the strength to make any impression as he attempted to shuffle himself upright in the bed. Margarita rushed to his side, gently manoeuvring him forward to plump his pillows before nestling him back against them.

'Thank you,' he said warmly as she turned and walked out of the room, bottom lip quivering as she closed the door behind her.

Joyce raised a bony blue-veined hand to beckon Pinkie forward. 'Take a seat,' he smiled, his teeth set huge in his wizened face. Once tanned skin, now waxy and yellowed, stretched over protruding cheekbones. Pinkie was shocked at the change in him since she had met with him only weeks before. She hadn't thought he looked a well man then, but now he looked positively cadaverous.

She did as he asked and pulled up a chair, the cloying stench of sickness filling her nostrils.

'How are you getting along with my grandson?'

'Well, I think. He seems to like me, and I'm doing my best to keep him busy as you asked,' replied Pinkie, her tone as breezy as she could muster in the circumstances.

'I haven't felt up to sitting on the balcony for the last few days, but I can hear his laughter around the place, and I can only assume his newfound happiness is down to you.'

And the absence of his father, thought Pinkie.

'Me ... oh no, I'm sure I play a very small part. He's a naturally friendly boy; easy to like.'

'Yes, he is,' Joyce said, his pride at the fact plain to see.

Pinkie guessed this might be a good time to raise the subject of the cruiser.

'I hope you don't mind me asking but have you recently bought a boat?' She shuffled in her seat as she asked the question. She didn't want this to be an interrogation. Not with the man so ill. 'Sam told me you had, and I was a little concerned he'd made it up to impress the other kids at school. I know he wouldn't actively set out to lie, but he's so obsessed with cars and boats I thought it might be wishful thinking and might backfire. I didn't want it to get out of hand or for him to get in trouble for fibbing.'

'No, he's not making it up, although I'm disappointed he told anyone when I specifically told him not to,' said Joyce, his ragged cough punctuating every word.

'Can I get you some water?' Pinkie asked, rising from her seat to grab the jug on the table next to him.

'No, I'm fine,' he said, brushing away her concern.

'I'm sorry I didn't mean to get him into trouble.'

'It's not your fault or his come to that. I should have known better. It's just I enjoyed the look on his face when I showed him the picture in the brochure.'

Pinkie understood the sentiment. She, too, got immense pleasure from the child's infectious enthusiasm for all things mechanical.

Joyce reached for the mask from the hook to his right, declining Pinkie's assistance again as he placed it over his mouth and nose, filling his lungs before continuing. When finished, he laid the mask on the crisp white sheets in front of him, fingers trembling slightly as he turned the valve off.

'Cancer, stage four,' he said, 'pancreatic.'

'I'm sorry,' Pinkie sympathised. 'Wouldn't it be more comfortable for you in hospital where they could manage your pain?'

'Margarita does that just fine, and my doctor visits me here at home,' he added. 'I prefer to die in my own bed, and I've still got too much to do to give in quite yet. Anyway, enough about my decrepit carcass. What was it you wanted to talk to me about, the boat?'

She very much would have liked to talk about the boat and why a dying man thought he needed one, but she decided there were other matters more pressing.

'Actually, it's a couple of things. I need a place where Sam can fiddle with his bits of machinery without worrying about making a mess or having to clear away between sessions. I noticed there's an old summer house in the garden and wondered if it would be alright to use that. It needs some sprucing up, but nothing I can't do myself with a little help from the builders as they are already on site.'

Joyce had turned his head and was looking wistfully out the window across the garden towards the sea.

'It was my wife's place,' he said. 'Diane fancied herself as a bit of an artist. That's one of hers on the wall there.'

Pinkie's eyes followed his to the wall opposite, where a large painting generously daubed with vivid colour took up the majority of the space. It was of a garden, and its childlike naivety made her smile.

'I like it,' she said honestly. 'It's sort of … joyous.'

'I suppose it is,' said Joyce surprised, looking at it as if for the first time. 'Yes, you can use it. She'd be glad for you to. She never got to see her grandson. Gary was a child himself when she passed, and I sometimes think it's what made him so ... so angry.'

He chose his words carefully, but Pinkie knew exactly what he meant by them. Gary was a violent thug.

'I'm sorry.'

'When your time's up, it's up. We all wish we could change things, but there it is. Your second question?'

'It leads on from the first. I wanted to go into town to buy a few paints and glue along with some crafty bits and pieces to stock the place for Sam; some posters maybe for the walls and oilcloth for the table would be a good idea.'

'Make a list and Miguel will get it for you.'

'I don't mind going myself. I have the car, and I need a few personal things as well.'

The expression, temporarily bright when they were talking about his wife and grandson, darkened.

'I'd rather you didn't go into town on your own.'

Pinkie, indignant, said, 'I'll go on my day off if that's your concern?'

Joyce didn't answer. His hand reached for a buzzer to his side attached to a monitor like you might have alongside a baby's cot.

'Margarita, can you come straight away? I need the bathroom.'

Pinkie knew an excuse when she heard one, and only Joyce's frailty saved him from a comeback. As it was, she decided to leave it, knowing she had outstayed her welcome.

Chapter Twenty-Four

BACK IN HER ROOM, Pinkie retrieved the card Ewan had handed to her at The Yellow Gecko and rang the number. When someone answered, she said the one word written on it, 'BARFLY' and ended the call. Five minutes later, Ewan was on the phone.

'So, what's up?'

She was relieved to hear a friendly voice.

'Plenty. Something is very wrong here. Old man Joyce is ill, and Gary has barely shown his face since the first day I arrived. The gates are manned by Albanians, and there's a huge outbuilding going up in the garden. What's more, I'm a virtual prisoner. I can only get in and out of the place if I'm driven by Joyce's man. I've just asked if I could take a day off to go and buy a few bits and pieces in the village and been told I'm to make a list and they will be bought for me. I feel like some Victorian servant, bloody Jane Eyre. No, take that back, like Mr Rochester's wife, confined for life to my quarters.'

'Mr who?'

'Oh, never mind.'

'Take a breath. First, the Albanians. How do you know they're not just working on the property like the other guys? I told you Joyce was having work done.'

'Christ, Ewan, give me some credit. I might have been out of the game for a while, but I know the difference between a tradesman and a gangster when I see one. Criminal tats and a gun in the waistband of your trackies is a bit of a giveaway.'

'Okay, okay, I believe you, and what about Joyce? When you say ill, how ill are we talking?'

'Well put it this way, if I do manage to get Christmas off, I'm pretty sure he won't be around to carve the turkey. Cancer. He's on the way out. It looks to me as if he should be in hospital, but when I suggested it he said it was impossible. He had too much to do.'

'And the kid?'

'He's fine for now, but this isn't the place for him, a dying grandad and an absent junkie father. Before I arrived, I think he spent all his time either with the builders from the village or the housekeeper Margarita.'

'Anything else?'

'Isn't that enough to be going on with?' said Pinkie sarcastically. 'But okay, Sam Joyce's grandson told me this morning his grandad has just bought a Princess and get this, it cost over a million quid.'

Ewan let out a long whistle on the other end of the phone.

'Now you tell me what a dying man wants with a luxury cruiser when he can't even get out of bed.'

'Perhaps he's planning a Viking send-off; intends to have it set alight as he floats off to Valhalla or Vilamoura. Isn't that where golfers go when they die?' said Ewan.

'Oh, ha bloody ha.'

'Now don't bite my head off when I say this.'

'Go on.'

'I think we should call Matt. In fact, I know we should. I get the feeling we've been told half a story here.'

Pinkie paused. She hated this feeling of vulnerability. Her whole working life, she'd manoeuvred herself in and out of jobs under her own steam, but she wasn't stupid. That was then and this was now, and she needed help. She was in the midst of something rotten and, locked inside the gates of Joyce's villa, she was never going to get anywhere without help from the outside. If Matt was right about Joyce's involvement with people smuggling and God knows what else, she had to get out of there while she still could.

'He's bound to want to meet up with you. You up for that?'

She hesitated. 'I'm not sure I can get away.'

'Be sure. I think he has information you need to know.'

'What information?'

'I don't think we should talk about it over the phone.'

'You don't know, do you.'

'No.'

'You're such a dick, Ewan.'

'So I've been told, but I'm your dick ... hang on, that came out all wrong.'

'No shit?'

'Okay, okay, but it doesn't alter the fact if Matt asks for a meet, you need to touch base with him as soon as possible.'

'What do you suggest?'

'Don't ask me. You know the people you're dealing with better than I do, but if Joyce is as ill as you say, I reckon, despite all his rules, he's not going to be up to keeping tabs on you. Even you come pretty low down in the list of priorities for someone on his death bed.'

'Yes, okay, call him,' she said, trying to keep the anxiety from her voice. The truth was that contrary to every professional rule in the book, she didn't have a clue who she was dealing with or how they'd react. She was angry with herself for getting carried away with Ewan's scheme when she hadn't done her homework.

'Okay, I'll talk to Matt and get back to you later.'

'Will you be there when I meet Matt?'

'Why, don't you trust yourselves not to kill each other if you're left alone?'

'It feels awkward, that's all, after so many years.'

'That's exactly why I won't be there. My old games teacher drummed it into me to always be a player, not a spectator and certainly not a referee. That's a thankless bloody job. You two are grown-ups or claim to be, so play nicely. I don't know what Matt's up to or what he might be asking you to do, and I'd rather not know. I've got a really bad feeling about this one. It doesn't sit right with me, none of it. If I didn't know better, I'd think you've been lying and are working for someone, and this Lionel Joyce is your target, and I can tell you right now Matt's probably thinking the same way.'

'I am working on something but not in the way you think,' said Pinkie. 'Look, I promise I'm not under contract. If I was, I'd have told you when we met in Lisbon. More than that, I would have called you in on it. What would be the point of risking it when Joyce is on his last legs? All I'd have to do is let fate take its course.'

'If you say so. You and Matt sort it. Just leave me out of it. I'm looking for an easy life these days, and you two have never been easy.'

'But let him know I'm here for one reason only, to get Sam away. I want nothing to do with whatever it is he thinks the Joyces are involved in.'

'So that's why you're here, to take the boy. I never had you down as a kidnapper.'

'It's not kidnapping if you're taking him home.'

PINKIE KNEW Matt would be all over this the minute Ewan called him, and if she was honest, despite her misgivings, she was glad she'd be getting some answers soon. Until she had the whole story, how could she decide on whether to stick with her plan or draw a line under the whole thing, even if that meant leaving Sam behind? She couldn't bear to think about that. She never broke a promise, even those like this one made to herself. She had to think of something, some excuse to get out of there without raising suspicion or challenging Joyce, but what? She could feign illness, gyppy tummy or the flu, maybe, but knowing her luck, Joyce would offer her an appointment to see the doctor who visited him at the house.

The smell of baked apples drifted upstairs from the kitchen and it gave her an idea. Not ill, she didn't need a doctor; a dentist, she needed to see a dentist. She could say she had a toothache, say one of her molars was playing up. No one would stop anyone with toothache from seeing a dentist, and they never did home visits.

To appear genuine, it needed to have been bothering her for a couple of days, not something likely to go away of its own accord. There was no time like the present to start the deceit.

Chapter Twenty-Five

PINKIE MADE her way down to the kitchen to join Margarita for lunch. The table was laid for two, a steaming cast iron pot centre stage.

'Sit ... sit please,' beckoned her host.

'I hadn't realised he was so sick,' said Pinkie reflecting on her meeting with Joyce that morning.

Margarita's eyes were fixed on the earthenware plate she was loading with chunks of fish, spicy thick tomato sauce and thinly sliced potatoes, deliciously crispy at the edges.

'Shouldn't he be in hospital?' pressed Pinkie.

Margarita lifted the breadboard to offer a hunk of warm cornbread, only meeting her guest's eye when she knew she had been served.

'I have said so too, but he will not listen. He says he wants to stay here as long as he can.'

'Surely Gary should be here, doing his bit to help.'

Margarita's dark brows knitted in disapproval. 'That boy is no good. He has no respect for his father. Gary is interested only in himself. He was a spiteful child, and he is a selfish man.'

Pinkie was taken by surprise; she had no idea Margarita had been with the family since Gary was small.

'You've worked for Mr Joyce a long time?'

'Since he first bought this place. I was eighteen when Mrs Joyce first employed me.'

Pinkie was curious. 'What was she like? Mr Joyce showed me one of her paintings this morning.'

Margarita got up and opened one of the drawers, rummaging for a second before returning to the table with a photograph.

She pointed to a fair-haired woman wearing white bell-bottom jeans and a stripy top, touching heads with a boy about Sam's age sitting on her lap, arms wrapped around her neck. Both grinned as if they'd just been told a joke or maybe tickled each other. Standing next to them, smiling stiffly for the camera, was a slight, shy-looking teenager with dark waist-length hair. She was beautiful.

'Is that you?' Pinkie asked

'Yes, hard to believe, isn't it.'

'No, I didn't mean … it's just you look so young.'

'And tiny too,' she said, sighing. 'Mrs Joyce was a wonderful lady. We were all sad when she died.'

'When was that?'

'She fell sick after they'd been here a couple of years. Gary was about eight then.'

'And was the villa always called Margarita?'

The woman blushed and looked much younger.

'No, it was little more than a shack when they bought it and the land. None of the houses around here had been built. Once they had built a new property on the site, they took me on full-time. Mrs Joyce liked my name, so she used it, and it's been Villa Margarita ever since. It was still a small place back then. I used to clean and help with the cooking for Mrs Joyce and stay over whenever Mr Joyce came across from England as he often brought guests and there was extra to do. The property has grown over the years, with the pool and the gym and now with all this work going on in the grounds.'

Pinkie took the cue to ask the question on her mind for some time.

'Was it planned before Mr Joyce fell ill?'

Margarita stood to fetch a pitcher of water from the sideboard.

'I have no idea. Perhaps,' she said, pouring them each a tall glass. 'Paolo tells me it has a kitchen and a bathroom, so maybe. He finds the stairs difficult these days.'

'Paolo, is he one of the workmen?'

'Yes, he is. He is also my son.'

'Your son. I'm sorry I didn't know you were married. I assumed as you lived here you were single.'

'You were right to think so. I never married. My son was brought up by my parents in the village.'

Pinkie flushed with embarrassment at having inadvertently stumbled upon something so painfully private. This woman was possibly her only ally in the household. The last thing she wanted to do was alienate her.

'I'm so sorry, it's none of my business.'

'It's okay,' Margarita reassured, 'it's old news and no secret. The whole village knows … have always known. At least you do not look to judge, the way they did.'

Pinkie changed the subject. 'Margarita, tell me, are the men who were at the gate the day I arrived working on the building too?'

'Why do you ask?'

'They seemed out of place, that's all. The rest of the builders are local, and the way they questioned me, it was almost as if they were guarding the villa.'

'It's not my business. I don't ask questions, and I don't think you should either.'

Margarita turned to lift a cake from the oven. 'I have kept it warm.'

'It smells delicious,' praised Pinkie, the promise of cinnamon and caramel spicing the air. 'I would love some, only I'm trying to avoid sweet things at the moment. I've had a nagging toothache for a couple of days. I was up half the night with it.'

'Toothache … nothing is so painful. I have some óleo de cravo in the pantry,' said Margarita heading for the alcove off the kitchen where she stored provisions to retrieve a tiny brown bottle which she passed to Pinkie. 'Dab a little on your gums around the tooth that hurts.'

'Thank you,' said Pinkie, grimacing as she unscrewed the lid and felt the unmistakeable sting of cloves assault her nostrils.

'You will have to see a dentist. There's a good one in town who treats the tourists. He speaks very good English and takes emergency appointments. My cousin's daughter works in one of the hotels, and they send guests with problems to him.'

Pinkie didn't want to appear too keen. After all, they were talking about a trip to the dentist. It was human nature to want to put it off.

'I'll try this first,' she said, lifting the oil of cloves. 'Hopefully, it'll do the trick.'

'Maybe for a little while, but you should get the tooth seen to as soon as you can.'

'I will.'

'Make sure you do. I don't like cooking for people who don't eat my food.'

Pinkie forced a smile. 'Thank you. This has been so nice.'

'You are very welcome. I'm pleased you're here. It's nice to have some female company and Sam is so much better since you came.'

'Sam ...' Pinkie looked at her watch. 'I really must go; I need to pick him up from school. I don't want to be late.'

'Go ... go. Tell him to come see me for some cake when he gets home.'

'Thanks again,' Pinkie shouted over her shoulder as she headed for the driveway where Miguel was waiting in the car, engine revving.

The text from Ewan pinged on her second phone while she waited outside the school gates for Sam.

> Tomorrow. 2pm. Museum of Archaeology behind the Fisherman's Beach.

THE FOLLOWING MORNING, Pinkie arrived for breakfast looking even more pained than she had the day before.

'That tooth still bothering you?'

'Afraid so,' she winced as she sipped her coffee. 'The stuff you gave me helped. I got a better night's sleep, but you were right, I need to see a dentist.'

'I thought so,' said Margarita, sliding a note across the table.

'I looked up the number after you left yesterday. Call them. Best get it over and done with.'

Pinkie took the note, pulled her mobile from her pocket

and dialled the number, walking away from the table to look out onto the garden so that Margarita would not see her cancel the call before anyone answered.

'I need to book an appointment, please. I've had chronic toothache for a couple of days. I'm worried I may have an abscess forming ... this afternoon? That's great ... 2.30 yes, that's perfect. No, I don't mind waiting. I appreciate your fitting me in. Can you tell me how long the treatment's likely to take? I see, no ... no, that's fine. Yes, I'm privately paying, I'm not on holiday I work here. Smith ... Patricia. Yes, my mobile number ... is 07338343466.'

'There, I told you he'd fit you in,' smiled Margarita as she came off the phone.

'He has an extraction first thing this afternoon, but the receptionist said if I am prepared to wait, he'll see me before the end of the day. She said to arrive at about two o'clock.'

'Good, Miguel can take you and pick you up later when he goes to collect Sam from school. Hopefully, by tomorrow evening, you'll be ready to eat my puddings again.'

Chapter Twenty-Six

PINKIE HEADED for the door of the Clinica Déntaria. Peering through the vertical blinds of the outer foyer, she waited for Miguel to drive away before pulling a cotton sun hat and a pair of sunglasses from her bag, leaving before the receptionist looked up from her screen.

Sticking to the shady side of the street, she followed the directions on her phone.

Walking fast, head down so as not to make eye contact, she soon reached the cobbled alleyways of the Old Town with its tightly packed houses shuttered to the afternoon sun. She headed towards the Praia dos Pescadores, the fisherman's beach, its cafés and seafood restaurants crowded with the lunchtime trade. The smell of fried food made her nauseous, and the glimpse of cobalt sky through one of the paint-peeled archways gave only temporary respite from her mounting struggle to hold down the contents of her stomach. She was not prone to nerves, but this was different. The thought of a reunion with Matt, something she would never have countenanced only days before, had sent her off kilter.

Her head was pounding in the sticky breathless heat, and she longed for a long cool drink in one of the courtyard bars fringing the square but couldn't risk it. Snaking through the huddle of souvenir shops selling fridge magnets and posters of Ronaldo, she reassured herself provided she kept things strictly professional, didn't let herself be drawn into discussions about her private life or Matt's for that matter, she could keep it together. Like it or not, she had questions only he could answer, and this might be her only chance to ask.

It was with relief she spotted the sign, 'Mûseu Municipal de Arquelogia'.

Once inside the single-storey building, she pulled off her hat and prized the damp strands of hair free from her forehead. She paid the entrance fee, forking out for a guidebook at the same time, not wishing to look as if she was loitering without intent.

The place was airy and deliciously cool, although practically empty, and she wondered whether many beach-happy tourists bothered enough about the town's cultural heritage to venture through its doors despite the cheap one-euro entry fee. From the guide plan, she could see the tiny museum was divided into four sections, the first dedicated to prehistoric times.

At the end of the room, a small group of school children aged ten or eleven gathered around a frieze running the full length of one wall depicting man's progress from ape, via several millennia, to modern man. She could hear the teacher telling her charges the original version of the chart, The March of Progress, was now out of date, no longer reflecting the scientific opinion that evolution was less linear and more tree-like with its forking branches.

She was impressed by how rapt the students seemed,

hanging on their teacher's every word, but wondered if they'd be quite so engaged if she took charge of the lesson. History was, after all, the recounting of other people's experiences, and in her experience, some humans had made more progress than others. She had met some who had hardly evolved at all; vicious knuckle-dragging Neanderthals with psychotic tendencies who would beat their enemies to death for fun. Hopefully, it was a lesson in evolution these kids would never have to learn first-hand.

She looked around; still no sign of Matt.

She thought it best not to stray too far away from the main entrance in case they missed each other, so she didn't follow when the group moved on into the Roman section. Instead, she circled the display of megaliths taking pride of place in the centre of the room, running her hand over their ancient chiselled surfaces.

She sensed his presence before she saw him and, for a second, wished she'd shuffled on behind the school party. She could have skulked behind the display cases, seen him first and bounced without fanfare if she didn't feel up to this, but now it was too late. His critical stare pinned her to the spot. She'd always tried to keep history where it belonged. In the services, unburdening to a psychologist had been part of the debriefing process, but she'd never really engaged, and since then, she'd become her own therapist, adept at diffusing the past, so it didn't blow up in her face. The exception was those episodes featuring Matt. His name was synonymous with anger and pain. She could not, would not forget Rob. She missed him too much but found it hard to remember him without thinking about his death and Matt's role in it. In Matt's case, the past cast a long shadow and here, standing within his icy orbit, it felt like it had finally caught up with her.

Nevertheless, she knew she had no option but to face him.

'You found it then?' he said.

She turned. Hands sweating, she gripped the guide, trying to slow her breathing.

For a moment, she was thrown, her mind playing tricks as she tried to equate the man before her with the man she had once agreed to marry. She'd imagined the years would roll away but instead, they were stacked high between them, every bit as solid and immovable as the monoliths next to her.

'It's well signposted,' she replied, mouth dry.

'You look well. You've hardly changed at all,' Matt said, not sounding overly pleased about it.

She said nothing, not wanting to acknowledge the compliment, well-meaning or not.

He sensed her reticence, his body tensing.

'Shall we find somewhere to sit?'

There was nowhere in the first section, and the guide hadn't mentioned a café.

Matt took the lead. He'd been here before.

It was strange seeing him in civvies. In her mind's eye, he was always in uniform. She knew it was illogical. She'd seen him in jeans and a t-shirt often enough. Come to that, she'd seen him stark bollock naked, but the image that stuck was the last one at Rob's funeral.

Although he was broader, his tanned neck thicker, he'd retained the bearing of a military man, straight-backed, his steps solid and decisive. His hair, no longer regulation short, was grey and thinning at the back. Had she met him in the street, would she have given him a second glance? Probably not. The old him, or rather the young him, had been the focus of her fury for so long, yet she felt nothing towards this stranger.

She'd never subscribed to the school of thought that you could eradicate bad deeds if you hid away for long enough. She'd never felt sympathy for octogenarian Nazi war criminals fighting extradition. Yet the animosity she had felt and, if she were truthful, nurtured for so long suddenly seemed hackneyed and self-indulgent. Rob was dead. It was a fact that couldn't be altered. He had been a soldier like Matt, and had he lived, he would be like him, old and spent and probably disillusioned just like every other retired serviceman she met these days. She didn't know if it was this place, the idea of man's history condensed into four small rooms or the anti-climax of seeing her old lover in the flesh, but suddenly her anger felt pathetic. She had placed Matt on a pedestal and judged him against those lofty standards but now, with his thinning hair and sagging jowls, he was nothing special. He was no longer a fallen hero.

Rob, on the other hand, would sparkle in the firmament with all those who died before their time, forever valued for their unlived lives; their unfulfilled potential. She followed him through to the Roman section past the amphora lined up like soldiers and a small votive alter until he halted at a bench opposite a display about food preservation in Roman times. They sat her at one end, him at the other. She stared at the frieze of olive trees and sheaves of corn and hoped their meeting wouldn't prove to be a failed harvest, a fruitless effort, with empty plates at the end of it. She was under no misconception he had the clout to send her packing, and all she'd risked coming to Lisbon would have been a complete and utter waste of time. She would have to go back to the UK without Sam, and on top of it all, if Trenear was on to her, she would lose everything precious to her. Her little house, her garden, those hard-won friends she'd been able to make and her liberty of course, the thing she had always valued the most.

She let him speak first, heart too heavy all of a sudden to take any initiative.

'When I heard you'd retired, I was relieved,' Matt said, staring straight ahead. 'Then I get the news you're back in harness, and what's more, you're on my patch.'

She felt herself bristle and knew her face would be red.

'I'm no such thing. I told Ewan this is not a job, and I meant it. This is a favour for a friend, nothing more. I had no idea Joyce was under surveillance.'

'Well, he is, and now you're slap bang in the middle of my operation. I could have killed that Welsh git when he told me he'd fixed you up with the nanny's job.'

'Well, perhaps if you'd confided in your oldest friend in the first place, he wouldn't have. We both know he would never have crossed you to help me had he known.'

'You and I know if he hadn't got you inside that gate, you would have found your way.'

'Maybe, well, I'm here now, so for the sake of damage limitation, I suggest you let me in on whatever you're up to.'

'First of all, you must confirm you are not here to kill either Gary or his father.'

I'm not. I'm here to try and reason with them, petition them on behalf of a friend. I have no intention of killing them.'

Matt looked relieved. 'What has Ewan told you?'

'Nothing other than it's a joint task force operation headed by Europol, and it centres on trafficking.'

'Correct but not the type you both imagined. We're not talking about refugees looking for a better life. This is about the illegal movement of organised gang members.'

'How exactly is Joyce involved?'

'We believe they're using his villa as a safe house, a place to haul up while they wait for their papers, fake of course, and in the meantime to train.'

'Train, for what?'

'For war.'

'Against who?'

'Anyone who looks to stop them.'

'But I haven't seen anything like that.'

'What about the pair you mentioned to Ewan.'

'Okay, yes, that was odd. They seemed to be guarding the villa, and one of them had prison tattoos I recognised.'

'Short blonde hair, scrawny-looking. We know him. He's a minor player, muscle for one of the Fis we believe to be involved with Joyce.'

'Fis?'

'Family ... clan.'

Pinkie suddenly felt hopelessly out of touch with a world she had once occupied so comfortably. The little knowledge she had about the Mafia Shqiptare had been acquired in the nineties when she'd been aware of their growing influence following the fall of the iron curtain and the chaos that followed. There had been rumours of widespread racketeering and corruption of local officials in the country; a free for all. Those willing to oblige had got rich, and those who weren't got murdered. The intelligence forces back then had been understandably concerned both the state and the police were compromised. The potential lawlessness was a real threat to the peacekeeping forces trying to retain control of the region. From what Matt was saying, it would seem things had only got worse.

'The Albanians control the majority of illegal activity coming into Europe via the Balkans through Turkey. They started with trafficking for sex, prostitution, then cocaine and now, you name it, they run it. Europol has real concerns about the inroads they've made in such a short space of time. Their growth is phenomenal. There are thousands of members in each group spread across the world. They've established allies with other crime organisations but remain independent and impossible to infiltrate. They operate under an archaic family system based on *Besa*; trust to you and me, and outsiders are unwelcome. The discipline is rigid, and the punishment ruthless. While the structure is unsophisticated compared with some of the other crime families who've been at it longer, the tech they use is second to none. They've infiltrated financial systems with bogus workers to commit financial and identity fraud on a massive scale, and there is a danger they are slowly but surely acquiring the technical know-how to bring a country to its knees. They are set up to survive losses, even severe ones. Any men they lose can be replaced easily by the population who, through family ties, are beholden to the organisation wherever they are. Add to that a history of national service within living memory and shed loads of money, and you can see we have a big problem.'

Pinkie didn't need a diagram.

'How did Joyce become involved?'

'We think originally through his friendship with Jerome Fielding, a sleeping member of a London firm hanging out in your neck of the woods. He drowned a year or so ago. Before his untimely demise, Fielding planned to build a casino in Penzance, and that's where Joyce came in. He was on the planning committee. Fielding ran call girls through his lap dancing clubs, many of them sex-trafficked from Eastern Europe. We know he was involved in extortion, and we think he probably had something on Joyce. The councillor was certainly instrumental in passing several very suspect decisions. They raised a few eyebrows at the time, but nothing came of it. It got interesting later, though, when the police pulled off a sting in Penzance, arresting a key member of the same London firm trying to import a huge volume of cocaine into the country through Cornwall. You might have seen it on the news. Well, luckily for us, that member, a career criminal called Theo Morgan, decided to throw his lot in with us rather than swallow what was bound to be a long stint of risky jail time. He's on witness protection. The information he's fed us over the last year or so has completely changed our perspective, but most of all, it's made us realise we are unprepared for the threat the Albanians pose.'

Pinkie remembered the case. A teenage girl had been dragged from the water. Fielding was the main suspect in her kidnapping. She'd always thought Cornwall a haven from many of the vices infecting elsewhere. She'd been naïve to think anywhere was immune these days, but at least the girl had survived the ordeal if she remembered correctly. It was in the paper, a local policeman ... Trenear. It hit like a brick. The photograph of Ross Trenear with his family, the hero of the piece. He was no slouch then, this detective. He was tenacious and willing to take risks. Just her bloody luck.

'Are you okay?' Matt asked. He had swivelled to face her.

'Yes ... yes, why do you ask?'

'You look pale, that's all.'

'It's the heat, and I didn't have lunch.'

Matt reached into his man bag and brought out a power drink; the type Pinkie had seen in the vending machine at the gym but never thought to buy. He unscrewed the lid and handed the bottle of vivid blue liquid to her. She read the label.

'God, if it can do all that for you, I wonder why people need the likes of us anymore.'

'Just drink,' said Matt. I don't need to tell you; you must stay hydrated in this weather, and the caffeine will keep you going.'

She took a glug of the sickly-sweet drink, wrinkling her nose as she screwed the lid back on. 'Ugh, it sets your teeth on edge.'

'Better get yourself back to the dentist then,' Matt grinned, shoving the bottle back into his bag before continuing. 'Fielding was brought out of semi-retirement for that gig, though we believe the daft sod was stupid enough to try and cypher off some of the product for himself.'

'And it got him killed?'

'Seems likely.'

'So, Joyce still has connections with this London gang through his history with Fielding?'

'It's the most likely explanation.'

'And the Albanians?'

'They're connected with the same London firm at the trafficking end. They supply people, not only sex workers and muscle, but ordinary run-of-the-mill workers, labourers on building sites across the capital, plumbers, electricians, and brickies. It's a regular industry with an unexpected outcome none foresaw, especially the homegrown OCGs. They now rely on these boys as suppliers. Without them, the semi-legitimate enterprises they use to launder money like Mr Fielding's development projects, come to a grinding halt. The Albanians have manoeuvred themselves into a position where they can hold the other OCGs to ransom.'

Pinkie watched him talk. He was so immersed. She

remembered what it was like to eat, sleep and breathe a mission like this, where every waking moment and even your dreams were plagued with details of the case you were working on, the men you were chasing.

'The problem is their demands for a bigger slice of the cake have met with resistance.'

'And their response is to take over the bakery.'

Matt smiled. 'Exactly.'

'And these men you're talking about, these Albanian mobsters, are being trained to flood the UK in significant numbers.'

'Mobsters is the right word. The grasp for power and territory we are seeing is more akin to something you would have seen during prohibition in the US. We can't afford open gang warfare on the streets of our major cities. The prospect of a major recession and all the fallout, let alone the problems in the Met, means there's no extra cash for policing this kind of crap. We need to kill it at its roots so it can't grow. We cannot let them take hold; we might never get back control. Think of Naples and the Camorra.'

An image of officials being bombed, judges threatened, children kidnapped, and innocents shot in the street newsreeled through Pinkie's mind.

'Look I get it, but I've not seen anything, and Joyce is dying. Maybe whatever you think was going on has been called off because of his condition.'

'The builders are still arriving every day, aren't they?'

'Yes, but the housekeeper, Margarita, hasn't got a clue what the new building is for, and that's odd because she knows everything that goes on in the place. She's been with Joyce for ages, and her son is one of the builders, but despite that, she has no idea. If Joyce was planning to build a barracks to house Albanian gangsters, surely she'd know?'

'He's hardly going to advertise something like this to the world. I would expect him to want to put some space between the builders and the new arrivals. He won't want talk in the village.'

Margarita had said the work would be finished that week.

'Hang on, are you telling me you expect that building to be housing Albanian gangsters anytime soon? Because if you are, I'm out of here, and I'm taking Sam with me.'

'Ah yes, the kid.'

'I know Ewan would have told you it's why I'm here.'

'I know you intend to leave with the child, and I know why too.'

Her throat tightened. God, he didn't know about Carlisle, did he?

'Gary Joyce is a prize prick if ever there was one. Anyone can see he has no business being in charge of the boy, but his mother's dead, committed suicide when he skipped the country with him, but you know all this, don't you, because you're friends with the grandmother.'

Her heart was thumping now.

'You're here to take him back to Cornwall to her. She's the friend, and he's the favour. I'm right, aren't I?'

She needed to keep calm. She needed to keep calm. Matt wasn't shy. If he knew more, he'd say. She was as certain as she could be he didn't know about Carlisle.

'Yes.' She heard the tremor in her voice.

'Okay. Then I'll make a deal with you.'

'I'm listening.'

'You act as my eyes and ears inside the villa. Let me know when the men arrive, and I'll see to it you get Sam back to his grandmother. What's more, I'll make sure Gary Joyce doesn't bother your friend or the boy ever again. You don't need to say yes now. Ewan will call tomorrow for your answer. Sleep on it.'

'I don't need to. I'll do it. If this lot are arriving as soon as you say, I'll be watching them anyway. Old habits die hard. But I want a guarantee at no time will that little boy be in any danger. If there is any chance of that, I get to know in advance so that we can get out. I don't know what you're planning, but I do know we need to get out before it happens.'

'Agreed, so where do we go from here?'

'I provide you with surveillance equipment. I want you to install it in Joyce's room so we can hear his conversations. We need to know who visits him and who he talks to on the phone. These guys are clever. We've got people on the team who speak Albanian, but the texts and calls between the man we're tracking and his Mik are becoming increasingly confusing. We need context, and we can only really get that with someone in situ.'

'Mik?'

'A sort of liaison officer in charge of coordinating operations on the ground. In this case, an underboss called Niko Kurti. I'll send you a photo so you can let me know if he turns up.'

Pinkie hadn't seen any regular visitors other than the builders and the cleaners.

'Are you sure it's not Gary who's involved with these people rather than his father?'

'Trust me. No one would deal with Gary Joyce. He's a fool and a junkie.'

'But where is he? Don't you think it's suspicious he's gone to ground?'

'He's not gone to ground. He's been living on that cruiser the kid told you about.'

'You mean to tell me he's been down in the Marina, ten minutes away from the house, and he hasn't bothered to visit his sick father or his son?'

'What can I say? He's a prick. He's been too busy flashing the cash around, inviting girls aboard. A couple of nights ago, he had a party that ended with him beating one of them up. He's been in the local nick ever since.'

'No one's bailed him out?'

'No. He contacted the house to speak to his father but was told by the housekeeper he was too ill to come to the phone. Gary was furious, but without his dad's help, he's stuck there.'

Pinkie looked at her watch. 'I need to make a move. I'm meant to meet Joyce's driver at the school to pick Sam up.'

'I'll drop you off.'

'I wouldn't want to be seen.'

'I'll drop you around the corner. I'll get the car. You follow me out in ten minutes.'

She did as he asked. He was waiting outside for her a little way up on the other side of the road. She headed for the car and slid into the passenger seat next to him, waiting for him to start the engine.

'I need to tell you something.'

She'd managed to keep the meeting strictly professional and hold herself together until now, but the tone of his voice told her all that was about to change.

'It's about Rob.'

Her brother's name sounded wrong in his mouth. He had no right to say it, not to her, not to anyone. Her scalp prickled as she resisted the urge to raise both hands to cover her ears like a child.

'You never got to hear the whole story. Ewan told me he'd spoken to you about what happened, but he didn't know the half of it. I tried to make contact after the funeral, but you wouldn't take my calls. You were grieving, I got that, so I left it. After that, the opportunity never arose. I've thought about ringing you too many times to count since, but in the end, I chickened out. However, I'm going to say my piece now whether you like it or not. This could be my last chance, and you need to know the truth.'

'I don't have to listen,' she said.

'You do, you know you do.'

She pursed her lips. Her show of defiance wouldn't stop him, and if she left without hearing him out, she knew in her heart it wouldn't be the end of it. She'd be wondering what it was he so urgently needed to tell her for the rest of her days and, let's face it, what could be worse than what she already knew?

She slumped down in her seat, her sigh his cue to carry on.

'That night ... the night of Rob's birthday, I'd managed to get in a couple of crates of lager and some vodka, and six of us set about getting smashed. It started off a good night, you know, squaddies a long way from home, letting off steam. Rob was on good form but at some point in the evening, I can't remember how or when the conversation turned to our wedding.'

Pinkie felt sick.

'It started with the usual banter, you know the old ball and chain stuff; how life was all downhill from here on in. Good humoured until Rob started.'

She imagined the pause was there for her to engage, but she was determined not to make this easier for him. He wanted to rake this up, not her. She said nothing.

'He started saying things about you, personal things.'

She shot him a look.

'What things?'

'Nasty, spiteful things.'

'Brothers do that,' she snapped. 'Only children like you wouldn't understand.'

It was a mean thing to say, she knew.

'Not like this. This was embarrassing. He wouldn't shut up and the more I objected and tried to laugh it off, treat it like the brotherly banter you're talking about, the worse it got.'

'Go on then, you're obviously dying to tell me. What did he say that was so bad, that I sold his record collection; beat him at Ker Plunk?'

'Look, it doesn't matter. Forget it.'

He moved to start the engine.

'Turn it off. You don't begin a conversation like this and then walk away from it. Tell me what he said.'

'He said I should steer clear of you. That you'd only make me unhappy. He said you were a self-serving bitch who had always got what she wanted, including me, but now you'd soon get bored and drop me like a ton of bricks.'

She stared at him, wide-eyed and incredulous.

'That wasn't the end of it either. Things got lewd. He started saying foul, disgusting things about you. He said you were "a whore on heat", his exact words. By then he was ranting, reeling about the room with a bottle of vodka in his hand. "You don't think you're the first, do you?" he taunted. "Every wet behind the ears recruit I ever brought home for Sunday lunch has been there before you. You're the last in a long line of horny bastards who got their end away.'

Pinkie swallowed hard. She couldn't believe it. 'That's not true ... I never.'

'I know, I know you. It was total bullshit, but the rest of the boys didn't know where to put themselves. They could see this was getting out of hand. If it had been anyone else but Rob saying those things about anyone's fiancée, someone would have punched his lights out. I knew it was a lie, and this wasn't him. I tried to calm it down, laugh it off, but he wouldn't shut up. I practically had to carry him back to the barracks. He was so off his tits. I managed to sit him down on the bed and got his boots off. I started to take off his jacket, and that's when he …'

She braced herself. She could tell from Matt's face it was bad.

'What?'

'He grabbed me … you know, there.' His eyes drifted down to his crotch. I pushed him away, not hard but hard enough for him to fall back on the bed, thinking he won't get up now. I told myself this was some sort of public schoolboy shit. I thought he'd sleep it off and not remember a thing, but he didn't stay down. He was up in seconds and coming after me as I headed for the door. He tackled me to the floor, trying to kiss me; "Don't leave me, Matt, I love you. I love you more than she does."

'I didn't know what to do. I was scared someone might come in. I pulled away, and when he came at me again, I thumped him, and he went down. I told him he disgusted me, that I was going to marry you and he could forget about being my best man once I told you what he'd done. He started to cry and make excuses, and that's where I left him on the floor, begging me not to say anything to you. When I went back in the morning to pick him up for our duty he'd already gone, and the rest, you know.'

She sat silent, trying to unscramble his words.

'I didn't care he was gay. You have to understand that. Had he come to me and told me, I wouldn't have given a monkey's, but I was angry at what he said about you and embarrassed at what he'd said to me. I'd planned to tell him so. I would never have told you. I'm only telling you now so …'

'So, you look like the good guy,' she said, turning to face him, teeth bared as she spat out her contempt. 'You didn't have to say a fucking word. You could have left me with the brother I thought loved me. But it's okay. I absolve you. That's what you want to hear, isn't it, that it wasn't your fault, that in some way Rob was damaged goods, unhinged, a raging queer? You make me sick,' she said, tears pricking.

'I'll take you back now,' he said calmly.

Had she been anywhere else, she would have got out of the car, but she was already running late and was in a state.

Matt did a three-point turn, heading in the opposite direction towards the school.

'Tell me when to stop.'

As soon as Pinkie recognised the road leading off from the school, she began to undo her seat belt. She felt light-headed. She needed to get out of the car quickly.

'This will do fine,' she mumbled.

'Under your chair is the box containing the listening device. The instructions are inside.'

She stared at him.

'Don't worry, you can send the information remotely; you won't have to see me again. You'll also need this.'

Matt leaned across her, she thought to open the passenger door, but instead, he popped the glove compartment.

'Here, I need you to take it,' he said, grabbing a brown velvet dust bag from which he pulled a Glock 19.

'I don't need that,' she choked, looking at the gun.

'Have you been listening to a word I've said? I picked it because it's small enough to fit into your handbag.'

She didn't have the energy to argue. She took it from him, knowing her first task on arriving back at the villa would be to hide it in the summerhouse under the stove where no one would find it. She reached beneath her seat for the box, opened the door and stepped onto the pavement.

'One more thing,' Matt said, leaning across the passenger seat to talk to her before she slammed the door. What kind of electric gate is it? Keypad? Or is it radio operated?'

'No, keypad. Joyce's cars have been fitted with gadgets, but guests and tradespeople have to speak into the microphone and Margarita lets them in. Why do you ask?'

'No reason. I intend to *blow the bloody doors off* anyway.'

The Michael Cain parody did nothing to relieve the tension.

'Fine,' she said, slamming the door shut without a goodbye.

PINKIE WAS WAITING for Miguel at the school gates when he arrived to pick Sam up. Despite everything, she'd made it with five minutes to spare.

'How's the tooth?' he asked as she slid into the passenger seat.

'Sore,' she said, making the effort to feign slack lips, numb with anaesthetic. I must avoid hot drinks for a couple of hours.'

'You'll need to drink wine, then.'

With Sam safely in the back seat, they made their way back to the Villa Margarita.

Her head was full of Rob.

Chapter Twenty-Seven

PINKIE COULD SEE something was up the minute the gates opened. Gary's car was parked haphazardly, half on the drive, half on the lawn, passenger door wide open. He was being held over the bonnet, feet off the ground, by one of the builders, a man younger than Gary with a halo of dark curls. Short and stocky, the rip in his t-shirt revealed a muscular torso unlikely to be challenged by the emaciated addict.

'Drive around to the garage,' said Pinkie, not wanting Sam to see his father brawling.

'What's Paolo doing to Dad?' asked the boy.

So that was Paolo, Margarita's son; what on earth could have angered him enough to threaten Gary?

Miguel paused. 'Shouldn't I stop to help?'

'No, do as I say,' ordered Pinkie. This didn't need to turn into a free for all.

Miguel drove around to the side and parked, helping Pinkie marshal Sam through the door leading from the garage to the store room off the kitchen.

'I think I'd better break it up,' Miguel said, seeking Pinkie's approval to leave.

'Stop that. Stop it right now.'

It was Margarita's voice.

'She's beat you to it,' said Pinkie. 'Sam, upstairs. Put your uniform in the laundry basket. You won't need it at the weekend. Once you've changed, we'll go down to the beach for a swim. How's that for a plan?'

Sam bundled up the stairs, schoolbag swinging, leaving Pinkie to meander through to the kitchen into the hall and join Margarita at the front door.

Gary's car had gone. Margarita and Paolo were standing looking out across the drive at the muddy scar gouged in the lawn.

As soon as Paolo spotted Pinkie, he walked away.

'What was all that about?'

Margarita spun round, eyes bright with tears.

'Nothing.'

'It didn't look like nothing to me.'

'Gary was drunk. I told him he shouldn't come to the house in that state, upsetting his father and Sam. He told me to mind my own business. He said, "when my old man finally kicks the bucket, you'll be out of here". Paolo heard him shouting and came to defend me.'

'As any good son would,' said Pinkie reassuringly. 'I'm sure Gary didn't mean it. Like you said, he was drunk. None of us could manage without you.'

'I don't think so. Gary has never liked me and now with Mr Joyce the way he is, I need to face facts and start looking for another job.'

'But this is your home.'

'Not for much longer.'

The woman shrugged her placid acceptance and walked back into the house without another word.

Pinkie thought of the conversation with Matt. Maybe Margarita getting out of there was no bad thing. This place was going to change whether she liked it or not. If Matt was right about the men who would replace the genial gang of builders, this was no place for her. Perhaps she should try and talk to Paolo to see if his mother could stay with him or another family in the village.

'I'm ready. Can we go for a swim now?' Sam was standing in the hallway in his trunks, wetsuit and towel tucked under his arm.

'Yes, of course we can,' she said, 'give me two minutes to get changed.'

Upstairs she changed into her costume before slipping on a pair of shorts and a t-shirt. Grabbing her beach bag, she threw in a bottle of sunscreen and then walked to her handbag to retrieve her sunglasses and the brown velvet bag holding the Glock Matt had given her. She intended to hide it in the summer house on her way back from the beach.

Her hand shook a little as she thrust it under her towel along with her second phone. Sunglasses perched on top of her head, she checked herself in the mirror before swinging the bag over her shoulder and heading back downstairs where Sam was helping Margarita cut out biscuits from a roll of dough.

God did this woman ever stop feeding people?

'I've told him not to eat before he swims. I put some of the baked ones and a sandwich in the bag there. He can have them when he comes out of the water. I expect you can't eat yet?'

Pinkie looked blankly before remembering her tooth.

'No, not for a couple of hours and no hot drinks.'

'I thought not. I've put some iced tea and a bottle of water in there too.'

The woman handed the bag to Sam, bending to kiss him on the forehead as she did so.

'No jumping off the rocks.'

The boy dropped his head, reddening a little.

Pinkie searched Margarita's face. 'Are you okay?' she asked, thinking of the altercation with Gary.

'I'm fine. I'm used to Gary, and as you said, he probably didn't mean it. You two go and have a good time.'

Pinkie reached out and touched the woman's shoulder. She couldn't help but feel sorry for her. She hadn't seen her out of her apron since she arrived. She guessed she must have had time to herself before the builders arrived and before Lionel became ill but still, she couldn't get the image of the slight young girl with the shy smile out of her head. She'd been tied to the family and this house all these years. To someone like Pinkie, who valued her freedom, it would have been an unbearably claustrophobic life.

She joined Sam on the patio. 'Shall I carry that for you?' she said, taking the bag from him.'

He nodded.

'Come on then, let's go and have some fun.'

The boy slipped his hand into hers. It was the first time he'd done that, and she didn't know what to make of it. Perhaps he was learning to trust her, or maybe it was just a kneejerk reaction to the sight of his father. The turmoil that man inflicted every time he turned up like a bad penny. Either way, it felt surprisingly good.

Seconds later, he pulled away to run on ahead.

'Don't open the gate until I get there,' she shouted after him.

The saline breeze blew her hair across her face. It felt so

different up here, away from the stifling heat of the town. Such a shame no one other than the gardener ever seemed to bother to visit this part of the garden. You could see the ocean from the house, of course, Lionel Joyce had a great view from his balcony, but all the senses needed to engage for the full effect. Only here on the clifftop did you appreciate how special this place was.

Sam was waiting at the gate for her.

'Go on then. You can open it. You can probably walk the path a lot quicker than me. I'll follow you but don't go in the water until I get there. Wait on the beach.'

'Okay,' Sam beamed. 'I will.'

The steps, to her surprise, were not the treacherous uneven kind she was used to in Cornwall, where you had to constantly look down at the ground because your feet were apt to slip away from beneath you. These were timber and had a rail. They looked newer than the fencing on the cliff edge, and she wondered whether the work had been done as a bid to make them safe after Sam had found his way down to the beach whilst his nanny was otherwise occupied.

Someone had taken the trouble to install lighting along the edge of the steps. She couldn't see a switch and guessed it must be solar. And why not in this climate? But it was a lot of trouble to go to for a little boy. Surely it would have been cheaper to read him the riot act and tell him he wasn't to ever go there alone again. Yet from what she'd seen so far, whether something was expensive or not didn't factor in the Joyce household. Neither did common sense.

Sam had wriggled into his wetsuit and was standing at the water's edge by the time she reached the bottom.

'Go on then, in you go,' she shouted, watching as he waded out. The sea looked perfect for swimming, although there was enough surf for body boarding, and she wondered if she asked, Miguel would buy the boy a cheap board from one of the beachside shops in the town. It would give him a hobby to take up when he returned to Cornwall.

Sitting down on the sand by the shade of the rocks, she rummaged in her bag for her phone. No reception. She expected Matt would text to check she got back okay. Not, she suspected, because he gave a damn about how their meeting had ended or how she was feeling, but because he needed to be sure his asset was in place and ready to work.

She zipped the phone and Margarita's picnic into the bag, discarded her t-shirt and shorts and ran down the beach to follow Sam into the water.

It was chilly, and she remembered this was not the Med. She took the plunge, surfacing close to the boy. He was a good little swimmer, happy to dunk his head under the water, whereas lots of children his age found that daunting. Her father had forced her and Rob to put their heads under, ignoring the protests, not to mention the splutters and gags until, eventually, they submitted to the salty sting in their nostrils. Her father called it tough love. She knew now it was sadism and control.

She felt something nip at her ankle and let out a small scream.

Sam popped up like a seal, giggling; the sun twinkling on his long, wet lashes.

'I thought you were a shark,' she grinned, playing to her audience.

'You don't get sharks here, not the sort you mean that bite you, more likely to be a jellyfish,' he said. 'They sting you with their tentacles. They leave big red marks and make you sick. I've seen pictures at school.' He said this with the sort of relish peculiar to small boys with a sense of drama and a love of gore.

'Wow, we'd better watch out for them then. What flavour do they come in strawberry or lime?'

He giggled, getting the pun.

'Okay, clever clogs, how about you stay away from my ankles?' she said. 'Although I must say you're a very good swimmer.'

'I know.'

'Who taught you?'

'Paolo.'

'In the pool?'

'Sometimes, but mostly here on the beach.'

Pinkie was surprised. 'When?'

'Every day last school holidays.'

She knew Paolo had taken an interest in the boy and let him hang around while he was working but had no idea they were this close.

'So, you never come here alone?'

'No, I'm not allowed.'

'Is that after you came down here alone when your other nanny was still in charge?'

'No.'

'I thought—'

Sam interrupted. 'Oh, you mean when Grandad thought I was lost, but I was with Paolo?'

'Did your dad know that?'

'Yeah, of course. He had a row with Paolo about it.'

'A row?'

'Yeah, on the beach.'

The boy, bored by her questions, swam away.

'Don't swim out too far,' she shouted after him, lowering herself back into the water so it lapped over her shoulders.

Why hadn't Gary told his father the boy was with Paolo when it looked like his girlfriend was going to get the sack? Paolo was Margarita's son, after all, and she was practically family.

Sam had stopped swimming to wave at someone on the shore. She spun around to see who.

A tall, dark-haired man was making his way down the steps towards the beach.

'Who are you waving at?' Pinkie shouted across the breakers to Sam.

'Grandad's doctor.'

Though Margarita had talked about Lionel's doctor, she had only once caught the briefest glimpse of him entering his patient's bedroom. Why on earth was he here, had something happened? If it had, she needed to get to him before Sam did. He'd suffered enough loss in his short life already and would need to be handled carefully.

'I'm cold,' she shouted. 'I'm going in to dry off. You swim for a bit longer if you like. I'll get your sandwich and drink ready for you for when you get out.'

The boy didn't need a second bidding to keep having fun.

She waded out of the water, reaching her towel just as the doctor stepped onto the sand. Wrapping it around her shoulders, she set off towards him, but before she had time to take more than a couple of steps, he'd turned tail to head straight back up the way he'd come.

She hollered after him, wondering if perhaps he hadn't seen her, although it was unlikely in her bright red costume, and Sam had been waving. Not to mention they were the only ones there.

He carried on walking.

Rude, she thought. Why on earth was he here if not to

speak to her or Sam? Unless it was some weird exercise regime to walk up and down those steps, or maybe he'd been looking for someone else. It was a private beach, so it had to be someone from the villa. Paolo? He was the one who usually took Sam swimming.

'Out you come, Sam,' she shouted, gesturing for the boy to follow.

She lifted the sandwich from the bag along with the water and biscuits and took a long gulp of the iced tea from the flask Margarita had packed for her.

Sam joined her, and after she'd helped him out of his wetsuit and dried off, he tucked in. She was conscious the clock was ticking, and despite Sam's protests, when he'd finished, it was time to go.

The ascent back up the cliff was certainly more arduous than the walk down, and it struck her the doctor had been taking his own medicine. He'd practically galloped back up the steps, never once using the handrail.

On reaching the lawn, she told Sam to run ahead and give the wet sandy towels to Margarita to wash so she could take a quick detour to the summer house to hide the Glock.

The garden was rippled with the orange hues of late afternoon, leafy shadows playing across the grass. The summer house was stiflingly hot. She opened a window, pausing to check Sam hadn't doubled back. It was his favourite haunt, after all.

The components of his latest project - cardboard boxes, an ashtray full of corks and an empty pop bottle - were strewn across the table. He'd finally managed to prize a bottle of vinegar and a pack of baking soda from Margarita's pantry to complete the homemade rocket he aimed to launch. This was Mark 4. The others had all failed miserably.

Certain she was alone, she retrieved the velvet bag holding the Glock. She checked the chamber to reassure herself it was empty. She never trusted anyone else to handle her guns, let alone choose them for her. She liked the 19 well enough. It was reliable, with the fewest moving parts of any military issue sidearm. Compact and easy to conceal, as Matt said, it could fit in her handbag, but it wouldn't have been her choice. It was the gun you gave a novice. If you couldn't manage to hit a close-range target with a Glock, you had no real business holding a gun, let alone firing one. It was the trigger safety she couldn't stand. To someone like her, used to the feel of a gun, the two-stage safety trigger felt inelegant. True, it wouldn't fire off if you accidentally dropped it, shooting a random passer-by, which was useful if you were an amateur or a policeman under public scrutiny, but she was no amateur and Matt's choice smacked of paternalism. She walked to the stove.

Once again, with her full weight against it, she was able to shift it enough to reveal the gap beneath the charred floorboards. She was pleased with her choice of hiding place. The stove was too heavy for Sam to move and too filthy for anyone else to want to go near. She knelt down and, with the gun in her right hand, felt around until she found a place to wedge it so it wouldn't fall through below the building. Satisfied, she slid the stove back, making sure she replaced it exactly where it had been, rubbing away any marks she had made with the heel of her trainer.

She'd decided to spread her bets and stash the ammunition behind the headboard in her room.

Her hands were filthy, but she'd have to wait until she got back to the house to wash. There was a paint-splattered sink in the summer house from Mrs Joyce's time, but the water had been disconnected long ago.

When she got back to the villa, Margarita was sitting on the patio sipping a glass of the same iced tea she'd enjoyed on the beach. There was a young woman with her.

'Good to see you with your feet up for a change,' Pinkie said, trying her best to hide her grubby fingers.

'I'm waiting for the doctor to finish with Lionel so I can go up with his food, not that he eats much these days. Oh, I must introduce you,' she said, looking towards the strikingly good-looking twenty-something next to her. 'This is my niece Angelina, the one I told you about who works in the hotel.'

Pinkie racked her brain.

'The one who recommended the dentist to me.'

'Oh yes, of course,' gushed Pinkie, 'thanks for that. He was excellent, fixed it in no time.'

The girl flashed a dazzlingly white smile as if to say, "I know what I'm talking about when it comes to teeth, lady."

'He came to the beach, you know,' said Pinkie wanting to change the subject.

'Who?'

'Lionel's doctor, earlier on, I think he was looking for someone.'

'I can't think who.'

'I thought Paolo, maybe?'

'Paolo,' she said, straightening her back, wide-eyed, 'why would he be looking for Paolo?'

'Sam said Paolo was the one who took him down to the beach to swim sometimes, and I thought maybe someone had said Sam was there, and he got the wrong end of the stick.'

'No,' Margarita said sharply, pushing the chair away. 'Paolo is not here today.'

Pinkie, sensing a raw nerve, didn't press it further. She

wondered if it had something to do with the row Sam said Paolo and Gary had on the beach. It would have been just like Gary to delegate responsibility for Sam to someone else, then twist it, so the nanny's sacking was somehow Paolo's fault.

Margarita walked towards her, defensiveness morphing to concern as she frowned at Pinkie's hands. 'You've had a tiring day. Why don't you go take a long soak in the bath and get an early night? I'll bring your food up if you like, say around seven. I can look after Sam. We can watch a movie,' she said, pulling at Sam's salt-spiked hair. 'You can help me deliver your grandad's tray. He'll be pleased to see you before he goes to bed.'

The offer of a relaxing soak in a hot bath without any distractions was too great a temptation to resist. She wanted to be alone with her thoughts; not have to make polite conversation. 'If you're sure, and it's not too much trouble,' said Pinkie, truly grateful for the housekeeper's kindness.

'Of course not. You go on up. I'll be there with your tray once I've seen to Lionel.'

'Nice to meet you,' Pinkie nodded to Angelina.

'Likewise,' smiled the young woman. Then as Pinkie turned to walk away, 'Glad the toothache has gone.'

Chapter Twenty-Eight

TRUE TO HER WORD, Margarita knocked on her bedroom door at ten to seven with homemade Gaspacho and a tempting foamy white dessert.

'Did you have a nice soak?'

'Wonderful,' Pinkie said, looking down at the tray.

'I didn't want to give you anything hot just in case,' she said, 'and I left the bread off the tray. This time of day it's not so soft, and I was worried your tooth might still be tender.'

'Thank you. This is perfect. It smells so good.'

'I hope you like plenty of garlic. I follow my mother's recipe.'

'I love it,' Pinkie smiled. 'What's the pudding?' she asked.

'*Natas do Céu*, it means heavenly cream. Enjoy.'

Pinkie took the tray from her.

'Just leave it outside the door when you've finished, and I hope you sleep better tonight.'

As soon as she was gone, Pinkie made herself comfortable on the bed, the tray on her lap. Though emotionally drained by the day's revelations, she was starving. How did the saying go, feed a cold and starve a fever? They could add eat your way through an identity crisis to the homily.

The spicy tomato soup was deliciously refreshing and the custardy pudding aptly named. When finished, she placed the tray outside the door and then, exhausted, changed for bed.

Matt's revelation Rob was gay had been no revelation at all. She'd known deep down not because he'd ever said anything; the homophobic rantings of her father had throttled any conversation he could have had about his sexuality with her. She imagined his pain, living the lie and then on top of it all, when he confides in his best friend, the only other person he is close to, he's rejected. She imagined how he'd felt all those months watching her and the man he loved fall for each other, slowly becoming the third wheel. It must have been agony.

She pulled the covers up to her neck. She was overtired and also, she guessed, suffering from the heat. Matt was right. It was important to make sure you drank enough in this weather. The heady sensation she'd struggled with all afternoon was more than likely down to dehydration. She finished off the bottle of water next to her bed and turned off the light. Listening to the trill of cicadas beneath her window, she plummeted into a deep sleep.

Her dreams were unusually vivid. She was back in Cornwall sitting on a blanket on her lawn, or rather a red and white chequered tablecloth like the one Margarita threw over the garden table when she fed the builders. She never sat on the lawn anymore. Who did? Everyone she knew had at least one set of patio chairs. Even in her dream, it felt odd. She kept thinking she should get up and return the cloth to the kitchen before it got dirty.

It was summer or the beginning of it. The rhododendrons had gone over, but the roses were at their blousy best. She could smell the patch of lemon verbena in the bed to the left where bees hovered around the lavender; the English kind they seemed to like better than the fancy French variety. She looked up. From the sun's position, it was about midday, and she felt for the floppy cotton sun hat she'd worn that afternoon in Albufeira. But she wasn't in Albufeira, was she? She could hear the buzz of a lawn mower next door. It must be Saturday. Agnes always mowed her lawn on Saturdays in the summer months. Her neighbour was a stickler for routine. She lay back and let the golden light wash over her. The sun felt so good on her tired limbs. *Just a little longer,* she whispered. She'd have to go pick up Sam from school soon. Then again, if she'd brought him back with her to Cornwall, surely that was Liz's job now. She had just begun to relax when a shadow crossed her face.

'You never stop, do you, cogs always turning, trying to work it all out.'

She pulled herself up onto one elbow, shading her eyes to see the face of the figure standing over her.

'Rob?'

'Come on, let's take a walk.'

Her brother held out his hand. She took it, and he pulled her to her feet.

'Rob, what are you doing here? Are you on leave?'

He kept a tight hold of her hand as they walked down the path, past the greenhouse full of plants.

'But I burnt you all,' she said.

'It doesn't matter,' said Rob, tugging her to move faster.

'But you don't understand. I killed a judge.'

'I know, isn't it wonderful?' he said, his broad smile lighting up his young face.

She began to laugh, too. They passed Joyce's summer house, and she realised they were no longer in Cornwall. If this was her garden, they would have reached the end of it by now.

The psychedelic flowers swayed and waved as they passed. 'Who taught them that?' she asked.

She tried to blink the images away, knowing they weren't right, they couldn't be right. She glanced back over her shoulder at the winking hibiscus and began to giggle. Her house was still there, the greenhouse, the pile of rocks behind the shed waiting to be transformed into a rockery. Yet, she could hear the sea, and she didn't live by the sea; couldn't afford to.

'Come on,' said Rob tugging at her arm.

'I don't want to,' she said, trying to pull away. I need to water the rosary pea.'

'Come on,' he said.

She looked at him. It was no longer Rob pulling her. It was Matt.

She let go of Matt's hand. Spinning around, she called out, 'Rob ... Rob, where did you go?'

Matt grabbed her around the waist. He was dragging her now, nearer and nearer to the fence, and the more she tried to struggle, the closer they got to the cliff edge and the sheer drop to the sea below.

Chapter Twenty-Nine

PINKIE WAS FLUNG BACK into the waking world by the hollow chime of scaffolding poles being thrown into the back of a pick-up, the racket making a lie-in impossible despite it being Saturday, and technically she was not on duty until ten. It was the one day of the week Sam was allowed to play video games and watch TV, and generally, he would get up at eight, have breakfast, and then be glued to the screen until she dragged him away.

She'd flung off her covers. Her pyjamas were damp with sweat. Her pillow was wet where she'd drooled. She might as well get up.

She shuffled across the room and pulled back the curtains. Upturned wheelbarrows, off-cuts of timber and tools littered the lawn waiting to be loaded into a string of vans blocking the drive. The builders, who never came on weekends, seemed unusually disorganised, and it crossed her mind they may have been under the impression they had more time to pack up and leave. She remembered what Matt had said; Joyce would want to have some space between their exit and the new visitors' arrival. Had the dates been brought forward?

She felt groggy, her mouth sour. She remembered her dream, or rather her nightmare. It was unusual for her to remember either, and even on the rare occasion she did, she never seemed to conjure the psychedelic wonderland variety she'd experienced last night. Perhaps it was the caffeine-loaded drink Matt had given her or just the stress of meeting him and learning about Rob. Whatever the reason, it had been bizarre, and she felt like crap this morning. She wanted to crawl back under the covers but knew she couldn't. There was too much going on.

Summoning the effort, she headed for the shower.

The breakfast dishes had all been cleared by the time she'd dressed.

'Margarita?'

No answer. She made herself a coffee and headed for the lounge expecting to see Sam, cross-legged in front of the TV, ear-phones in playing his Nintendo. But he wasn't around either. Perhaps they were outside saying their goodbyes to the workmen. She reached in the top pocket of her shirt, remembering it held Margarita's oil of cloves. It would stain if the bottle leaked, not to mention the stink. She wandered across the hall back to the kitchen. She'd better put it away in the pantry. She wouldn't want Sam finding it. It wasn't dangerous, but if he opened the bottle and got it on his hands, it might just end up in his eyes, and then he'd know about it. She was opening the pantry door when Margarita came in with the boy in tow.

'Do you need something?'

'No, I'm fine. I was just bringing this back,' she said, holding the tiny brown bottle aloft.

Margarita took it from her and shut the pantry door.

'I'll put it away later,' she smiled. 'We've been outside with the builders, haven't we, Sam?'

'Yeah, they've left me lots of cool stuff. I've got a toolbox, screwdrivers and chisels, and they've left me a drill and something called a spirit level so I can make things straight. Oh yeah, and a hacksaw.'

'Wow, that does sound cool,' said Pinkie.

'I told them to put it all in the summer house along with the few offcuts of wood they've left for him so you can sort through to make sure there's nothing too dangerous,' said Margarita, eyebrows raised.

'It's fine; it's not an electric drill,' said Sam. 'I'm not a baby.'

'Okay, how about we go and have a look?' Pinkie said, hand on his shoulder steering him towards the door, turning to ask the question before she followed.

'Did you know the builders were leaving today?'

Margarita looked at her, exasperation laddering her face.

'Why would I? No one tells me anything around here anymore.'

———

HOUR ON HOUR, the cacophony grew, reaching a crescendo of hollers and horns at midday as the cement mixer was loaded, and with the thud of a door, the last van rumbled down the drive and out of sight. The builders had been there since she arrived, the symphony of men at work, an ever-present accompaniment to daily life around Joyce's villa. Their presence had lent a veneer of normality. With the silence came foreboding and the stark realisation what lay ahead was about as far from normal as you could get.

Leaving a delighted Sam to rifle through the box of goodies the men had left for him, Pinkie wandered away from the summerhouse to where the new building stood.

It took up most of the far corner of the garden. There were no nods to Portuguese design; nothing charming or quaint to draw you in. It had a brutalist quality Pinkie would have found unsettling even had she not known the purpose for which it was built. It looked incongruous amongst the palm trees and bougainvillaea with its corrugated roof and small single-paned windows. It was as plain as day to anyone who had ever served in the military. This was a barracks.

The door was ajar and she entered. Inside it was surprisingly large. The exposed rafters gave extra height not obvious from outside. The place smelt of freshly sawn timber. The builders had done an excellent job at tidying up. It was impeccably clean.

The space was subdivided into three distinct areas. From the stack of plastic-covered mattresses propped against one wall, she guessed she was standing in the sleeping quarters. She counted the mattresses, eight in total. The space would just about accommodate eight metal framed beds, but there was no way anyone would go to the trouble of building something like this for a one-off enterprise for such a small number. This was going to be used more than once. Any fool could see the eight were to be the first of many.

The adjacent room was of similar dimensions and housed a basic gym, a small pool table and a TV along with built-in seating along one wall. Next to that was a wet room and separate loo. The kitchen area was at the very end of the building. There was a table and chairs and little else. It was spartan even for a barracks, and Pinkie assumed the rest of the equipment hadn't arrived yet. There was a small run of melamine worktops housing a sink, toaster, kettle and microwave, but no cooker.

She was startled by Margarita's voice from behind, echoing the observation.

'From the look of this, I'm expected to do the cooking. I thought things would be a little easier once the builders left but clearly not.'

'Do you know when they're arriving?'

'No, no one has told me how many or who they are. I'm just the one who has to feed them,' she said, peeved at the prospect.

Pinkie couldn't blame her. Planning rations for eight men who presumably would need feeding three times a day was no mean feat.

'I counted eight mattresses.'

'Me too, but some must be spare surely. You cannot expect to cram eight guests into such a small space.'

Pinkie couldn't bring herself to tell her you could if they were soldiers or men used to coping with the confines of a prison cell.

'Paolo said I should go and ask Mr Joyce for some help or at least a pay rise, but he is so ill I just can't bring myself to bother him. I don't even know if he's sure what's going on, not really.'

'You mean Gary might have arranged this?'

'Maybe. Perhaps he has let it out for money. Who knows? I haven't seen him since he fought with Paolo.'

A true friend would tell this woman the identity of the men who would soon be invading their lives. She should be allowed to leave while she could. Who knew what could happen once they arrived? At the very least, life would be difficult, at worst, downright dangerous. No doubt she'd be seen as useful for the time being as cook and cleaner, but after that, who knew what the future held? If these men thought for one moment she might be a risk, they would kill her. Pinkie was certain of it. Matt had been clear; these people took no prisoners.

Then again, if she told Margarita the truth, not only would she potentially wreck Matt's operation but also risk both their lives. She could, she supposed, encourage Margarita's growing dissatisfaction with the state of play while still keeping her in the dark, but she doubted the woman would countenance leaving unless she could convince Joyce to leave too. She didn't give a flying fuck about Joyce, whether he died here or in hospital, but Margarita did and would never leave him. She'd have to pick her moment, but Margarita was already at the end of her tether, and the threat of Gary arriving with a bunch of boozy coke-sniffing mates might well be the straw to break the camel's back.

'Do you want me to talk to Mr Joyce for you? I really don't mind.'

Pinkie expected a wave of relief to sweep the woman's face, but instead, she looked even more fraught. 'No, it's okay. I'll talk to him.'

Chapter Thirty

DESPITE MARGARITA'S insistence that she would handle things herself, Pinkie decided there and then she would make it her business to intervene on her behalf. She didn't know what, if anything, she'd achieve other than perhaps glean valuable intel on when their guests would be arriving and the opportunity to surreptitiously plant Matt's recording device in Joyce's room.

Margarita left shortly after lunch for what Pinkie supposed was a pre-emptive trip to the supermarket, whilst Sam had swapped Team Houston in the summerhouse for Team Lego in his bedroom.

She'd already texted Matt to let him know the builders had packed up and left that morning. She checked her phone for a reply, but she had no notifications.

She knew time was limited. Margarita would be gone for a while, but Sam was bound to come looking for her sooner or later. There was only so much self-entertaining a seven-year-old could be expected to provide.

From her underwear drawer, she retrieved the small

brown envelope Matt had handed her the day before and shook the tiny metal object free. Things had certainly moved on a pace since her day. The device was minuscule, barely two inches long and whisper-thin, resting as light as a feather on her palm.

She pressed the switch on the side to check it was charged. According to the blurb, the highly sensitive stereo microphone was voice activated and supposed to be able to pick up conversations fifty feet away. She didn't have fifty feet or the time to test it. She hoped Matts's team realised this was too risky to fuck up.

Slipping it into her blouse pocket, she made her way along the corridor to Joyce's room. She knocked, waited, and then knocked again. When no one answered, she let herself in.

As before, the curtains were pulled. The only light in the room was cast from a small table lamp. The man was propped up a little in the bed, chin resting on his chest, eyes closed, and from the lack of movement, he was fast asleep. Lifting the recording device from her pocket, she looked for somewhere to place it; somewhere it could pick up people talking without being obstructed.

She balanced it between her thumb and forefinger. Its size meant it was unobtrusive enough, and its black metal casing made it robust. Nevertheless, she needed to make sure it was out of harm's way; that it didn't accidentally end up in the vacuum cleaner.

It could store over four hundred hours of audio, although its fifty hours of battery time meant sooner or later, she'd have to retrieve it for a recharge, so it needed to be relatively accessible. The plan was to plug the thing into her laptop and forward the recording to Matt remotely. At least it meant she wouldn't have to meet him again.

She scanned the room. The device was capable of cutting out ninety per cent of environmental noise, but she wasn't convinced it would manage to cut out the relentless hum of the machinery behind Joyce's bed. Anywhere around there would be a challenge.

There wasn't much furniture in the room, the wardrobes were built in, and the tables either side of the bed and the metal trolley were loaded with sick room paraphernalia and medication which she assumed was subject to constant movement. The central light fitting was a fancy wrought iron affair, all winding stems and floral finials, nothing to balance the thing on. There were no wall lights but then, her eyes rested on Mrs Joyce's brightly coloured painting. It was a permanent fixture, and the frame looked wide enough to accommodate the gadget easily.

Using one of the bedside chairs to step up, she ran her finger along the top surface of the frame to check for dust and was delighted when she found a thick layer. Dust was good. She knew the cleaners never set foot in here, and this was proof Margarita had more than enough on her plate without worrying about cleaning places no one ever got to see.

She shuffled the recorder about halfway along, happy it would function fine there.

She returned the chair, pausing as she did to take a better look at Joyce. The man's breathing was shallow and laboured, and he looked even more jaundiced than before. She slipped her hand around his wrist to check his pulse. It was weak and irregular. He didn't react at all to her touch, and she guessed the medication the doctor prescribed had knocked him out. She bent closer, thinking she might pull back his eyelids to see if his pupils were dilated but thought better of it. There was a faint sweet fruity smell around him she tried to place. Peaches, maybe, no apricots, that was it, like the jam she'd seen her friend Agnes use on the fruitcake at Christmas before she blanketed it with icing. There was an empty bowl on the table beside him, and she thought maybe stewed fruit was all he could keep down. Margarita would have made it her business to cook anything he fancied to tempt him; she knew that much.

She walked across to the steel trolly by the side of the bed. Amongst the various bottles of pills and supplements, there was a bottle of oral morphine for the pain. She reckoned if she shook him, he still wouldn't wake up, so any talk she was going to have with him would have to be put on hold. She'd have to leave it to Margarita to broach the subject of recruiting help.

She left quietly, joining Sam just as he was on the brink of placing the last brick in the reactor shaft in the Star Wars death star.

'Looking good,' she said, seriously impressed.

'I reckon I'll have it finished by next weekend. Then I'll be able to work on my rocket.'

'Good idea. I've got a feeling you're gonna crack it with Mark 4.'

'Me too,' he grinned, 'I need to wrap the baking powder in a tissue.'

'Makes sense,' she said, 'slow release to build the reaction.'

He nodded sagely. 'Can I have pizza for tea?'

'I'll have to cook it. Margarita isn't a big fan of pizza.'

He smiled. 'I don't mind. I trust you.'

'Well, I'll do my best but no promises. I'll have to pass it by the boss lady.'

She left him to it. On the way back to her room, her phone pinged with a text from Matt; a photo attached. She waited whilst it loaded. Revealing itself from bottom to top, it was a close-up of a man walking down a rain-slicked street, phone to his ear. The text read:

Niko Kurti

Pinkie recognised him immediately as the man she'd seen the day before on the beach; the man claiming to be Lionel Joyce's doctor.

Chapter Thirty-One

ROSS HAD SPENT the last week or so interviewing members of Philippa Floyd's gardening club. He would have liked to have been able to say it had been a fruitful and enjoyable exercise. However, it had been anything but. He'd suffered no less than four garden tours, been required to unblock a sink and had his leg rogered by an over-sexed Bichon Frise whilst its mistress cut him a slice of Victoria sponge. The whole thing was made worse by the fact he had taken holiday to follow this lead; holiday he had not told Karenza about and lived in fear of her discovering.

The need to take this feckless course of action had come about largely because of the brick walls he'd hit trying to investigate Philippa Floyd through the usual channels. It started the minute he logged in to check her status, which these days began for everyone with social media. She had no profile whatsoever, no Facebook or Instagram and wasn't on Twitter or WhatsApp. He looked up Agnes Chenoweth. There she was, larger than life, scowling at the camera, daring anybody to friend her, but

Philippa didn't feature. It was odd for someone who'd been involved in the media, especially a journalist who worked with charities, both of which relied on publicity. He'd searched 'Philippa Floyd-Pen Name'; no joy there either. He trawled the sites of charities operating in Somalia, scanning countless project photographs and promotions, but she was neither mentioned nor pictured in any of them. He called up the census, and there she was at her current address, but when he searched the previous one, there was no trace and no further details on the electoral role other than she had stated her occupation as *retired*. She was too young for a state pension, so he headed for HMRC. He had her date of birth from her passport, the gold standard of IDs and thought he'd try to link it up with a tax reference or a National Insurance number, which he did manage to access via the Department of Works and Pensions site. It was there he found a record of a MOD pension. Thrilled he was finally making progress, he'd headed on into the site armed with her reference only to be bounced straight out again. He tried to circumvent what he assumed was a glitch and was met with *you do not have the authorisation to access this information.* After trying every other trick he knew and getting the same stock reply, he gave up. Hence, he was on his way to interview another middle-aged woman, hopefully dog-free, to see if he could get any useful information on the elusive Pinkie.

He was a little more hopeful with this one. Several of the other candidates had told him Liz Hosking was a particular friend. Whether that particular friend was able to remember a conversation months ago about Carlisle was another matter.

He pulled up outside the address. The garden, as anticipated, was a picture. He was becoming quite the expert on summer bedding.

The woman who answered the door was younger than some he'd met previously, one of whom had forgotten he was coming and thought he was the man from Dyno-Rod. He hadn't had the heart to disappoint, hence the unblocked sink and the dry cleaning bill for a pair of suit trousers.

'Mrs Hosking?'

'Come in, come in and call me Liz, please.'

Ever the policeman, he scanned the furnishings for the number of bums on seats in the household.

'I've got coffee on the brew if you'd like one?'

Already awash with the stuff he wanted to decline but was not one to offend.

'Lovely, black please, no sugar,' he smiled.

He looked around the room; family photos, a daughter and grandchild, he guessed. A photograph of a younger Liz with a man on holiday, the Arc de Triumph behind them. They looked happy, but he'd noticed no obvious sign of a man in the house. He might be wrong. Some of his sex, unlike him, were tidy enough, although in his experience, very few retired men failed to leave their mark. Coats or muddy boots in the hall, rolled up newspaper down the side of a chair, remote resting on the arm poised for *Pointless*.

'You said on the phone this was about Philippa?'

'That's right. Her neighbour,' Ross made a show of flipping over the page of his notepad, 'Miss ... Chenoweth has reported her missing.'

The woman frowned. 'Missing, are you sure?'

'She hasn't been seen for several weeks, and Agnes, Miss Chenoweth, says it's unusual for her not to have said where she was going or how she could be contacted.'

He was on first-name terms with Agnes these days. It

was hard not to be when she had you on speed dial. She checked in most afternoons to let him know she had nothing to report, the conversation lasting at least ten minutes each time. To her, they were a team; Cagney and Lacey, Dalziel and Pascoe. Ross was slowly losing track of which of the dynamic duo he was meant to be but was pretty sure in Agnes's eyes. He was the sidekick.

'I just assumed she was away. It's been difficult to keep track of people since COVID. Lots of the members don't come to the club anymore, and we've not picked up on our lunches since. A couple of our group have elderly parents, so we have to be careful.'

'So have you had any contact at all, telephone … text maybe?'

'Not phone, not for a few weeks. I'll have to check if there have been any texts I've missed.'

'That would be helpful,' said Ross, not holding out much hope.

Liz returned with her phone. Scrolling down to the last text message she received from Pinkie, she showed it to Ross.

'Not recent, I'm afraid.'

> So nice to talk today. I hope it didn't rake up too many unhappy memories.

'Unhappy memories?' asked Ross.

'Family stuff.'

'I see … that's a nice photo,' he said, pointing to the snap of Liz and the man he assumed to be her husband.

'Thank you. It seems a lifetime ago now. It was taken the year before my husband died.'

'I'm sorry.'

'Don't be sorry. It's nice to talk about him. I've got used to being alone. Like a lot of people, I've had to.'

'Have you got family close by?'

'No, unfortunately not. I had a daughter, but she passed away several years ago.' Liz paused. 'Actually, that was the conversation the text refers to. My Rachel committed suicide, you see.'

Ross felt dreadful. This poor woman didn't need any more grief. Giving her Philippa Floyd's disappearance to fret about on top of everything else was plain cruel.

'I'm so sorry. Look, I'll get out of your hair,' he said, placing his coffee cup down on the table. 'If Miss Floyd should make contact, could you give me a ring?' He stood and handed over his card, his mobile number handwritten on the back.

Liz hadn't got up. 'It was good to talk to Philippa about it all. She's a very good listener, you know. I expect that comes from all her years as a journalist. She was genuinely interested in my grandson. She didn't shy away from embarrassment like some who've heard the story before. She was even interested to know about my daughter's custody case and the judge who handled it. Most would have found the court stuff dull but not her. She allowed me to vent.'

Ross sat down again.

———

AN HOUR LATER, he was back in the car, more convinced than ever Philippa Floyd was his prime suspect in Carlisle's murder. Finally, he had his motive. He also had another name to focus on; one he'd come across plenty of times before when investigating Jerome Fielding, one of the gangster's cronies from the golf club, a man the force had always suspected of malfeasance when he was a planning officer but had never been able to get enough dirt to stick. Councillor Lionel Joyce. What's more, he knew where Joyce was, and his son, and if Liz was right, his grandson too. The Joyce dynasty was in Portugal, in the villa all that graft and laundered money had paid for and if his hunch was right about Philippa Floyd, passport or no passport, she had skipped the country and was camping on their doorstep waiting for an opportunity to chalk up her second victim. Bloody hell, he was sounding more like Agnes every day. Where was his evidence? He ought to backpedal a little just to make sure he wasn't heading off in completely the wrong direction. Then again, if he put the brakes on now, he was likely to fly over the handlebars and land on his ass. He could, of course, take his feet off the pedals and freewheel and see where it took him. After all, he was on his holidays, and there were cheap flights from Newquay to Faro leaving every day.

Chapter Thirty-Two

AFTER CALLING MATT, Pinkie settled by the pool, trying to make sense of what she knew while watching Sam swim laps.

She could tell from Matt's reaction he was every bit as surprised as her to learn Nico had been posing as Joyce's doctor for weeks but had concluded he'd done so to be able to come and go without attracting unwanted attention from the builders. His view was that Joyce knew very well who Kurti was. Once he'd got a handle on the situation, he was more than satisfied with this explanation and ignited with the implications. It meant he was right about Joyce. He was actively involved with the enterprise. What's more, now she'd successfully planted the listening device, they'd be getting first-hand intel from here on in. At no time did he ask her how she felt about it all.

Had he done so, Pinkie would have told him she felt the opposite. She was struggling to process the information and to see where this left her and her plans. If Joyce's doctor was not his doctor, then who was treating Joyce? Matt had brushed her concerns aside, implying Joyce might be feigning illness. Pinkie didn't wear it. The man would have to be an Oscar winner to pull off the kind of stupor she'd seen the evening before. Ruling out pretence, she had to consider what else might explain his condition. The morphine would cause his semi-conscious state, but it didn't explain the rapid deterioration. Pinkie knew a dying man when she saw one.

She felt bad for Margarita, this poor woman who yet again had been duped. She was labouring under the misapprehension her beloved employer was in the capable hands of his physician. She'd followed the doctor's regime of medication, no doubt to the letter, when in fact, it was an elaborate scam. Whilst Lionel's pain was being managed, she doubted he was being treated at all. Why not? Who would benefit from Lionel being out of the picture?

Gary.

It made sense. Joyce was out of it most of the time. There was no way the man she'd seen the night before could be planning anything. He could not have held a conversation with Nico, even with a gun to his head. The more she tried to rationalise it, the clearer it became. Gary had to be the protagonist here, not his father.

She heard Margarita's car coming up the drive.

Sam was stretched out on the grass, reading his book.

'Are you okay here for a while? I'm going to help Margarita with the shopping.'

Sam nodded, too engrossed to answer.

Margarita was in the kitchen unloading the bags around her feet.

'I'll give you a hand with this lot,' offered Pinkie. 'I thought you were taking a long time. Now I know why.'

'I've been told the visitors are arriving tomorrow. I needed to get a big shop in before they turned up.'

Pinkie wondered who had told her. She'd been in the dark earlier when they'd spoken, and she knew first-hand Lionel Joyce hadn't been in any fit state to phone her when she was out.

'Mr Joyce finally let you in on his plans then?'

'Not Lionel. Gary called me to say eight of his friends are arriving tomorrow morning.'

Gary; so, Gary was up to his neck in this.

'He's coming home then?'

Margarita hesitated, a can of tinned tomatoes hovering above the kitchen shelf in her hand.

'No, he said he wouldn't be here when they arrived. He has other plans.'

'What other plans?' asked Pinkie, frustrated by the man's elusiveness.

Margarita looked flustered.

'I don't know. Why do you keep asking me these questions when I've told you no one tells me anything?'

Pinkie was taken aback by the ferocity of the response.

Margarita slumped down into a chair.

'I'm sorry,' said Pinkie, 'I'm just naturally nosey, I suppose. I've barely seen Gary since I arrived. He's Sam's dad, and he doesn't seem to care at all about his son. I can't help but feel he could make more of an effort.'

'I'm sorry,' Margarita sighed. 'I didn't mean to snap. It's not your fault. I'm worried about Lionel, and with Paolo gone and these men arriving … I feel nervous when it comes to Gary.'

Pinkie understood. Gary didn't inspire confidence. If he was involved with something, it was a foregone conclusion it would be a shit storm.

'You sit there. I'll make you a cup of tea. Let me wait on you for a change.'

The housekeeper didn't object. She stared into space, running the long till receipt from the supermarket through her fingers.

Pinkie plopped a tea bag into the cup and reached up for the sugar bowl. Margarita took her tea black and sweet.

Sam shouted from the patio, 'Someone's coming up the drive.'

Margarita got to her feet. 'It'll be the meat delivery. I saw the butcher in the village and told him I'd leave the gate open,' she said wearily.

The sugar pot was empty. Pinkie scanned the table for a new pack, then rummaged in the grocery bags but couldn't see any.

She could hear Margarita chatting at the door to the butcher in Portuguese. Perhaps there was some sugar in the pantry. She walked to the alcove and pulled open the double doors to reveal shelves stacked with provisions, flour, rice, pasta of every shape and variety, large cans of olive oil and an entire shelf of herbs; marjoram, thyme, sage and more exotic ingredients star-anise, saffron, the latter reminding her of saffron cake and Cornwall.

She noticed a small tub of rose petals and next to it a larger one labelled *Folha de Louro*; bay leaves. She had a couple of topiary bays standing sentry outside her front door, and suddenly, overcome with longing for home, she unscrewed the lid and lifted one of the leaves. It didn't look the same as the ones she was used to, and she wondered if it was a different variety. The ones at home had a serrated edge which made them lethal if they were caught in the back of the throat when left in a dish. She used them in her homemade minestrone but was always careful to remove every last one before she served it. These were long and thin, almost spiky. She held the leaf between her fingers, lifting it to her nose, expecting the familiar herbal scent, a little like oregano. She tried to crush the leaf between her palms to release the oils; nothing, almost no aroma at all. Bay was a member of the laurel, but this wasn't bay or any other culinary ingredient. Pinkie believed she knew what this was, and as she held it, her thoughts swarmed like flies around roadkill.

She heard footsteps coming through the hall into the kitchen. Thrusting the leaf into her pocket, she grabbed an unopened bag of sugar, closed the pantry door and headed for the kitchen where she went back to making the tea. Margarita was leaning over the table, pulling parcels of meat from a plastic tray and ticking them off her list. She didn't look up until she'd accounted for every one and signed the butcher's chitty, handing him an envelope of cash as he took his leave.

'There you go,' Pinkie said, placing the sugary tea on the table. 'Did Sam go up to his room?' Her mind was racing.

'No, he headed down to the garage. Miguel's working on one of the cars and he wanted to watch. I checked with Miguel. He said it was fine as long as he didn't get under his feet.'

'We won't see him for a while then,' Pinkie said, helping Margarita load the meat into the freezer. 'If you don't need any more help, I think I'll go back outside to catch some sun and read my book.'

'I'm going to be planning the meals for the next few days so I can get a head start.'

'I'm afraid I can't help you there unless you intend to dish up pasta every meal.'

Margarita laughed. 'You're not much of a cook then?'

'No, I suppose I've never got into the habit. I've always been in other peoples' houses working, so I've never really had the chance to learn.'

'Your mother never taught you?'

'God no, she was hopeless.'

It was a lie. Her mother had been a decent cook, basic but tasty stuff, and back home in Cornwall she enjoyed cooking for her friends, albeit she wasn't too adventurous and still hadn't mastered how to crimp a pasty or debone the day's catch.

Outside she picked up Sam's wet towel, draping it over the sunbed to dry, then, checking no one was watching, took the leaf from her pocket. Nerium oleander, the same variety used to hedge Joyce's villa and the boundaries of many of the neighbouring properties.

Unlike the ubiquitous privet and dreaded leylandii, oleander was a show stopper. Its carnival crimson flowers sang of summer holidays and Sangria, but behind the glamour lurked something darker. Its stems, leaves and even its starry flowers were poisonous. They contained not one but four deadly toxins. The first symptoms included general lethargy or feebleness often accompanied by blurred vision, haloes around objects and general irritation of the mucus membranes. The lethal dose was around four grams, but smaller amounts over an extended period could be equally punishing on the body, causing nausea, diarrhoea and severe stomach cramps. Confusion, depression and disorientation followed along with excruciating headaches. What killed you, though, were the cardiac glycosides slowing your heartbeat and lowering your blood pressure to an unsustainable level. People generally died through accidental ingestion, having chewed the leaves or the petals of the flowers or, strangely enough, through inhalation of toxic smoke. There was one story of men from Napoleon's army using the branches as skewers to barbecue meat, inhaling the smoke and never waking up. Others, tired of life and, with a sense of the dramatic, brewed tea and killed themselves. Oleander tea was a deadly beverage in the hands of those who wanted to do harm, and it smelt of apricot.

The assumption was there to be made. Margarita was poisoning Joyce, but why?

She had nothing to gain from his death. In fact, quite the opposite. Once her employer passed away, Gary would be in charge, and he'd been crystal clear about his plans for her when it happened. Other than rare individuals like herself who were professionals in the field, poisoners generally had one of two motives - money or revenge. A man like Lionel in regular contact with his lawyers would have surely made a will, and it was equally probable, given her years of devoted service, Margarita got a mention, but it was unlikely to be more than a gesture. He had Gary and Sam to think of, and from what Pinkie had witnessed, whilst there was mutual respect, the employer and employee divide was always maintained. There was nothing to warrant more than a modest legacy; a pension, perhaps. In any case, Margarita was not the avaricious type. She never showed the remotest interest in anything other than her kitchen. That left revenge. Why would Margarita want to punish Lionel Joyce?

She decided she'd have to box clever. The woman had flown off the handle earlier because she'd asked one too many questions. It was probably best if she made herself scarce, didn't appear over curious about Joyce and his doctor or the new arrivals when they turned up. Miguel had talked about taking Sam for a spin to buy the body boards she'd asked for. She decided to persuade him to postpone the trip until tomorrow so she could go too. It would get her away from the villa for a couple of hours. She'd suggest they stop for lunch to save Margarita the bother of cooking with everything else she had going on. They could head to one of the restaurants fringing the Marina; her treat. Miguel was delighted. She guessed as it wasn't his weekend off, he was glad for something to do and for some adult company. Joyce never required his services these days, and he generally seemed at a loose end. Her motive was not unselfish. She wanted the opportunity to get a better look at Joyce's yacht and to check if Gary was still around.

Chapter Thirty-Three

ROSS ARRIVED at his hotel room, pleased with how smoothly everything had gone, all things considered. He looked at his watch; just gone midnight. The two-and-a-half-hour trip from Newquay had literally flown by. He'd intended to use the time to plan, but he'd barely opened his file and ordered his coffee before he'd nodded off. He'd been woken by the announcement they were approaching Faro airport and the temperature was a balmy nineteen degrees.

He grabbed a beer and a carton of peanuts from the mini-bar. He knew he'd be stung for them, but it was late, and he had no intention of going out again. To his surprise, he'd had no trouble getting a room, although he'd had to book for five days even though he could only possibly get away with a couple at most.

He'd told Karenza he was on a job and would be holed up in a barn on Bodmin Moor for most of the weekend trying to catch a gang of pikey sheep rustlers who had been making a nuisance of themselves. He'd said he couldn't be contacted, and even if he could, the signal was patchy and he'd ring in tomorrow or sooner if they got lucky and caught the perpetrators. He'd picked something dull enough not to raise interest but even he'd been surprised when she'd barely looked up from serving her customer at the bar to say goodbye as he threw his backpack over his shoulder.

He'd been relieved at the time but was beginning to worry her short shrift stemmed from suspicion or miff he was making excuses not to help out in the pub. He was a crap liar, especially where she was concerned, and any doubts she had could easily be checked if she rang the station and asked for him. If she did, some bright spark was likely to ask how the holiday was going.

Sweat gathered around his collar at the thought of it despite the air conditioning, which seemed to be set somewhere between midwinter and arctic. He walked over to the control panel, randomly pressing buttons until the fan cut out.

He slipped off his trainers and hopped onto the bed. Lifting his phone, he resisted the urge to call home for reassurance and pulled up Google Maps.

Joyce's villa was just outside of town. It would only take him twenty minutes in the hire car. He planned to head there tomorrow afternoon. Straight after breakfast, whilst it was still relatively quiet, he intended to visit the hotels he'd shortlisted to see if anyone recognised Philippa Floyd from her photograph. He'd prepared a list in advance, picking the smaller places rather than the ones offering free entry to the local nightclubs or all-inclusive package deals for families. The woman he'd met would want serenity rather than as much sangria as she could neck in one sitting. A single woman of a certain age would stand out like a sore thumb in one of those places, and if he was right about her reason for being there, she would want to keep a low profile. At present, his plans were limited to finding her. What he'd do with her if he did was another matter.

Chapter Thirty-Four

ROSS SPENT a long and unproductive morning foyer-hopping his way around the Old Town. The final hotel on his list, the Villa Martino, was adults only, overlooking the beach and described on TripAdvisor as 'boutique'. A lot of hotels back in Cornwall referred to themselves as 'boutique' these days. He understood it meant they were small and select, hoping to cater to guests who were a little more discerning, but it still seemed a strange word to describe a building to Ross. It made him think of bellbottom trousers and the psychedelic Biba dress Karenza had bought one year from a charity shop to wear to a seventies fancy dress party.

Ross walked through the white-tiled lobby, trying not to feel envious of the bloke in his board shorts, the words Nazaré 2018 blazoned across his t-shirt. He resisted the urge to walk over and talk to him. Nazaré, with its record-breaking waves and surf museum housing the boards of the biggest names in surfing history, was number one on Ross's bucket list; its sixty-foot waves the Holy Grail. If this were

September when the first big swells were hitting the Lisbon coastline, he would have made sure he'd been there to see it and sod the consequences.

The attractive young woman manning reception was pointing at a map unfolded on the counter.

'If you head inland, you can take this route through the Serra de Monchique up to the village here,' she said, leaning in to point. 'You can have lunch there and visit the ruins, or there is a very old and beautiful church. The roads are a little narrow, but it is well signposted.'

Ross hung back until she'd refolded the map and handed the man the keys to the hire car before approaching.

'Good morning, sir, can I help you?' the girl welcomed.

'I hope so,' said Ross adopting his most persuasive smile, before pulling the photograph of Philippa Floyd from his pocket.

'I wonder if you have seen this woman? I think she may be a guest in your hotel?'

The girl barely glanced at the photo. Her eyes fixed on him, the smile still there but more hesitant. 'I'm sorry, sir, but I cannot say either way. Our guests are entitled to their privacy. I'm sure you understand.'

'Yes, of course, but perhaps you've seen her around here at one of the other hotels or in one of the cafés or restaurants?'

'Sir, I think I have made myself clear. You can talk to my manager if you wish, although I'm sure he'll tell you the same thing.'

'I understand,' said Ross, 'but the English lady in the photograph is missing. I am a private investigator hired by her family to try and find her. They are, as you can imagine, extremely anxious. We have reason to believe she may well be here in Albufeira.'

'She must be a very important woman for them to pay for an investigator to come all the way over here.'

He sensed the girl might be fishing for a name he did not want to give at this stage, not until someone recognised her.

'Yes, she is ... to her family, that is.'

The girl lifted the photograph from the counter to take a closer look.

'No,' she said emphatically, handing it back.

'The hair is grey in the photograph, but she may well have dyed it. It may be dark now, brown or black even.'

The girl looked again, and Ross thought he saw a glimmer of recognition, but it passed as quickly as it arrived.

'I'm sorry to appear rude, and I hope you find your lady, but I really must get back to work.'

'Of course, please don't let me hold you up. Thank you for your time, and if you do happen to see her in the street or somewhere around, maybe you could give me a ring? I'm only here for a couple of days. I'm staying here if you need to contact me.'

The girl had already turned away to speak to another guest.

Ross slipped the note with his hotel details across the desk towards her and left.

Despondent, he sauntered across the road to a bar overlooking the beach and ordered a beer. On reflection, cold calling the hotels had been a lame idea. Without his warrant card, he had very little power even in the UK, let alone here. Setting aside the confidentiality issue, it was also the height of the season. All the staff he'd tried to engage in conversation had made it clear they were too busy to stop what they were doing to talk to him about some random middle-aged woman he was looking for. If it had been a teenager, things might be different, but showing them a picture of a grown woman and saying she may be in disguise had to come over as odd. He'd sensed several hadn't believed his story, and he couldn't say he blamed them. They were right to be cautious. He could be a stalker or working for an abusive husband trying to track down his errant wife for all they knew. He wouldn't be at all surprised if one or other of them called the police after he left.

What to do next was the question. The choices were limited. He could turn around and catch the next flight home, give up on finding Philippa Floyd, or he could head for Joyce's villa. He wasn't sure what he was going to say when he got there. He'd never met Joyce personally, but the councillor had been bosom pals with Jem Fielding, and so the odds were he knew of him, if not before, certainly after the coverage he'd got in the local press following Fielding's death. There was no doubt in his mind Joyce was connected, and if his intel was right the man certainly wouldn't need Devon and Cornwall's best to protect him. No matter which way he looked at it, his evidence was not sufficient to put Philippa Floyd at risk. If he was wrong about her, he would have alerted a man with ample reasons and criminal connections to the existence of a woman he might choose to deal with personally.

He'd have to stick to the pretext he was looking for a missing woman from Cornwall who was in the region and ask if Joyce could put out a few feelers amongst his ex-pat friends just in case she'd turned up somewhere. He could hint at criminal activity, embezzlement, a cashier who'd run off with her employer's takings, something vague like that.

It wasn't perfect by any stretch, but it would have to do. He might have to visit a few neighbouring properties with the same story just in case Joyce asked around. If he'd seen her, he would know for certain he was right and would call in help. If he hadn't, then his so-called holiday was coming to an end.

―――

ANGELINA GLANCED towards the revolving door to check the investigator had left before turning back to the newly-weds wanting to book a couples' massage.

'There you go, I've booked you in for three this afternoon and applied your twenty per cent honeymoon discount. There will be a complimentary glass of champagne for you after. Enjoy.'

She waited until young love's dream entered the elevator, then, pocketing the sheet of paper torn from the hotel notepad, picked up the telephone, dialled an outside line and when the phone wasn't answered, left a message. 'Niko, we need to talk. I think we have a problem.'

Chapter Thirty-Five

THE MARINA WAS BACKED by hotel and apartment blocks and fronted by waterside restaurants and upmarket gift shops and galleries.

'Where do you recommend?' Pinkie asked as Miguel parked.

'Depends what you're looking for.'

She glanced over her shoulder at Sam in the back seat.

'Burger and fries?'

'Yep,' he grinned.

'I know you so well,' she smiled back.

The marina was a popular place to hang out at weekends. Many of the swankier restaurants were already full, the tables on the decks outside popular.

Miguel paused at the entrance of a place about halfway along the dock called 'The Lazy Dog'.

'This place is good for burgers and basic stuff. Not too expensive either,' he added, clearly worried about the budget.

'I told you; this is on me.'

They managed to bag a table outside as another party was leaving. Sam and Miguel ordered American-style cheeseburgers and skinny fries, while Pinkie decided to opt for torpedo-shaped cod fritters served with a generous bowl of peri-peri dipping sauce.

Sporadically a cheer would echo from inside where a small group of locals were drinking beer and watching a football match playing on the big screen. Pinkie noticed Miguel nod to one of them as they walked through to the deck. She also clocked the pool table at the far end of the restaurant.

She thought she might have difficulty persuading Sam to stay with Miguel if he knew she was going to attempt a closer look at his grandfather's yacht. The good news was she didn't think he had a clue it was berthed at the Marina. If he had known, he would have been on the edge of his seat on the drive there, desperate to board and have a look at the navigation instruments. Likewise, Miguel hadn't mentioned it. It made her wonder if the Princess or Gary come to that, were still there.

She sat back in her seat, glancing nonchalantly at the yachts on the water.

'How the other half live, eh?'

'I don't envy them their boats,' said Miguel, pulling the lettuce from his burger bun and placing it on the side of his plate. Something she knew he wouldn't dare do at Margarita's table.

'I prefer my transportation to have four wheels. Gary asked me when he was last at the villa if I'd crew for him and his friends when they came to stay, and I told him no. It's not in my job description. What's more, I don't swim.'

So, they did intend to use the boat to get away.

Sam glanced up, briefly scanning the water before

returning his gaze to his plate. 'They're mostly for sailing. I quite like that one,' he said, pointing a skinny chip at a catamaran moored straight ahead. It's an interesting design.'

'But not as good as Grandad's?'

'No, Grandad's is ace.'

Pinkie had read up on the marina. It had more than four hundred berths. She certainly couldn't see all of them from where they were sitting. The potted hedging dividing them from the adjoining restaurant and the jaunty angle of the turquoise sail shades flapping above their heads obscured the view on either side. She guessed each establishment had paid a premium for their slice of the scenery and wasn't going to share it.

'Have you ever played pool, Sam?' she asked, changing the subject.

'No.'

'I noticed there's a table inside. I'm sure Miguel would be happy to show you how when we've finished eating. If that's okay with you, Miguel?'

The driver's eyes had strayed towards the big screen more than once during the meal, and she guessed he would be only too happy to join his friends inside to watch the game.

'Yeah, sure.'

'It's all about strategy; planning the angle of trajectory, and getting the ball to do what you want by aiming your cue at exactly the right spot. Just the sort of thing you enjoy.'

The boy suddenly looked interested.

'Okay,' he shrugged.

Miguel pushed his chair away from the table. 'Are you playing too?' he asked Pinkie.

'No, I'll settle the bill, then I thought I'd wander along the front. I've been meaning to buy Margarita a little something for being so welcoming, and I noticed a few nice gift shops. I won't be long.'

'No problem,' said Miguel, placing a hand on Sam's shoulder, 'take as long as you like.'

The larger yachts were berthed in the second tier of quays. Unlike many marinas, there were no gates and access wasn't limited to those with a pass. Many of the boats were fairly modest in the nautical scheme of things. A few advertised fishing trips beyond the breakwater or tours of the Benagil caves, with the promise of snorkelling the crystal-clear waters. One she noticed even boasted a marine biologist to answer questions during a two-and-a-half-hour dolphin-watching adventure. Sam would have loved that one. It was a pity they'd been tethered to the villa by Joyce. She guessed the boats were a valuable draw for the tourists, many of whom wandered around taking selfies.

It didn't take her long to spot Lionel's cruiser. The Princess stood out amongst the other vessels with its sleek s-shaped canopy and its eye-watering price tag. The lack of canvas covers suggested it had been in recent use. Two young girls of about fifteen were posing with the lack of self-consciousness exclusive to the young. Taking turns to snap each other, Pinkie wondered just how many photos of teenage pouts a girl needed before it was enough. Although they'd obviously taken great care to pick this particular yacht, the proximity of the photographer and the angle they were using meant they'd capture little more than a streak of white fibreglass. She had to get rid of them.

'Would you like me to take one of both of you together?' she offered.

'That would be goat.'

Pinkie was about to ask whether that was a yes or a no,

when the girl with the camera seeing her bemusement, explained.

'GOAT; Greatest of All Time.'

The two posed; sunglasses on, sunglasses off, hats on, hats off, fake kissing, fake dancing, fake smiles, while she snapped, ending with one they promised would be the last, with arms around each other, heads tilted so they touched, their free hands raised in a double-fingered peace sign. Pinkie thought if the gesture was heartfelt, it really would be GOAT, but she doubted it. Eventually, they skipped off, examining her handiwork as they headed back towards the shops, no doubt wondering why she'd bothered getting so much of the boat in shot.

When she was sure they weren't coming back, she took a lingering look at the beautiful vessel so aptly named. She really was a princess.

She knew the yacht's stats almost as well as Sam. It boasted four double cabins, each with a bathroom plus accommodation for three crew. More than enough space for the eight men scheduled to take up residence at the villa, but it was hardly low-key. Then again, perhaps that was the point. They were unlikely to be stopped by anyone on this thing. They'd be viewed as just another charter of rich young men living the dream, and unpalatable as it was, wealth intimidated even those in authority.

The open plan lounge with its cream leather seating and glossy rosewood surfaces screamed luxury. The attention to detail was mind-blowing. There was certainly no expense spared. It was a far cry from the vessels she'd trained on, where tight budgets and the threat of overrunning maintenance contracts had fostered an ethos of make do and mend.

She listened for signs of life. She'd already decided if

anyone challenged her, she'd tell them the truth. She was looking for Gary. She was his son's nanny; they'd had lunch in one of the marina restaurants, and she was wondering if she should bring the boy down to see the boat.

Only the clink of wire halyards against the neighbouring vessel's mast and the gentle lap of water disturbed the hush.

The salon dining table was cluttered with bowls of half-eaten snacks. She counted no less than four empty champagne bottles, one thrust upside down into a bucket of melted ice that had toppled, spilling water across the table and onto the cream carpet beneath. Gary was certainly not averse to having a good time at his father's expense. She wondered if he was sleeping this lot off down below.

She headed down the shiny aluminium staircase. The doors to the cabins were open, the beds freshly made up, ready for guests.

Satisfied there was no one about, she headed back upstairs to the main deck, to where according to the layout plan she'd saved on her phone, the master suite was located.

The door was shut. She knocked and listened. Met with silence, she took a deep breath and entered, half expecting to find Gary and a couple of playmates out for the count.

The cabin, like the others, was unoccupied, but that was where the similarity ended. It was a mess. The bed was unmade and by the state of the sheets, hadn't been touched for days, if not longer. Every surface was cluttered and filthy. As she walked further into the room, her foot hit yet another empty champagne bottle which rolled across the carpet, wedging itself under a chair strewn with dirty laundry. The place stank of sweat and smoke and something else rancid and sweet. Pinkie lifted a can of deodorant from the dressing table and sprayed. If anything, it made matters worse. She coughed as the dry powdery vapour caught the back of her throat.

The bathroom door was a couple of inches ajar.

She pushed it, thinking it would open, but something was stopping it.

Putting her full weight against it, she shoved again, managing to open it just enough to allow her to reach her hand around to the light switch.

The wall-to-wall mirror above the sink unit lit up. No longer in darkness, she could see vomit just inside to the right, which explained the stench, but she still had no visibility to the left to see what was blocking the door.

This wasn't what she'd expected. Her muscles twitched under her skin as she tried to prepare herself for the unknown.

On TV, the hero met with a scene like this generally kicked down the door, but in the real world, such reckless action could have disastrous consequences for someone lying injured behind or with a gun to his head; not to mention what it could do to the ligaments in her knee unless she caught the door just right. She took a deep breath and, with one final shove, pushed again. This time she managed to shift the object behind the door just enough to create a big enough gap to squeeze through.

Sitting with his legs wide apart, his back against the door, was Gary. Without stooping to check, Pinkie could tell he was dead.

There was no sign of foul play other than the self-inflicted kind.

The remnants of three lines of coke powdered the lid of the shiny black toilet seat.

Rewinding the scene, it looked as if he had knelt to

snort a line and then fallen back against the door. Pink spittle crusted the stubble on his chin and had dribbled onto his t-shirt, already splattered with vomit. If she had to hazard a guess how this had played out, she would say the vomit was down to the booze and the coke had been a pick-you-up. Like all overdoses, it would have been an undignified death. His breathing would have slowed, and his lungs flooded with the liquid, which mixed with carbon dioxide had bubbled up into his mouth. There was irony in the death, she supposed. Given where it happened, the obituary could, without contradiction, say Gary had drowned at sea.

How long has he been dead, she wondered? The trendy ambient lighting distorted the colour of everything in the bathroom, but she could still see livor mortis had set in. His bottom half had taken on blackberry stain hues where his blood had settled when his heart had stopped doing its job. His lips and fingernails were blue. Though the smell of vomit and stale urine was overpowering in the small enclosed space, there was no hint of decomposition yet. The rigid set of his neck suggested although rigor mortis had begun in the smaller facial muscles, it had not progressed to the rest of the body. So, he'd died within the last six or seven hours. She guessed the early hours of the morning after whoever he had been partying with had left.

The position of the door suggested she'd been the first on the scene; the first to nudge the body out of its final position.

Gary had no time to call for help even if he'd had a phone on him and the ability to use it. She had to conclude she was the only person in the world who knew Gary Joyce was dead. She had no intention of keeping the secret to herself. Neither did she intend to follow what anyone sensible faced with such a situation would do and call the police.

Sidling her way out of the bathroom, she pulled her burner from her bag and punched in the second of the only two numbers on it. She was ready to call Ewan's contact if Matt didn't answer, but by the third or fourth ring, he picked up.

'It's me.'

'I know, what's up.'

'It's more who's down; Gary, he's dead.'

There was a longer than expected pause at the other end of the phone.

'Matt are you still there?'

'Yeah, yeah I'm thinking.'

His voice was panicky and she wondered if he'd been at a desk too long, that he'd lost that edge that came with being in the field. She knew what they felt like those moments of hesitation like the ground was crumbling away beneath your feet but indecisiveness could get you killed.

"Where… where is he?'

'On the yacht.'

'That's something I suppose we'd be fucked if this had happened at the villa?'

'Don't you want to know how he died?'

'Yes …of course.'

' Well, are you going to enlighten me?'

'Overdose of cocaine.'

'How can you be so sure?'

'Because I found him. I'm here with the body right now.'

His voice rose an octave.

'Fuck. Does anyone else know …does anyone know you're there?'

'No and no.' she replied calmly. Part of her, the bitter and twisted part, was enjoying listening to him squirm. She knew he was a pen pusher and she had the advantage over him in that respect but his floundering surprised her.

'Why the hell were you meeting him?'

'I didn't say I was meeting him. I wanted to get away from the villa and decided to come down to the Marina. I just thought I'd check out the boat that's all.'

'You need to get out of there and tell no one about this. I'll get someone to take care of it.'

'Surely, if you're right about his involvement he's going to be missed.'

Matt hesitated.

'We'll cross that bridge when we come to it. We'll have to hope The Albanians regarded him as much of a loose cannon as we did and assume he's gone on a bender or got cold feet about the whole thing. Like I said before we don't think Gary's the main man …that's his father. Gary at best is an extra in this play.'

Pinkie wondered if he'd heard that line in a film.

'O…kay,' she said trying to stifle her amusement.

'If the authorities find out Kurti is bound to abort his plans. He intends to use that yacht but won't be able to if the police are carrying out an investigation. They'll impound the thing. Gary fucking Joyce has really balls things up for me.'

'I don't suppose he's too thrilled with the fact he's dead either.'

'Just get yourself out of there PDQ.' Then as an afterthought, 'you haven't touched anything have you?'

'Of course not.' she said indignantly', what do you take me for.'

'Good…good. Get yourself back to the villa. I need you

there to confirm the men are in situ and all looks good. I'll send someone in to clear up this mess.'

Pinkie ended the call. She had thought of divulging her suspicions about Margarita had the opportunity arisen. It hadn't, and now she wasn't at all sure she trusted Matt to know what the hell he was doing. How on earth could he think the Albanians would carry on with their plans faced with Gary's disappearance and Joyce's illness. These were seasoned professional criminals. They did not take unnecessary risks. The government did not pick up the tab for their cock ups the way they did for Matt. They paid for their mistakes with their lives.

Downstairs in the lounge area, she stooped to look out of the window, to check no tik-tokin tourists were milling about the boat before exiting the way she had entered.

Her legs felt heavy as she headed back along the quay. She should be pleased. One of the obstacles to her getting Sam home to Liz was gone for good and his grandfather wouldn't be far behind if she was right about Margarita. She should be jumping for joy. Her job had just got easier but how could she face the little boy knowing this and what effect would it have on him when the truth came out, as it had to eventually. Granted Gary wasn't much of a dad but the poor kid had already lost his mum and she didn't doubt his fondness for his grandad. Could Liz's love make up for all that loss? Either way, she had no choice but to stick to the endgame. In theory, it was in sight but who knew what she'd face back at the villa. She was still not in control much worse she wasn't sure those who were meant to be were either. Matt was an opportunist. Maybe had things gone to plan at the museum and she'd reacted as he'd anticipated; fallen in his arms and forgiven him, things might be different. Then, he might have her best interests at heart but now she wasn't so sure. She had sensed a diffidence. He'd spoken to her with a hint of contempt as if she was one of his operatives, not someone doing him a favour. There was no denying operatives were valuable, it was why they were referred to as assets but just like any other assets you owned you could choose to neglect them; allow them to crumble into disrepair and abandon them to the scrap heap. She needed someone watching her back; someone she trusted with the information she had about Margarita; someone she trusted with her life. Ewan. From now on she'd trust no one but him.

She headed back towards the restaurant only to find Sam and Miguel had gone leaving a message behind the bar for her to meet them at the car.

She was greeted there by an excited Sam and a fraught-looking Miguel trying to manoeuvre a brightly coloured bodyboard into the boot of the car.

'He said you agreed to buy him one, I hope he hasn't played a trick on me. He's already beat me at pool.'

Sam beamed.

'He's right I did say he could have one but I didn't expect you to get it here today.'

'He spotted it in the shop a few doors down from the restaurant, and was insistent.'

She looked at the boy, his face full of exuberance and thought of his father lying dead, in a pool of his own vomit.

'I think a champion pool player deserves a prize, don't you?'

Chapter Thirty-Six

THE 4X4S WERE PARKING as they arrived back, black with tinted windows and chrome so shiny it dazzled. Exactly what she'd expected. OCGs seemed to have a universal compulsion to wear their ill-gotten gains where it showed. Members, even those high up the food chain were prepared to live around the corner from the crack houses and brothels they ran. They shat on their own doorstep on a daily basis. Pinkie guessed they felt comfortable there where they were known and no one questioned their authority. Most, in her experience, were chippy and fitting in didn't come easy. So, despite the huge volume of cash moving through their fingers they lived small lives. The compensation was the bling. They couldn't resist the flash cars, the bottles of Crystal, the holidays in Dubai. Anything that yelled money. It was as if career criminals had to have constant reminders to hand that the violence, fear and degradation they inflicted and suffered was worth it because they could walk into a swanky restaurant and the maître-d would take one look at the special edition Rolex and know they could pay the bill, better still they would leave the biggest tip of the night.

Two men got out. They wore jeans and tight-fitting black t-shirts. They weren't armed.

Unlike the two on the gate the day she'd arrived who had used their scrawny menace to intimidate, these men sported finely hewn bodies, used to punishing physical workouts. They pulsed with barely suppressed violence the kind always alert to threat, set to unleash at the slightest provocation. They didn't need to be packing hardware to prove they were dangerous men not to be messed with the confident swagger was enough.

Margarita called after her as she headed up to her room.

'Did you see our guests have arrived?'

Pinkie paused.

'They're hard to miss. Have you met them yet?

'Not yet but Lionel's doctor has spoken to them.'

I bet he has. thought Pinkie.

'Lionel's doctor; I thought they were Gary's friends. How does he know them?'

'Oh, he doesn't but he speaks their language. They're Albanians apparently and he's Eastern European himself; didn't I say that before?'

'No,' said Pinkie, 'no you didn't'

'He only moved to Portugal once he'd retired. Lionel met him at the golf club and instantly took a liking to him.'

Was this woman so naïve, or was this show for her?

'I've invited him for dinner this evening. Paolo is coming to help with settling the men in and he's bringing my niece, Angelina, the one you met the other day with him. She's excellent with languages. She has to be working in the hotel.'

Margarita's anxiety had turned to excitement. Pinkie could tell she was enjoying having a full house and the fact it provided an excuse for Paolo to return to the villa. She'd probably managed to get him back on Joyce's payroll. Pinkie couldn't blame her for wanting to make the most of the gravy train before it ended and Gary stepped in even though she knew it would never happen now Gary was dead. Pinkie acknowledged her respect for Margarita had cooled since finding the Oleander leaves. She knew it made her a hypocrite given her history but it was what it was. Try as she might she couldn't help but see her in a different light. It would no doubt be the same if her friends in Cornwall got to learn the truth about her. She had to wonder what the woman's agenda was and whether she had plans for her too. The other night after Margarita's Gazpacho she'd been ill; she'd had that weird dream about Rob and felt like death warmed up the following morning. Could that have been down to Oleander. Did the woman see her as an obstacle too?

'Okay, I'll be down the usual time.'

'Maybe a little later about eight- thirty so Sam will have gone to bed.'

'That's fine,' said Pinkie.

Back in her room, she phoned Ewan. It took a good twenty minutes to fill him in on what had happened since they had last spoken. She told him about her meeting with Matt at the museum, her suspicions about Margherita and finally Gary. She barely paused for breath and he barely spoke at all, which was a first for him. What he did say was he would be there as soon as he could. It was all she needed to hear.

EWAN SAT on the bed looking at his phone for several minutes contemplating why he had just agreed to drop everything and head to Albufeira. He'd promised himself he wouldn't get involved and had stuck to his guns until now. He'd assumed she and Matt would pick up where they'd left off. He'd never heard her like this before. She was usually so together; then again, what Matt had told her about Rob would have shaken the most stoic. He was finding it difficult to take in. It would be so much harder for her to accept the implication that Rob had chosen to go out there alone that morning, had known what would happen if he did, and wanted it. Why had Matt felt the need to come clean after all these years? It was selfish and cruel. This kind of heartache was difficult to cope with at the best of times and could render her vulnerable. She'd certainly sounded different. He didn't know the ins and outs of Matt's mission. He wasn't part of it, and that had been fine, but it sounded as if Pinkie was in the thick of it. Added to that, things had taken an unexpected turn. The Albanians were already there, and she was having dinner with the main man that evening. It was all a little too close for comfort in his book.

If he set off now, he'd be there in two and a half hours. He'd stop and sleep in the car once he was near the town and deal with his accommodation in the morning.

The only real question was whether he should tell Matt what he was doing. If he were truthful, he wasn't sure he was up to handling anything this big solo. Once maybe, in his prime, he would have given it a go without a second thought, but his older self was a little more circumspect. His body demanded it. It was not as resilient as it had been. These days he feared injury. On his last visit to his GP, he'd been told in all likelihood, he'd need a hip replacement before he was fifty-five because of excess wear and tear.

That was one word for it. He couldn't afford broken bones or broken teeth from a punch in the mouth, for that matter. The very thought of dental implants made him feel queasy. Jesus Christ, why couldn't the woman have stayed safe and sound in Cornwall? If the pair of them got out of this alive, he'd tell her to pack it in once and for all. Retirement wasn't such a bad thing, especially with the right companion. Whether he'd have the nerve to tell her if he was ever going to settle down with anyone, he'd like it to be her was still up for debate. For now, he needed to fill the car with petrol and get on the road.

Chapter Thirty-Seven

MARGARITA'S GUESTS were already seated when Pinkie entered the room. The two men rose in an unexpected gesture of chivalry.

'This is Lionel's doctor, Niko. And Niko, this is Patricia, little Sam's new nanny.'

Pinkie offered her hand.

'I've heard a lot about you,' said Niko.

'All good, I hope,' said Pinkie, pulling her hand away from a grip a little too tight for comfort. She tried to place the accent. It was Albanian but a completely different dialect from the one spoken by the men on the gate the day she arrived.

'Mostly,' he grinned.

'Someone's been busy,' she said, turning to Margarita, anxious to divert attention away.

The cook looked red-faced and flustered.

'It's a special request from our guest. Niko helped me put the dish together.'

'A man of many talents,' said Pinkie, pouring herself a glass of water from the jug in the centre of the table.

'You haven't tasted it yet,' said Niko pulling her chair out for her before sitting opposite.

Angelina let out a girlish giggle, the kind to curry favour. It wasn't surprising. Pinkie couldn't deny Niko Kurti was handsome. Despite knowing what he was, she found herself disarmed by the laughter lines wrinkling the corners of his eyes and his broad, easy smile. He was in his early fifties, she guessed, well-built but not musclebound. His hair more peppered with grey than it had appeared at a distance and in Matt's photo. There was confidence in his movements; his hands as he reached to pour her wine, were tanned and dexterous. There was nothing uncouth about him. He was a class act; someone used to being the most important player in the room.

'Thank you,' she said, taking a sip to steady her nerves.

Paolo seemed unusually quiet. He sat next to Angelina, scowling into his glass. Angelina, on the other hand, seemed effervescent with chatter.

'It's been hell at the hotel this week. One complaint after another. People wandering in and out asking questions. I'll be glad when this season's over. I'm thinking of taking a vacation myself. Where do you recommend, Niko? You seem the type of man who has travelled.'

'I'm the wrong person to ask. I like it right here. It's why I've made my home in the Algarve.'

'Oh yes, me too, but I'm young. I need to spread my wings; South America or the States, or what about the Emirates, Dubai maybe? I've heard a lot about Dubai. There are a lot of wealthy guys there. I could find myself a rich husband and not have to work anymore.'

Paolo's chair scraped the tiles as he leaned back to grab another bottle of wine from the rack behind him.

Kurti ignored both of them, turning his attention back to Pinkie.

'Would you like one?' he asked, pinning her with his steady gaze as he passed a bowl of shiny black olives in her direction.

'No, not for me, thanks,' she replied, resisting the urge to look away. To let this man take control of the space between them would be a mistake.

'Have you ever felt the urgent need to escape, Patricia?'

The question sounded barbed, although for the life of her Pinkie couldn't think why.

'Not really. Whenever I've travelled, it's generally been with the family I'm working for, so it's never been a holiday as such, but I've always enjoyed it nonetheless.'

'Good ... good,' said Niko staring towards Angelina, eyebrows raised. 'So not everybody hates their job.'

Angelina slunk back in her chair.

The conversation halted as Margarita approached with a large blue and white tureen in which swam chunks of meat in grease-slicked gravy. It was a curious-looking dish boasting both brown and white meat. The latter Pinkie guessed must be chicken. Next came a large platter of rice and a smaller, equally unappetising dish of what looked like chopped garlic in water.

It certainly wasn't one of the culinary delights usually gracing this table. The muddy stew lacked colour; the glossy peppers, aubergines and tomatoes so vibrant in Margarita's recipes.

The cook looked understandably worried.

'Niko, would you serve, please?'

'Of course,' he smiled.

Pinkie held out her plate.

'It needs to be eaten with the rice to soak up the gravy,' he grinned, serving everyone around the table before helping himself to a large portion.

'Is that garlic in the water bowl?' asked Pinkie.

'It's in white vinegar. You add it as a condiment, like you English add mint sauce, to cut through the fat.'

'I see,' she said, sprinkling a generous spoonful over the stew.

Angelina poked her meat around her plate, her lip curled in disgust.

Paolo had not yet lifted his fork, but Pinkie noticed he had poured himself another large glass of wine.

'Come on, eat … eat, it's delicious,' Niko bellowed down the table at them.

Angelina smiled, not a real smile this time; contrived, showing too many teeth, then lifting her spoon, took a tentative sip of the gravy.

'Ah, well. In for a penny in for a pound,' Pinkie said, scooping up a piece of white meat from the broth. The texture was denser than she'd expected, more like tofu than chicken. She swallowed hard, the afterburn of garlic and vinegar overpowering every other flavour. She noted she was the only one other than Niko who had added the sauce and wished she hadn't.

Angelina seemed committed to eating only rice but not one to be outdone, seeing Pinkie take a piece of meat, did the same.

'It's good … no?' said Niko, enthusiastically forking a large chunk of the dark meat into his mouth.

Margarita stared hopefully at him as he chewed.

'What's in the dish?' Pinkie asked her.

'Carrots, celery, onions,' she replied, still staring at Niko as he chewed.

'You're missing the best bit out,' he said.

'And lamb,' she said, looking away.

'Ah,' said Pinkie, slightly relieved. 'And the white meat?'

'Brain,' said Nico, voice booming with enthusiasm.

Out of the corner of her eye, Pinkie saw Angelina spit the meat back into her bowl before lifting her napkin to her mouth.

Margarita looked mortified.

Niko laughed.

'Come on … where's your sense of adventure?' he chided. 'You'll have to do better than that if you want to be a globe-trotter. They eat stuffed camels, not to mention sheep's eyes, in Dubai. You have to burn the eyelashes off, of course, so they don't stick in your throat and choke you. This is tame in comparison. Albanians eat Paçe for breakfast. We're trying it out so Margarita can feed it to those strapping young men next door every morning. It has enough calories to keep them going all day. It took a bit of persuading to get her to buy the sheep's head from the butcher and boil it whole, but with a bit of encouragement, she entered into the spirit.'

He lifted his glass to toast the chef. Margarita smiled nervously back at him.

'Why aren't you eating?' he shouted down to Paolo. 'Don't you have the stomach for honest working man's food? Your mamma spent time cooking it. The least you can do is try it.' His tone was raucous, convivial even, but with a prickly underbelly, they all felt.

Paolo reddened. Pinkie saw Angelina surreptitiously touch her cousin's clenched fist. There was no mistaking Niko's taunt for anything but a challenge. Paolo, eyes down,

The Poison Promise

shoulders hunched, lifted his spoon and scooped up the rice and stew, holding the unappetising mush in his mouth before washing it down with a generous gulp of wine.

Satisfied with this small victory, Niko turned back to Pinkie.

'So tell me about yourself. You have family back in England?'

'There's really not much to tell,' Pinkie replied, making a conscious effort to put her creeping paranoia on the back burner. This was their first meeting, after all, and didn't everyone begin with this kind of banal chit-chat? 'I have no family to speak of. I never married and both my parents and my only brother are dead, a few cousins scattered about, but that's about it.'

She noticed Angelina staring at her, her mouth pinched as if dying to say something.

'So, no one to tell you where to go; no one wondering where you are or what you're up to?'

Pinkie was unclear if he was trying to draw a comparison with her and Angelina's employment dilemmas or whether this was a genuine question.

'No, no one, and that's just how I like it, but listen, you're far more interesting than me. Angelina said you were well travelled, and with your knowledge of food, it seems she's right. Then there's your day job. Where did you train as a doctor?'

There was hesitation, and she thought for one moment she might have overstepped the mark, that he might think she was fishing and become suspicious.

'Kosovo on the battlefield, the best practical education a medic could wish for.'

Pinkie didn't know what to say, and given the deafening silence, neither did anyone else around the table.

Had she been able to be herself, they could have had a meaningful discussion, comparing notes.

She knew the history, both the written and the unreported. The plight of the Albanian minority. The ethnic cleansing of Muslim Albanians by the monstrous Milosevic. The Serbian fight against the Kosovo Liberation Army and the UN Peacekeeping Force that delivered independence to the tiny province, only to bring to power a prime minister later accused of organ trafficking and of being connected to OCGs involved in prostitution and arms smuggling. She could say none of this without risking her cover, so said nothing.

Perhaps aware he had killed the conversation, he did not elaborate.

The rest of the dinner was relatively uneventful until Margarita produced a fabulous, caramelised flan which she served with ice cream and which, in this instance, they all had room for. Even Niko, who had eaten two helpings of Paçe, looked tempted but eventually declined.

'It looks delicious, but if you will all excuse me, I need to look in on my patient before I leave,' he said, wiping his mouth with his napkin as he rose from his seat.

Margarita rose as if to go with him.

'No, you stay here. You will want to clear up, I'm sure. Angelina, as you have nearly finished your food, perhaps you can come help me with the patient.'

Angelina immediately dropped her spoon and pushed her plate away.

As soon as Niko and Angelina were gone, Paolo got up and, without a word to either Pinkie or his mother, left, slamming the door behind him.

'Is everything okay with Paolo?' asked Pinkie.

Margarita shrugged.

Pinkie helped carry the dishes to the sink, pausing on the way to scrape the leftovers into the bin. 'Well, that was quite a meal.'

'Have you ever tasted anything so bad?' Margarita grimaced.

'No ... I haven't,' said Pinkie finding it hard to suppress a laugh, 'and when Angelina spat out the meat ... oh my God ...'

Margarita laughed too; both women squealed at the thought of the girl's face.

'Brains,' said Pinkie mimicking Niko's accent.

Tears rolled down Margarita's face.

'He actually wanted me to ask the butcher for a goat's head at first.'

That finished them both off.

They were still in hysterics when Angelina walked back into the room.

'What's so funny?'

'Nothing,' said Margarita flashing a sideways glance at Pinkie, who was biting her lip as she loaded the last of the cutlery into the dishwasher.

'I'm off. I have a busy day tomorrow,' Angelina said curtly. 'Thanks for dinner.'

It was as much as they could do not to start the giggles again.

ONCE THEY'D CLEARED everything away, Margarita made them coffee.

'He's a strange one,' said Pinkie.

'You get used to him, and he is a good friend to Lionel.'

'You said they knew each other before Lionel fell ill?'

'Yes.'

'And is he the only one treating Lionel now he's decided not to go to hospital?' Pinkie had to ask. If not now, when? She'd sensed a camaraderie with Margarita this evening and was sure the woman felt it too. They had been able to laugh together despite the strange circumstances they found themselves in and was pretty certain if the housekeeper was going to confess anything, she would do so now. If she waited, she might never know if she was poisoning Joyce, as she suspected. It was best to get straight to the point.

'I know you're feeding Lionel oleander tea.'

Margarita's eyes widened.

'Don't deny it. I know you have been giving it to him for some time. I found the leaves in a jar in the pantry when I was looking for sugar for your tea.'

'Why would I want to deny it?' Margarita said, placing the plates down on the table.

Pinkie was surprised by her candour.

'I'm helping him.'

'It's a poison. Oleander is deadly. You're slowly killing the man.'

'It's no such thing, not when you use it correctly. I think we need to sit down and talk.'

Pinkie sat.

'Lionel's dying. He has stage four cancer, and there is no hope, none whatsoever, as far as his doctors are concerned.'

Pinkie thought the pessimistic diagnosis was hardly surprising if Joyce was relying on Niko for medical advice. Margarita's next comment confirmed he was not the only source of the prognosis.

'I went with Lionel to Lisbon when he was first diagnosed. I was with him through all the tests, and when the consultant told him there was nothing to be done, no operation, no treatment, only pain relief. That man would have booked him into a hospice that very day if he'd had his way, but Lionel wouldn't hear of it, and neither would I.'

Margarita's jaw was set with a fierce determination Pinkie hadn't witnessed before.

'We came home and made a plan. We started looking for help elsewhere, alternative therapies, anything that would give him more time. I went to the library and took out every book I could find. Meditation, crystals, faith-healing, but realised most of what I was reading was nonsense. I am a Christian. I prayed. I lit a candle every mass, but Lionel didn't have enough time to wait for God to intervene or to waste time experimenting. I needed to be looking for alternative treatments that had a scientific basis. It seemed hopeless. Then one evening, I watched a TV programme about the dark web, about all the crazy stuff out there. I realised I'd been looking in the wrong place. I needed to reach out to others as desperate as us, those who had tried the treatments, use them as guinea pigs. So that's what I did. I reached out and found that the people who'd had the most success holding back their disease were those taking Oleander. Luckily for us, it's almost a weed here. I learnt how to prepare it and started giving it to Lionel. That was eighteen months ago, and Lionel is still alive when his doctors had given him six months at most.'

Pinkie didn't like being wrong, but in this case, she was relieved her judgement was off.

Margarita walked to the kitchen counter and picked up her phone. She scrolled down and handed it to Pinkie.

'Take a look for yourself if you don't believe me.'

Pinkie took the phone.

It was an article in an American medical journal.

"Nerium Oleander: A Pharmacological Analysis of Use in the Treatment of Cancers."

The article recorded that the drug had been used for centuries for healing and how, in the sixties, an extract had been patented by a Turkish doctor as Anvirzel and was still being used in Africa in the fight against hepatitis and HIV. Oleander had also been used in the treatment of cardiac congestion, heart disease and cancer and was found to be a powerful immune stimulator.

Margarita had highlighted the next bit.

"A modified extract of N. oleander administered daily via oral gavage was seen to strongly inhibit the growth of human pancreatic cancer."

'I read that and, for the first time in weeks, felt there was hope. I had to find out how to extract it safely, which, as it turned out, was relatively easy. There were so many people out there only too willing to share.'

Margarita walked to the drawer and pulled out a laminated sheet of paper; a laboratory method for extracting Oleander to administer as a medicine, including quantities, timings and a recommendation to strain the broth when boiled through four layers of coffee filters. Finally, it recommended preserving the liquid with cider vinegar or vodka.

'After about five hours, this is what you get,' said Margarita placing a bottle down on the table in front of Pinkie. The contents looked like cough medicine; the dark syrupy type your grandmother insisted was best and then held your nose to make you swallow.

'I started as they suggested with first a quarter, then half a teaspoon, building Lionel's tolerance until he could manage more.'

Pinkie handed the sheet back to Margarita. She remembered her greenhouse and the tortuous preparation of the

Rosery Pea to kill Carlisle. This was so different; this was a labour of love. She was ashamed she'd tarred this woman with the same brush.

'I'm sorry. I shouldn't have jumped to conclusions.'

'Most wouldn't have recognised the leaves, let alone known they were poisonous.'

Pinkie grappled for an excuse.

'It's the job. I'm always on the lookout for potential dangers to the children. One of my charges a long time ago had to have their stomach pumped after eating laburnum seeds. They were fine, but it taught me a lesson about children and plants.'

It had been Rob who had swallowed the seeds when he was young. Pinkie had forgotten all about it until now.

'That explains it, and I suppose as an outsider, you thought I had good reason to murder Lionel. All these years running around after him. I've watched those English films on television where the butler did it, but you see, I'm not just a servant. I am much more than that. Lionel and I love each other.' The woman's voice had taken on a wistful tone, 'And of course, we share our son.'

Pinkie couldn't hide her confusion. She had always assumed from the story Margarita told her about her parents taking care of Paolo and how she respected Lionel's wife, Paolo was the product of a teenage indiscretion with a boy from the village. It never crossed her mind Paolo was Lionel's child.

'Oh, I know what you are thinking. He took advantage of me, that I was a naïve young girl, an employee. That he had a sick wife who couldn't,' she hesitated, 'satisfy his needs, so he forced himself on me. But you're wrong, so very wrong.'

It was exactly what Pinkie was thinking, but she wasn't going to own it.

'Lionel adored Diane and had no idea what to do with his grief. It begins before someone passes, you know. The diagnosis snuffs out your future just as surely as it snuffs out theirs. Fear takes hold as your days together become numbered and the anxiety is crippling. I know how he felt now he's dying, and I'm forced to go through the same. But unlike me, he was no good around sickness; some people just aren't cut out to be carers. It's not their fault. He talks about when your time's up and all that, but he was scared then and he's scared now. I fully admit the first time we made love, it was partly out of pity on my part, but I don't regret my kindness. He needed love and I gave it to him.'

Pinkie watched Margarita's eyes drift to the window and the garden beyond.

'I made the first move. I won't accept I was a victim. I loved his love for Diane. I know it sounds crazy, but I came from a home where my mother was little more than a skivvy, someone to cook and clean and have babies. I'd never seen that kind of love, and I had certainly never seen a grown man cry. Lionel was never a handsome man, not the sort to turn a young girl's head, but it was what was inside I fell in love with.'

Pinkie was finding it hard to equate the heroic character Margarita was painting with the man she knew Joyce to be. Then again, if the woman had never known that side of him, if she had only seen him in this place when he was a relaxed, loving husband and successful generous employer, why wouldn't she have a polarised view?

Nobody revealed their whole self. The version of yourself you let people see was the one you selected for them. She had been many things to many people, often with the sole aim of deceiving them. She was not the person to judge this woman for falling in love with a man like Lionel Joyce. This had been no teenage crush; it had proved itself over the years to the point Margarita was still by Lionel's side, trying to keep him alive. Not because she needed the job or was worried about losing her home, but because she could not envisage life without him.

'Why didn't Paolo come and live here with you?'

Margaritas smiled the sort of smile people give you when they are reconciled to something that once gripped their heart like a vice. 'At first out of respect for Diane, then after she died out of respect for my parents. My father was outraged when he learned about the baby. He said he would forbid my mother to ever speak to me again, cast me out of the family if I brought the boy here to live with me. The village was already talking, and he said if I brought Paolo here, it would be obvious Lionel was the father. It was bad enough I had fallen pregnant, but to a married man when his wife was dying? Instead, it was decided they would tell everyone I'd had a short relationship with a boy working as a waiter in town that ended when he returned to university in Lisbon. It was a common enough scenario not to be challenged, and I was stupid enough to go along with it. Lionel agreed to pay for Paolo's keep. If I'm truthful, I think he was relieved. He felt he owed Gary his full attention after Diane died, and to bring another child under this roof could make the boy worse when he was already a handful. When he and Gary were back in England, sometimes for months on end, Paolo came here to live with me; a small concession by my father. My cousin, Angelina's mother, came to stay sometimes too. Angelina's father worked away a lot. She helped me around the place, and it meant Paolo had Angelina for company.

Those visits with my son in this house made everything bearable.

'What will you do now, I mean when Lionel passes?' Pinkie needed to know if she needed help.

Margarita, sensing her concern, reached out and touched her hand.

'Please don't worry. I know it will come soon. The medicine bought us time, but he is failing fast. Lionel bought my parent's house when my mother died years ago. I let it out to holidaymakers, but I will go back there to live when Gary inherits all this.'

Pinkie thought of Gary lying on the bathroom floor.

'What about Paolo? Hasn't Lionel left him anything?'

'If you mean in his will, then no. What would have been the point of secrecy for all these years just to let the world know Paolo is his son now? There is a trust fund; set up when Paolo was born. It's managed by the bank, and there's provision for me too. We have all we will ever need.'

The realisation suddenly hit. Now Gary was dead, the villa and all Joyce's other assets, including the Princess would pass by default to Sam. Money added a complication she had never anticipated. She would be delivering a millionaire in waiting back to her friend in Cornwall, and that kind of money brought a wealth of problems with it.

Chapter Thirty-Eight

PINKIE SAID her goodnights and headed up to bed. She had one job to do before she slipped beneath the sheets. She needed to retrieve the device from Joyce's room and send the recording to Matt. She wondered if Matt would want her to plant something similar in the barracks, now they were occupied. He had another thing coming if he did. She didn't intend to go anywhere near the place if she could help it.

She and Margarita had watched Niko's tail lights disappear down the drive fifteen minutes after Angelina left. So much for camaraderie. For all his macho talk of battlefields and real men, he had no intention of slumming it with his crew.

Margarita had looked dead on her feet when she'd left her. Pinkie knew once she heard her switch off the hall light and close her bedroom door, that was her for the night. Then would be a good time to sneak into the old man's room.

She lay on her bed waiting for what seemed an age as

the housekeeper clattered about the landing, shutting windows and cupboard doors, until finally, all was quiet.

Pinkie didn't intend to loiter. Tired herself, she couldn't wait for her head to hit the pillow. She crept out of her room and along the dark landing.

Outside Joyce's room, she felt for the handle and let herself in. The room was in total darkness. She'd expected the bedside lamp or the glow from Joyce's machinery at the very least. She paused in the doorway, waiting for her eyes to adjust and the blackness to turn to shades of grey but with the blinds pulled, not even the filtered light from the drive penetrated the room. She reached into the pocket of her dressing gown, pulled out her mobile and turned on the torch, nearly jumping out of her skin as the beam hit Paolo, sitting silently in the darkness beside Joyce's bed.

'Paolo. I didn't expect to see you. What are you doing here?' she stuttered before she had time to think how inappropriate the question was given Margarita's revelation he was Lionel's son. The only reassurance was he didn't know she knew his history. Feeling the need to justify her presence before he had time to answer, she added, 'I thought I heard a noise in here. I didn't want to wake Margarita. She's had such a busy day.'

Paolo didn't answer.

'Ah well, I must have been mistaken. I'll get off back to bed. Goodnight, Paolo.'

She looked over at Joyce, wondering if he was awake and if she should wish him goodnight too, but the man was fast asleep, a mask covering his nose and mouth to assist his night-time breathing.

She left the room, not stopping to take stock until she had bolted her bedroom door behind her. Leaning with her back against it, she wrestled with the uncomfortable truth she had been seconds away from being caught red-handed retrieving a listening device and what that might have meant for Matt's wretched plan, not to mention her.

Paolo had seemed sullen and distracted all evening. She'd put it down to Niko. Larger than life, he'd monopolised events. He might have been the guest, but he'd behaved like the host. It couldn't have been easy for Paolo knowing the ghost at this party, the real head of the household, was upstairs dying while his doctor held forth on the finer points of Albanian cuisine; an insult in itself to his mother's wonderful cooking. The whole episode had been made worse by Angelina's brazen flirting. It had been demeaning.

Pinkie felt for the young man who, unlike Gary, had never recognised his obligation to be at his father's bedside at this time, understood it was the decent thing to do. Having listened to Margarita speak so fondly of Lionel, Pinkie knew his actions would be of huge comfort to her.

Despite the ever-growing fatigue swaddling her, she understood she had no option but to stay awake until Paolo left and to try again.

To her immense relief, her unannounced intrusion had spoilt the moment and prodded Paolo to call it a night. Within minutes of her leaving, she heard Joyce's door click open and shut and the dutiful son's soft footfall on the stairs. She waited for ten minutes or so until she was certain he had gone before creeping back to the bedroom.

This time the lights behind the bed were dimmed as usual. Lionel was still asleep. Moving swiftly, she retrieved the device, checked all was how she'd found it and left.

Dizzy with the sense of relief, back in her room, she sat for a second before putting the machine on charge and loading the recording onto her laptop. She popped in her ear pods and poured herself a glass of water, ready to listen.

She could, of course, forward the thing to Matt and let him pick the bones out of it, but she wasn't a big fan of the *what you don't know can't hurt you* school of thought. In her experience, it could hurt you plenty. It soon became clear this could well prove to be a shorter task than she'd imagined, and she might actually get some sleep that night. She fast-forwarded the parts consisting of Margarita shuffling around the room and chatting about the mundane. There was only the occasional response from Lionel, who slept a great deal. If Matt was looking to gain access to the strategies of a criminal mastermind, he was going to be sorely disappointed. There were no incriminating conversations to scrutinise. As far as Pinkie could tell, there was not a single conversation with anyone other than Margarita. It wasn't unusual when undertaking surveillance to get nothing of merit, but in this case, the long bouts of silence, only the distant rhythmic pulse of Lionel's monitor breaking the monotony, rendered the whole thing a useless exercise. She finally reached that day's recording. Niko and Angelina had left to go to Lionel's room together. Neither was the quiet type, and she expected there would be something, anything, to break the boredom. She needn't have worried. What came next shocked her to the core.

'Why didn't you question her while you had her there?' said a voice she immediately recognised as Angelina's.

'Because it wasn't appropriate.'

'I told you about the investigator that came to the hotel. She's not who she says she is.'

'Who of us is?' replied Niko wryly.

'But what's she doing here?'

'Looking after the boy, exactly what she's paid to do.'

Niko sounded as if his patience was wearing thin.

'But she's not a nanny. She's hiding something.'

'She might have good reason to hide, but that doesn't mean it's anything for us to worry about.'

'But what if she's working with the police?'

'If she was working with the police, they wouldn't be drawing attention to her. She's probably avoiding an ex-husband or creditors. It's of no interest to me. She seems a perfectly ordinary middle-aged woman trying to do her job, and your aunt likes her, so what's the problem? My team will be moving out the day after tomorrow, and who knows, she might have similar plans, but until then, your aunt will be glad of some support when the old bastard dies.'

'Can't come quick enough as far as I'm concerned,' sniped Angelina, and Pinkie, for the first time, realised she didn't like this girl.

'I'm more worried about that cousin of yours. I hope we haven't got another Gary on our hands. We still haven't found that little fucker. We don't need another one going AWOL on us. We need Paolo to take charge of the boat. When I find Gary, he's a dead man, but I get the feeling Paolo would be less easy to get rid of. He has friends and family here, people who care about him. Although I could try lacing his wine. He was certainly knocking that back this evening. I got the feeling he didn't seem too happy about me being there.'

'He's a little jealous, that's all. Paolo's never been anywhere or done anything. He has no ambition. He was brought up by my grandparents and carries all their catholic guilt. They punished him for being illegitimate; taught him to be ashamed of who he was. You leave Paolo to me. I have always been able to control him; like a puppy dog, he's always looked to me to tell him what to do.'

'He didn't like you flirting with me, that's for certain.'

Angelina gave another of her simpering giggles, then nothing; dead air for seconds.

Pinkie wondered if there was a glitch with the recording until she realised what she was hearing was the silent prelude to sex and not the first-time kind. The fact they were doing this in a sick man's bedroom while he slept confirmed a disregard for Joyce bordering on contempt. Pinkie was too gobsmacked to be embarrassed by the frenzied pump of bodies punctuated with Angelina's muffled trills of pleasure, building until a groan from Niko signalled the climax.

The pair were in an intimate relationship, and it put a different complexion on things altogether. There was silence again, then shuffling as if they were retrieving discarded clothes.

Angelina was first to speak.

'I hear what you say, but it doesn't change the fact she's a liar. I rang my friend who's the receptionist at the dentists I recommended, and they hadn't heard of her. She never even made an appointment. I don't even think she had toothache.'

'What are you talking about?' Niko asked breathlessly. Sex with a woman half his age was a challenge despite his apparent fitness.

'Auntie rang me and asked for details of the dentist we use for the hotel guests because the nanny had toothache. She was supposed to make an emergency appointment. I met her here afterwards, and she said she'd gone, and the toothache was better, but she hadn't. I checked after that investigator called at the hotel to see if she used a different name, you know to access her dental records. They can do that from other countries, but she hadn't gone despite Auntie saying she'd been out all afternoon.'

Pinkie's heart was pounding so loudly she feared her ear pods might jump clean out of her ears.

'Okay ... okay,' said Niko, his tone less dismissive. 'Maybe we do need to keep an eye on her and find out more about this investigator. He knows who she really is. I'll have someone check him out. Have you got the piece of paper he gave you?'

'In my bag.'

Shuffling again.

'Trenear, an odd name. Must be real. No one would make that up.'

'Not like Patti Smith, you mean.'

'No, not like Patti Smith.'

Pinkie stopped the recording.

Trenear was in Albufeira, and he was looking for her, and there could be only one reason for it. She'd been right. He'd found something that day, something he believed put her in the frame for Carlisle's murder. Only one thing would do that, some remnant of the rosary pea. Nothing else would imbibe him with this level of confidence. She'd cleared up after herself, been meticulous in her preparation, but had she been quite so careful when she'd brought the plant into the greenhouse to take the seeds or afterwards when she'd carried it to the back of the garden to burn it? Since his discovery, the detective had no doubt fished around and uncovered the connection between Liz and Carlisle and, from that, Liz and Joyce. She had no choice but to tell Matt everything. It was the only way she could ultimately protect herself and warn Trenear. They were both in trouble and a long way from Cornwall.

Pinky retrieved the phone Matt had given her from

behind her headboard, but as she was about to call thought better of it. She had promised herself to trust only Ewan after Matt's attitude when she'd reported Gary was dead. It had seemed like a good plan then, and it still seemed so now.

She went through the usual process, and he called her back within minutes.

'Where are you?' she asked.

'I'm staying in a small hotel just outside Albufeira.'

'Does Matt know you're here?'

'No ... I mean, he knows I'm coming but not that I've arrived.'

'I need to tell you something before I tell him.'

'Right.'

Ewan sounded confused, and she didn't blame him. She swallowed hard.

'My cover's been blown.'

'When ... how?'

'In the last couple of days by an English policeman, a DI Trenear who's followed me here from Cornwall.'

'Hang on. You mean to tell me the police know you're here to kidnap the kid?'

'No of course not. If they did, they'd warn Joyce and alert the police at this end. Trenear's here because he thinks I killed someone back in Cornwall.'

'A hit?'

'No, not a hit. If it was, you know better than anyone, there wouldn't be a problem. There would be nothing to connect me. This is someone I'm linked to.'

'Linked in what way?'

'We swam together at a local swimming pool.'

'Seems pretty tenuous to me. Why does he think you killed this person because they beat you at backstroke?'

'No, because he found something at my house that incriminates me.'

'Why the hell did you let him search your house in the first place?'

'He wasn't searching my house. He came looking for witnesses. I think he found the evidence by accident when he was there.'

'What evidence are we talking about?'

'The murder weapon in my greenhouse.'

'He found your gun?'

'No, I think he might have found a seed.'

'Is this some kind of windup?'

'I wish it was.'

'And he thinks you killed this person with this seed?'

'Well, not that particular seed but one like it. The victim was poisoned.'

There was a long pause at the end of the phone.

'And did you ... do it?'

Her lip smarted where she'd been gnawing at it. Once she said the words, there was no going back. Their relationship would change forever. It was one thing to know your friend was a trained killer, quite another to know they were a poisoner; there was no honesty to it. The enemy who used poison was a cheat, and the friend who used it could never be trusted. You could forget they were capable of killing a man with a firearm or even their bare hands, as long as they never pulled any of that shit around you. But to worry every time they offered you a drink if you had upset them recently, there wasn't a friendship on earth worth that level of anxiety. Ewan would look at her the way she had looked at Margarita. It was why she'd never told him about the poisonings before.'

'Yes.'

'Fuck ... and are you going to tell me who this poor bastard was and what the hell he'd done to deserve this?'

'A judge. Judge Fenton Carlisle.'

'Jesus Christ, the one everyone thinks was killed by terrorists. The one on the news. So, it was a hit.'

'No, I told you, it wasn't.'

Pinkie's voice was little more than a whisper as she coughed away the shame. 'It was stupid. I realise that now. I'm not even sure why I did it. I kidded myself I was doing it for my friend, but if I'm truthful, I did it to see if I could, to challenge myself. I needed to know I could still pull off something complicated and risky, that I wasn't obsolete.'

'It's a bit excessive, don't you think? I bought a Ducati when I had my first midlife crisis.'

She had no excuse to offer.

'What did this judge have to do with your friend?'

'He's the one who took the boy away from Liz's daughter. He was a friend of Joyce. He started this whole thing.'

'And the policeman, he's here to bring you in as a suspect?'

'I don't know, maybe not officially. Surely the authorities would have gone public with this if I was on their radar. I think he's a bit of a maverick. Last year he was involved in a drug bust in Penzance when another one of Joyce's cronies, a cocaine dealer called Jem Fielding, drowned. The thing is, one of the men arrested in that operation is feeding Matt with intelligence on the Albanians. He's on witness protection. Matt's bound to think there's more to Trenear being here and that I'm linked somehow.'

'But you're telling me you knew nothing about any of this before?'

'No, honestly. I didn't.'

'Do you think this Trenear knows the connection?'

'No, I think he's deciphered my motive for killing Carlisle and maybe thinks I'm here to do the same to Joyce. I don't think he knows anything about the informant or Matts's operation. He needs to be warned.'

'Has he been to the villa?'

'Not yet.'

'Then how come you know he's looking for you, and more importantly, how do you know he's blown your cover?'

'He's been asking around. He called at the hotel where Margarita's niece Angelina works, asking about me. I don't think he mentioned my real name. She certainly didn't mention it when she was talking to Kurti.'

'Kurti knows about this?'

There was a fresh urgency in Ewan's voice.

'I heard them talking on the recording I made for Matt. Angelina is sleeping with him. I think she's up to her neck in all this. Kurti said he's going to do some checking on Trenear and if he's connected the way Matt says, it won't take him long to find out that he's a police officer. At least they don't know Gary's dead yet, which is one thing. Matt's team must have done a pretty good clean-up job. The men are leaving the day after tomorrow, and Paolo, Margarita's son, will be in charge of the boat.'

'I should never have suggested you go work in that house.'

'This was messed up long before you became involved. I could have said no or at least been honest with you. I owed you that much. Matt will be furious I didn't tell him any of this at the outset, but as far as I'm concerned, you're the only one I owe a thing. I've done everything he asked. I've told him how many men there are at the villa and about Kurti posing as Joyce's doctor. I reported Gary was dead, and I've retrieved his bloody recording for him. I'm done.

Now he needs to make good on his promise and get me and the boy out of here.'

'You and I know that will never happen if you tell him about the judge. You're the only asset he has on the inside. He'll hold Carlisle's murder over you until this mission is done, and the favours won't stop there.'

Ewan was right.

'I don't see I have any choice. If I tell him about Trenear, I have to tell him about Carlisle. He's going to want to know why a Cornish policeman has travelled here to look for me. The fact this policeman is the DI who arrested his informant is not going to be missed either. He's not an idiot. If I don't fess up, he'll think the whole thing is connected and somehow, I'm involved. He might even think I'm here to sabotage his precious mission. It's what he thought at first, and it won't take much to make him think that way again.'

'Look, he won't want anything ruining his plans. I dare say there's another promotion riding on this one. He'll know he has to make his move now before the whole bloody lot blows up in his face, and that'll be thanks to you. My concern is whether he's up to the job.'

It was Pinkie's concern, too, but there was no other option.

'I'll call him before I send the recording.'

'You sure? You could just wipe the bloody thing.'

'It won't change anything if I do. I'm at risk either way.'

'Okay, but follow your instincts. You sense things are getting too hot for you, get out of there tomorrow, don't wait for Matt. I'll be here to help you and the boy get away … I'm always here.'

Chapter Thirty-Nine

ONCE HE HAD SHOWERED and packed his bag, Ross headed out to find breakfast. He planned to drive straight to the airport after visiting Joyce and wasn't sure he'd get time to eat later. He made a B-line for the café next door. He'd picked up a voucher in the hotel foyer and wasn't going to waste it. His place didn't serve food, and he guessed it was part of an arrangement between the two rather than a recommendation of quality.

He could tell from the look of the place he was right and was going to be disappointed. The menu catered for tourists, a yellowing photograph of a full English taking pride of place on the plastic menu, but needs must. His stomach felt as if his throat had been cut.

The street outside was already teeming with locals carrying heavy shopping bags back from the Mercado Municipal. He'd passed an entertaining hour there the previous afternoon; time which would otherwise have been spent back in his dreary hotel room or in a bar blowing money he could ill afford.

Undercover and air-conditioned, with mosaic tiled floors and displays designed to show the produce at its best, he'd been drawn to a table stacked high with bright-eyed fish of every shiny scaled variety. The stand was a thing of beauty, more art installation than fish stall. Spider crabs so fresh they might shuffle sideways back to the sea at any minute. Ghostly squid, hovering between heaps of neon clams and barnacled scallops and above them a boggle-eyed octopus, speckled tentacles stretching to sucker in a shoal of sardines snoozing on a bed of bladderwort.

Leaning in for a closer look, he'd felt the rise of cool air from the lining of crushed ice and the waft of ozone, free for the first time since he'd arrived from the taint of suntan lotion and fried food.

He'd struck up a conversation with the fishmonger and taken a snap of a carapau, the king of mackerels, much bigger than the ones caught off the Cornish coast. He planned to send the photo to his father-in-law who had taken up fishing again since he'd retired, only to delete it, realising he'd have to say where he'd snapped it and you didn't find many mackerel, big or small, on Bodmin Moor.

He'd told the man he wished there was a market like this in St. Ives, but even as he uttered the words, he knew sadly it would never pay. Nearly all of the fish caught in Cornwall were sold abroad. The British weren't like the Portuguese. Even during lockdown with the bars and restaurants closed and things tight because so many relied on tourism, the locals hadn't wanted to fill up on fish, though the trawlermen were practically giving it away. His mother always maintained you could feed a family from the fruits of the sea if you knew how; no need for food banks. She was wasting her breath. The younger generations had forgotten how to cook it, let alone gut and fillet it. Rick Stein could rattle on as much as he liked how easy it was, most locals still preferred to get theirs from the Slippery Eel, the chippy on the quay. The pun the fishing industry *would soon be dead in the water* was a little too close for comfort.

He finished his scrambled egg and wiped the plate clean with a crust of fresh bread, which was the best bit of the whole overcooked thing. Giving the tea with tepid milk a miss, he left all his change as a tip for the waitress, who looked as if she never saw the light of day, pale moon face glowing under a frizzy tangle of dyed maroon hair.

He looked at his watch; nine-thirty. He'd get to Joyce's villa around ten, which seemed an ideal time. The locals went to ground around midday, not surfacing much until late afternoon. By then, he'd need to be back on the road.

He'd forgotten to park in the shade. It was hot and stuffy, and even at this hour, the steering wheel burnt his palms as he took hold of it.

He couldn't say he was looking forward to his meeting. His concerns about divulging too much in his eagerness to get information about Philippa Floyd hadn't waned. He needed to take things one step at a time and see how this unfolded. He wasn't even sure the man would be there or agree to see him if he was. He might be playing golf with his bank manager or whatever rich ex-pats with a chequered past did in this place. He half hoped Joyce wasn't there. He'd be able to go home knowing he'd dived in and come up empty-handed with a clear conscience. What's more, no one would need to know about this little venture. He could hand in the evidence on Floyd under the guise it had come to light post her reported disappearance. It wasn't a bad plan, come to think of it. He slowed down. He could turn the car around here and now and have done with it. After all, if he was right and she'd fled Cornwall, she was someone else's problem now. A sensible man would do just that. But if, despite all efforts, Floyd never surfaced, would he regret missing the opportunity to find her and bring her back to face justice? Probably. Then there was the niggling curiosity he'd carried since his investigation had been blocked in Cornwall. Who and what was Pinkie Floyd and was Carlisle her one and only victim?

He persuaded himself even if Joyce wasn't around, he might get to speak to someone else at the villa who may have seen Floyd hanging around. Or if not, he might at least get a glimpse of Liz Hosking's grandson and be able to give her a call when he got home to reassure her the boy was doing okay. He pressed his foot down on the accelerator. The sooner this was done, the sooner he'd be home.

He still hadn't called Karenza, although he'd sent a text. The last time he'd checked, she still hadn't replied. She was probably busy. He'd felt guilty this morning watching the waitress wipe tables, thinking of her at home doing the same, going through the early morning rituals so she'd be ready for the influx of hungry tourists on the hunt for pasties and cream teas. He usually dealt with the beer delivery at the weekends. He'd looked up the weather forecast for Cornwall on his phone. It was going to be a hot one. Karenza would need to put out the parasols, and the barrels would probably need changing before the evening shift. She'd have to call her father or one of the barmen to help. He felt bad about not doing his bit, although he had to admit he'd also checked what the surf was doing; two to four feet and clean. Perfect.

Driving out of Albufeira, he wondered why on earth Joyce had chosen this place over Cornwall. Granted, the climate was better, but it was so overdeveloped you could be anywhere. He thought of home, the cottage that had been in his wife's family for generations, squeezed in between the narrow thoroughfares leading down to the harbour. He imagined this place had once looked much the same. Luckily the Cornish were as stubborn and hard-faced as the granite they walked on and didn't take kindly to change, no matter how often they were told it was good for them. The parish council had already banned second homeowners from buying on new developments. He had mixed views. On the one hand, his son was courting a local girl and was desperate to get a foot on the property ladder. On the other hand, the pub depended on the tourists. He walked a tightrope that often ended in an argument whenever the news did a piece on rising house prices. For the moment, he was just happy his grandparents would still recognise the streets they'd played in as kids.

He didn't get a sense of that here. Why couldn't people learn it took years to create magic but no time at all to fuck it up? If this was what Joyce had planned for Cornwall, he was damn glad he'd retired to this neck of the woods.

Following the satnav, he turned into Joyce's road. Very nice, too, if you liked bowling green lawns. He was more of a wild meadow man, which basically meant he took the mower out of the shed if, and only if, the grass tickled his ankles.

A pickup carrying gardening equipment, including a mower and small tank marked 'Agua' pulled out from a driveway to his left and then stopped, forcing him to pull up behind it. The overall-clad driver jumped out, moved to the back to drop the tailgate and began unravelling a thick yellow hosepipe attached to the tank. He spotted Ross and raised his hand to wave him on, but there was no room to pass.

Ross wound down his window to ask the man if he

could move on a little, to where the road widened, but the whirr from the generator pumping the water was deafening, and he'd never hear him above the din. He was about to get out to tap him on the shoulder when he noticed a black Mercedes pull up close behind him. The passenger door opened and a swarthy young man dressed smartly in jeans and a dark blue jacket jumped out and began to walk towards the gardener, who by now was busy watering one of the large terracotta troughs lining the pavement. Ross was relieved. This guy would probably fare a lot better than he would.

There was a friendly exchange. The hose was turned off and Ross's foot hovered above the accelerator, ready to move off once the gardener got back in the pickup.

The young guy walking back to his car put his thumb up and Ross returned the gesture.

'He's just finishing off,' the man grinned as he paused by the passenger door, which to Ross's surprise, he then opened.

'Thanks,' said Ross, slightly taken aback. 'I was worried I'd have to give my limited Portuguese a go for a second.'

The man held out his hand. This sort of encounter would never have warranted an introduction back home, but here, people were more formal, and you couldn't knock them for being polite.

'Ross.'

Instead of releasing his hand, the man held on and slid into the passenger seat next to him.

This was beyond politeness, and Ross suddenly felt uncomfortable.

'Eduardo, nice to meet you, Ross.'

The man slipped his jacket to reveal a shoulder holster

at which point Ross's discomfort turned to blind panic as his heart began to race.

'I haven't got any money … if you've followed me from my hotel …'

'Sh … no one's going to rob you. We know you're not a rich man, not on a policeman's salary, eh?' he laughed.

Ross didn't feel like sharing the joke. How the hell did he know he was a policeman?

'You are to do exactly as I say. I want you to slowly turn the car around and drive back to the junction. I'll tell you where to go from there.'

Eduardo's voice was stern, his face deadpan as if the pleasantries were over and it was time to get down to business.

'But what is this all about?' asked Ross trying to keep the crack of fear from his voice.

'Just do as I ask. It'll soon become very clear.'

Ross looked in his rear mirror. The car behind had pulled back to give him room.

Ross manoeuvred the car through a gear-crunching five-point turn, his palms sweating so much he could hardly grip the wheel. He had to calm down but was struggling to string his thoughts together to open his mouth to speak. His stomach, tight as a drum, griped, and he swallowed the urge to bring up his breakfast. Lips tightly pursed, anything he had to say was swallowed too.

When they reached the junction, Eduardo ordered him to turn left and to keep driving until he told him to stop. Ross looked in his mirror. The Mercedes was following.

They'd travelled only a short distance before his next instruction.

'You see the layby up ahead? Pull in and park behind the van.'

Ross, knowing he didn't have a choice, did exactly as he was told, stopping a sensible distance from the van's bumper.

The Merc pulled in behind.

'Turn off the ignition and put your hands in your lap.'

Ross did as asked, watching with disbelief as his captor slipped a pair of handcuffs from his pocket and cuffed him.

'Are you arresting me? Are you police? Is this about me asking questions about the missing woman?'

He could hear the whine of desperation in his voice.

Edwardo didn't answer as he opened the passenger door.

'Now slowly get out.'

Ross lifted his bound hands to pull the keys from the ignition.

'Leave the keys where they are.'

The cab door of the truck in front opened, and a balding man in green overalls leapt out, loitering by the bonnet before jumping into the driver's seat the minute Ross was out of it.

'But my bag is in the back,' objected Ross, thinking about his flight home. 'I'm booked on a plane back to the UK this evening.'

Eduardo gave a wry smile, his eyes glistening with childlike glee. 'I admire your optimism, I really do,' he said before giving Ross a gentle shove by way of a reminder to get out of the car.

Ross watched the hire car drive away before being frogmarched to the Mercedes. The driver ignored them as they passed, only turning to look over his shoulder when Eduardo, holding the rear passenger door open with one hand, cupped Ross's head with the other to marshal him into the back seat. It was a gesture Ross had used many times himself over the years when ushering suspects into police vehicles but had never thought about the message it sent before now. *Don't mess with me. I'm in charge.*

Another shove from Eduardo in the small of his back tumbled him onto the seat.

'Don't try to get out that side,' said Eduardo, reading his mind. 'The child lock is on, and anyway, where would you go? We've got your bag, and I bet your passport and ticket home to the UK are tucked in the outside pocket, right?'

He was right.

Eduardo said something in Portuguese to the driver of the car and they both laughed. At his expense, Ross guessed.

Oddly his pulse had stopped racing when Eduardo pulled the cuffs from his pocket. If these were police, he could talk to them, persuade them he was one of the good guys, one of them, but suddenly he wasn't so sure. He scanned the dashboard for signs this was an unmarked police vehicle but there was no radio, no switch to trigger the lights in a chase and there was something about these men, the haircuts, the way they held themselves, Edwardo's confident swagger more military than police. He expected them to drive off, but instead, Eduardo reached inside his jacket and for one terrifying moment Ross thought he was going to unclip his gun and shoot. It would explain why they'd got him to drive; hadn't bothered to blindfold him or disguise their faces. They didn't expect him to be around long enough to identify them. Time seemed to slow. Karenza's face, his kids not like they were now practically grown but two or three years old, 'tackers' as they called them back home, eager eyes and lollipop-stained smiles. Before he'd let them down. He'd miss this second chance to watch them blossom, maybe even to take their children, his grandchildren surfing on Porthmeor beach, to show them what it felt like to ride a huge swell with the sun on your back. He was in a car in a foreign country with strangers one of whom had a gun and no one knew he was there. If these men, whoever the hell they were, killed him, no one would know. Karenza and the kids would think he'd left them in the lurch. There would be no one to put them right. There would be no body and no answers, other than the obvious one that he was a liar. He'd lied to his superiors, to his friends and family then fucked off without a bye or leave to God knows where. They'd all hate him, probably never utter his name again let alone grieve his loss. Everything would end here in this shitty lay-by. He braced himself for the inevitable, wishing to God he'd been wiser; a better father and husband, as he stared into his lap. His captor lifted his phone from his inside pocket and made a call. Again, the conversation was in Portuguese.

Ross listened for names, anything to give him a hint as to why these men had taken him. Then to his surprise, Eduardo handed him the phone.

Ross held it between his sweaty trembling fingers not knowing what to do with it.

'Go on speak…it's for you.'

Ross lifted the mobile to his ear.

'Hello…"

'What the hell do you think you're doing? Are you trying to cause a bloody international incident or are you just hell-bent on getting yourself fucking killed?'

The voice was unmistakable. His boss, DCI Luke Parish.

Chapter Forty

PINKIE WOKE, one thought pounding; to get her and Sam out of there before all hell broke loose. She had been awake most of the night, running through the plan again and again. Blinking away the sleep from tired, scratched eyes, she picked up her phone to check the time. Five fifteen, she had about an hour before dawn. She walked to the window to pull back the curtains. It was still dark, not pitch black but rather that sliver before daybreak when the sun's disk reached an angle of twelve degrees below the horizon, which they called nautical dawn in the navy. The moment when it was just possible to distinguish sky from sea well enough to navigate your way out of trouble.

That was exactly what she was aiming to do, navigate her and Sam out of the shitstorm about to happen. She'd spoken to him at bedtime the previous evening, told him they were going on an adventure and to set his watch alarm for five-thirty. She'd been scant on detail, telling him only that the start of the adventure was the Summer House, from where she needed to pick up something important before they left. Despite his naturally enquiring mind, he had not asked why it was a secret or where they were going. His only question had been whether he should take his laptop. She had told him he should only take things that were either useful or irreplaceable, and he had nodded sagely as if it was all the explanation he needed.

All she had to do now was collect Sam from his room, her passports and the Glock from the summer house and make a break for it. There was no point trying to get out through the gates, not with the CCTV, but she had found a place between the bushes at the seaward end of the garden where they could climb a tree and drop onto the grounds of the neighbouring property. It sounded so easy when she thought about it in the abstract, but she knew the reality was a different story. She was assuming Sam would be willing to do it for a start. Her brother had been up for anything. The more reckless, the better but on reflection, his bravado had been for her father's benefit, to always outshine her, to be the boy. Sam didn't give a damn about pleasing his dad. The incident in the pool was testimony to that, but he did seem to like to please her. She was banking on it.

Lionel Joyce's insistence his grandson should be physically active rather than glued to the TV or the latest games console was possibly the only sensible decision he'd ever made for him. The boy was strong and wiry for his age, and despite, or maybe as a result of, Gary's best efforts to chip away at his confidence had strength of character too. Whenever faced with a challenge, he rose to it, persevering until he got the hang of the thing. Pinkie would be proud of him if he was her grandchild; that was for certain, and if any child could pull this off, he could. She wasn't so sure the same went for her. She hadn't climbed a tree since she was about Sam's age, and recently back in Cornwall, when she had to get tree surgeons in to lop the sycamore in the garden, she'd stood watching with a mixture of admiration and horror as they dangled from the branches swinging their chainsaws with what looked to her the reckless abandonment of cartoon monkeys. Notwithstanding her misgivings, they had no choice. The wall was high, the smooth white render making it unclimbable, whilst the curved tiles topped with razor wire installed by Niko's men made it dangerous if you could. No, she had gone through it over and over again; their only option was to climb high enough amongst the branches to be able to drop clear of the wall into the garden next door. The good news was they'd be shielded by the thicket of shrubs on Joyce's side and hopefully cushioned by the spongy green lawn on the other. Ewan would be waiting for them with a car at the end of the neighbour's drive. It was only when she'd arrived at this part of the plan for the fourth or fifth time that she'd been able to finally drop off.

She imagined she hadn't been the only one to find sleep elusive. Kurti's men had been on edge the previous day. She had watched them packing and repacking their kit bags on the lawn to the front of the house and their intermittent breaks to work out their pent-up energy with a few sit-ups or a run around the garden. Since they'd arrived, the barracks had echoed with banter, some good-humoured, some broiling for a fight. Meal times had been loud, the music even louder, going on until the early hours of the morning. Gang members and criminals were night owls. They felt at home in the darkness, it was where they lived their violent lives. They caught up with the zzzs when the rest of the mugs who chose to work for a living went about their business. Confined to the villa, with little to keep them occupied, they worked out or played cards, the lights in the barracks rarely going out before three in the morning when Kurti wasn't around. Breakfast got later every day. Despite the fact it was hot as hell, and they were packed in the barracks like sardines, they had remained courteous to everyone, but tension and testosterone are a toxic combination, and yesterday a fight had broken out between two of the men at lunchtime, and some of Margarita's plates had ended up smashed. That afternoon and evening, things had been eerily quiet, and the lights had gone out at eleven.

Matt planned a dawn raid, the preferred method of SWAT teams the world over. He didn't have the imagination or confidence to deviate from a tried and tested model, and the timing made sense. There was nothing more disorientating than the sound of someone crashing through your front door at six in the morning, plus there were fewer civilians to get caught in the crossfire. The aim was to hit them before they got to the boat. Joyce's villa was a relatively self-contained location. Outside the gates was another matter. No one would give a damn if the authorities caught these men if their capture came at the cost of civilian lives or, worse still, multinational civilian lives. Civil suits and independent enquiries were not what Matt needed to progress his rise through the ranks. He needed a clean take.

The hope was if he panned up before the Albanians had dressed, had a cup of tea or a smoke, there was less chance of a running battle. A pretty sunrise could distract the most vigilant and kindle a false sense of security. Hopefully, by the time it happened, she and Sam would be on their way.

THE BOY WAS WAITING for her when she arrived in his room ten minutes later. He was fully dressed, backpack beside him on the bed.

'I set my alarm early,' he said triumphantly, holding up the bag. 'And I've packed everything I need.'

'Good, we're all set then. Let's go. Remember what I said last night? It's a secret, so we must be as quiet as possible so as not to wake anyone in the house. The same goes for outside. We don't want to disturb the men in the hut. It'll ruin things if we do.'

Sam nodded.

They crept down the back staircase through the utility room careful not to pause other than for Sam to slip on his trainers.

Once outside, they kept to the perimeter of the garden, Sam walking slightly ahead of her.

The grass was still dewy underfoot. The sun, an orange fireball about to rise above the horizon, had turned the misty garden a candy-floss shade of pink. She looked at her watch again; a quarter to six. Max's team should be in position by now, counting down the minutes. They would be a valuable distraction, drawing attention to the gates as she and Sam headed in the opposite direction.

Sam ran ahead. She followed him up the steps through the door of the summerhouse.

She felt a thud to the back of her head as, out of nowhere, rough hands grabbed her around the neck from behind, pushing her down onto her stomach, and straddling her so she could hardly breathe as the wooden floorboards grazed her cheeks.

She tried to shout, 'Sam ... Sam.'

She heard the boy yell out.

'Quiet.'

A woman's voice.

The bristle of a man's face close to hers, hot breath on her cheek as she recognised Paolo and behind him Angelina, holding a reel of silver duct tape and a pair of scissors.

'Quick, tape her feet,' Paolo said, holding her hands fast behind her back.

She tried to kick, but Paolo, strong and fit, pressed his whole weight down on her, so she thought her ribs would crack. Angelina gripped her feet and began to wind the roll of tape around her ankles again and again until she couldn't move them a centimetre apart, let alone kick out.

The girl then did the same to her hands, rendering them useless.

Pinkie knew better than to scream. It would bring Kurti's men running. Her only hope was this pair didn't intend to kill her, and she could wait it out until the cavalry arrived.

Paolo flipped her onto her back.

Angelina had moved to the table and was carrying a bottle towards them. Pinkie immediately recognised it as the same bottle Margarita had shown her in the kitchen the night she'd accused her of poisoning Lionel. Oleander.

'Pour it down her throat … quickly, hold her nose,' said Paolo.

'Why are you doing this?' Pinkie gurgled as the bitter mixture razored the back of her throat. She could hear Sam sobbing.

'Because you couldn't mind her own business. All you had to do was keep out of things that don't concern you,' said Paolo roughly, jettisoning himself from her as she coughed and spluttered, turning onto her side in an attempt to clear the contents of her mouth. She had misjudged this couple. This was not the young man she'd admired for being kind to Sam and looking out for his mother. This man was ruthless and cold. He was letting the boy watch everything without a thought for his wellbeing. Angelina was no better. She was enjoying this.

Paolo's mobile rang. He spoke only seconds to whoever was on the other end. He moved to the window. Speaking to Angelina in Portuguese, he handed her back the roll of tape.

'It's my mother. My father is worse. She's in a state and wants me there.'

'It's probably another false alarm. I'll go see what's going on. Tape her mouth. I'll check it out and come right back.'

Angelina stood over her, picking at the tape with nervous fingers, trying to find the end.

Pinkie stayed still. Paolo might come back at any minute. She had to look as if she intended to comply; act like the woman she had pretended to be for weeks in the hope she could talk her way out of this. She couldn't take any risks. She had to think of Sam.

'Please, please let me go?' she pleaded.

'Why would I do that? You know why you're here because you're a liar. You're working for the police.'

'I'm not. I have no idea what you're talking about. Why would I be working for the police?'

'Stop lying. We know all about you.'

Pinkie doubted that very much.

'Know what?'

'Niko gave you the benefit of the doubt, stuck up for you because he thought you were being chased, but I knew something wasn't right. I could tell that the so-called investigator who called at the hotel with your photo wasn't looking for a missing person. Well, turns out I was right. The man's a police officer.'

'Okay, okay. I wasn't being truthful. I am wanted by the police. If you let me go, I'll leave, and they'll be none the wiser. They'll never know I was ever here. I'll pay back the nanny's salary, and I won't bother you anymore.'

'It's too late for that, this Trenear might come sniffing around, and Paolo and I can't have that. My aunt told Lionel we didn't need another nanny, not after the fiasco with Gary and that little tart from the village. You would think with all the whores I've supplied him with over the years, the long-legged Eastern European teenagers Niko brings me, he would have better taste.'

So that was the connection. She helped Niko traffic girls for sex.

'Margarita offered to look after the boy herself, you know, but that wasn't good enough for his precious grandson.'

Pinkie tried to will away the creeping lethargy. Straining her neck, she tried to gather enough momentum to sit up but felt as weak as a kitten. Oleander … think, think. She couldn't gauge how much she'd swallowed. How many teaspoons … one … two … more? She had time, a couple of hours if she could get free. Her head was clear, although her stomach was beginning to cramp. She felt nauseous but knew she should avoid vomiting if she could.

'He didn't want the boy to turn out like Gary. He told her she hadn't tried hard enough with his son after his wife died,' sneered Angelina. 'He said if she couldn't raise Gary, why should he let her have another chance to cock it up with Sam? Can you believe that?'

Pinkie flinched at the loud rip as Angelina found the end of the tape. She had put the scissors down when she picked up the bottle and hadn't looked to pick them up. Her dark eyes were fixed on the wall above Pinkie's head as she vented her frustration, all the time unravelling the tape which stuck to her hands, although she didn't seem to notice.

'How could he expect her to love that spoilt brat when he'd made her give up her own son? We all hated Gary. I'm surprised she could even bear to look at the little monster when Paolo had to fend for himself without her.'

Head to one side, saliva thick in her mouth, it was difficult for Pinkie to speak, 'But your grandfather ...'

'Oh, she told you that bullshit, did she? About her father insisting Paolo live with him to try to save face for the family. What a laugh. Like anyone believed Paolo could be anyone but Lionel's, she'd never had a boyfriend, let alone a lover before him. It's not her fault. I think she's told the story of her and Lionel being in love for so long she believes it, poor old thing. I suppose when the truth is so ugly, you do your best to dress it up. That old letch raped her ... not at knifepoint. He didn't force his way into her room and rip off her clothes. He was way too clever for that. He groomed her in readiness for when his wife died. She was there to meet his every need, including his urge to fuck a teenage girl. I'm not saying she doesn't think she loves him. I'm sure she does, but that's all part of it, don't you see; the hold he has over her. Even now he controls her. He doesn't need her for sex these days. Now she's here to play nurse for however long it takes him to die. That's why you're here to look after Sam so she can give him her undivided attention; be chained to him until the very end.'

'I don't understand,' said Pinkie; she had to keep her talking.

'Someone needs to protect her. She can't be trusted to

protect herself from Lionel or Gary, so it's down to Paolo and me. We'll let nature take its course as far as Lionel is concerned; let Margarita have her tearful goodbye, but Gary won't be a problem for long. Niko's men will see to that when they find the cowardly little shit.'

'Sam?' Pinkie mumbled, suddenly aware she had not heard him for a while and fearing they might have given him the oleander too.

'Oh, don't worry about Sam. Paolo and I will look after him.' Pinkie followed her stare as she glanced for a second in Sam's direction before turning away in disgust. Pinkie's eyes, however, stayed riveted to where Sam was cowering under the table. He was fiddling with something. The Mark 4 rocket, pushing the roll of paper holding the baking soda Margarita had given him into a plastic pop bottle half-filled with vinegar and plugging the top with a cork.

'Paolo is his next of kin, after all, and he needs to be protected from those out there willing to take advantage of a child with the kind of money he's going to inherit when the old man dies. If you'd been who you said you were, we might have let you stay around to help out, but you're not, are you? Did you think Paolo and I would let you come in and ruin our plans? This place … using it as a safe house for Niko's men is our future. No more building work or pandering to fucking tourists for us.'

There was a massive explosion as the rocket shot up into the air, hitting the summerhouse roof before ricocheting to shatter the window, sending shards of glass across the room.

Angelina didn't see Sam shuffle out from his hiding place, but Pinkie was pretty damn sure from the scream she let out, she felt the scissors as he plunged them with all the force he could muster into her left foot, almost severing her big toe, so it hung by a single piece of shredded skin.

Angelina hobbled about, screaming obscenities, holding her foot as it spouted blood, finally staggering to the door and out into the garden.

'Sam, bring the scissors here,' Pinkie shouted to the boy who had retreated back to his hiding place.

He knew exactly what to do.

———

EWAN SAT in the car for as long as he could, palms gripping the steering wheel, ready to speed off as soon as she arrived with the boy. She was late, and she was never late.

If there had been a change of plan, she'd have given him the heads up one way or another. She would have sent a text knowing he'd pick it up. If she'd found herself without a phone she'd find another way. A scarf tied to the tree. They'd used that one before, on another mission years ago. It worked then, and it would now. He'd already been back to the wall a couple of times, just in case, but there was nothing.

He lifted his Beretta 92F from its holster and slotted in the magazine. It had been a while. It felt uncomfortable in the waist holster he never usually wore but made it easier to access if someone came to the car window and there was trouble. He was hidden well behind the gate at the end of the neighbouring property. Unlike Joyce's, theirs was not electric, and there were no security cameras. It had been easy to force the lock and gain entry. The place was empty. Pinkie had done her research on that front. The elderly couple who lived there never rented it out. They panned up each September and stayed until Christmas. The rest of the time, the place was shuttered, the gardener the only regular visitor.

He glanced at the clock on the dashboard. Matt's team were due to go in at any minute, assuming they were on time. He wanted no part in that pantomime. If he didn't go now, he might not be able to go at all.

Who was he kidding? It didn't warrant debate. Whichever way the wind blew, he'd never leave, not knowing whether she was safe or not. She'd said her cover may have been blown. If that was the case, things could only get uglier when the place was raided. Suspicions confirmed, she'd be singled out for special punishment.

Given the gates were off limits, he had no choice but to go for the fence, taking the exact route Pinkie had planned for her and the boy. It was less of a challenge from this side of the wall. The ground was slightly higher for a start, and this side was good old-fashioned brickwork without the fancy render, making it easier to climb.

He got out of the car and took off his jacket. He'd need to sling it over the razor wire when he got to the top to avoid slashing his hands to shreds.

It was a shame it was his best one. He wasn't remotely interested in designer labels, but he'd dressed up for her today, even had a haircut, having felt a complete slob the last time they met in The Yellow Gecko. His boots weren't ideal either, zip-ups with leather soles. The bricks would do for the toes.

He walked to the back of the car and lifted his leg holster from the boot, transferring the Beretta to its familiar position. If he was going to play Action Man, he might as well do it with conviction. The wall was more difficult than he'd thought. The bricks were smooth, laid level with the pointing; a burglar's nightmare.

He looked around for something to stand on but was out of luck. Scanning the length of the wall, he spotted a trellis a couple of metres down. On closer examination, he could see it was made of heavy-duty wire threaded through steel eyelets hammered into the wall and was just about sturdy enough to take his weight. Whatever plant it was meant to encourage to climb had died trying. He hoped he wouldn't do the same.

Folding his jacket to sling over one shoulder, he gingerly gripped the wire above head height and began to climb. He took it steady, testing each line of wire, finding his footing through the browning foliage until he could feel the gap between the razor wire and the tiled top of the wall. Heaving himself up, he checked there was no one on the other side. It was clear. He threw his jacket over the wire and, in one swift move, without giving himself time to think how much it might hurt, pulled himself on top of it before jumping down onto the grass on the other side.

The bloody boots had no real support, all style and no substance, and he wished he'd worn his Doc Martens as he turned his ankle. Scrambling to his feet, he took refuge in the shrubs to catch his breath, using the seconds to check out the tree Pinkie had intended to climb with the boy. There was no sign of her.

―――

'I'M SORRY, I'm so sorry,' Sam stammered. 'I should never have told Margarita about our adventure when she brought me my milk. She told them.' He sniffed back the tears as he snipped away at the tape with the blood-stained scissors, first freeing her hands, then her feet.

'Help me up,' she said, unsure if she could make it on her own.

Once upright. She held him by the shoulders turning him to face her.

'Listen to me. This is not your fault. None of it is *your* fault, and as for that rocket ... wow, that rocket was just ...?'

'I knew it would work, the old Mark 4.'

She smiled, hugging him close. 'It certainly did. It's about the best rocket I've ever seen in my life.'

The boy beamed.

'Now, help me move the stove.'

'The stove?'

'Yeah, it's where the treasure is. If you're having an adventure, there has to be secret treasure, right?'

The boy did as she asked, his eyes as wide as saucers as she pulled the Glock from its hiding place and checked the chamber before loading a magazine.

Her heart was racing now. She knew there was no way she would be able to climb the tree, and she couldn't risk the boy trying it on his own.

'Grab your bodyboard,' she said, 'hold it up in front of you with both hands and follow me out through the door. Make sure you stay as close as you can, and when I say run, run with it as fast as you can down to the beach.'

'Can I bring my bag?'

'No.'

'Can I take just one thing? It's something irreplaceable.'

'Okay, one thing, as long as it's not too big. It's got to fit in your pocket.'

'It does ... it will fit, I promise.'

'Go on then, quickly.'

He came back holding a pebble.

'My mum gave it to me before she died. She found it on

the beach in Cornwall where we used to live, and look, can you see … it has a stripe like an 'S' for Sam on it. She said it was lucky. It's irreplaceable, isn't it?'

Pinkie felt a lump rise in her throat.

'Yes, it is.'

Sam thrust the pebble into his pocket and picked up the bodyboard.

'Ready?' she asked, holding the Glock out in front of her.

Sam nodded.

The area around the summerhouse was all clear. Angelina's blood stained the steps and left its trail across the garden path towards the house.

'Okay, we're heading for the steps down to the beach. You lead the way. Don't look back and remember when I say run, you run, and when you get to the water, you paddle out as far as you can and don't stop.'

'Are we in danger?'

She wasn't going to lie to him. Fear was good now; it would keep the adrenaline pumping.

EWAN RELEASED the Beretta from its holster and felt his way along the wall through the undergrowth towards the house, knowing any minute now, Matt's team would blow the gates.

No sooner had he thought it than it happened. The ear-bleeding explosion sent a plume of flames and blue smoke high above the roof of the villa. He imagined the gates hanging off their hinges and Matt's forces heading through them, the pyrotechnics and smoke grenades there to confuse and lend valuable cover. The Albanian boys wouldn't know what hit them and when they did, it would be too late. That wasn't to say they wouldn't fight back. The acrid smoke caught the back of his throat. He could hear screaming from somewhere; a woman. Could it be her? He tried to get his bearings from the photographs he'd mulled over with Pinkie in the bar. If the gates were at the front, he was at the back of the villa, near the pool and the old summer house Pinkie had talked about in one of her calls. He headed in the direction of the screaming, trying his best to remain undetected. As he got nearer, he could hear the woman shouting obscenities in Portuguese. Not Pinkie. He didn't know whether to be grateful she wasn't hurt or concerned he still hadn't found her.

All hell was breaking loose at the front of the house. He could hear shouting now and rapid fire. He caught a whiff of CS gas. It always smelled like vinegar to him. He pulled his t-shirt up to cover his nose. He guessed Matt's men had lobbed a couple of canisters of tear gas into the men's barracks. They'd be staggering about, desperate to get outside, burning skin, burning lungs, tears pouring from their eyes to join the strings of snot running from their nostrils. Armed or not, that shit could render you useless if you weren't expecting it. It would be minutes before their eyes stopped smarting enough to see a thing let alone return fire. It was a clever move.

Keeping low, he crept forward until he was close enough to peer through the bushes and get a good look at what the woman was screaming about. She was lying on the slabs next to the pool, blood seeping into the concrete from a wound to her foot. A man about the same age was leaning over her, trying to comfort her with little success. She thrashed about as he tried to wrap a towel around her injury to stem the blood flow from what Ewan assumed was a gun wound. Neither looked armed, and he guessed they were from the house. He was about to return his gun to its holster and step out from his hiding place to ask where the nanny and the boy were when to his left, he spotted a beast of a man, thundering like a raging bull towards them. Tattoos etching both arms extended up his thick neck and the back of his bald head. He carried a semi-automatic in his right hand.

'It is bad. Those fuckers used tear gas.'

'I was in the house having a shit; the toilet in our place is—'

'I don't fucking care about your toilet. Where's my mother?'

For all his size and obvious power, the man took the reprimand.

'Inside with the old man.'

'Is she safe?'

The man shrugged.

'And Niko?'

'Gone.'

The girl began to cry.

This must be Paolo, Ewan thought. *Then the girl was Angelina.*

Paolo glanced towards the house as if wondering whether he should go to check, then seemed to change his mind.

'Help me carry her to the summer house. The nanny and the boy are there. We can use them as a shield. They won't shoot us if we have them. She's one of them, and they'll never kill the boy.'

Paolo ran towards the summer house, leaving the man mountain to lift the woman as if she was a toddler. Ewan shadowed the man from a distance as he crossed the grass to a low building he assumed was the summerhouse where Pinkie and the boy were. He drew his gun, ready to take advantage of the fact the only one armed in the group had his arms full, but before he had the chance, the housekeeper's son ran out.

'They're gone. She's managed to get free. The boy must be with her.'

The Albanian dropped the girl on the veranda like a sack of potatoes.

Ewan moved closer, still under cover of the bushes, thinking any minute now he was going to have to go in. Things were ratcheting up a notch. All around the sound of rapid fire, the smoke thicker. Helicopters circling.

'I see them. They're heading for the beach,' went up the cry as both men took off across the grass.

'Make sure you get that bitch …' shouted the girl after them.

Ewan skirted the back of the summerhouse, careful not to be seen by the girl who he could hear was on her phone screaming hysterically at whoever was on the other end of the line.

PINKIE AND SAM headed down the lawn towards the cliff edge, Sam running on ahead with his board and Pinkie following on behind, sweat pouring down her back as she tried to control her irregular heartbeat. The oleander was taking its toll. Lionel Joyce had built up his tolerance. She had not. She was struggling to breathe.

She kept one eye on the lawn stretching out behind them, ready to fire, if necessary, to protect the boy. She thought of Ewan sitting in the car waiting. If she wasn't there on time, he'd know she wasn't coming.

At the top of the steps, she reached for the handrail, only just avoiding a tumble as she lost her footing. She could hear shouting, much closer than before, and as she looked up, she saw Paolo with one of the Albanians, a man they called 'Ari', 'bear' in English, for obvious reasons. They were racing down the lawn toward them. Ari was armed.

'Run, Sam, run, and remember when you hit the water, paddle out and don't stop, not for me, not for anyone.'

Sam began to run down the steps as sure-footed as a young goat over the familiar terrain.

She rounded and fired a shot toward the two of them. She was too far away to hit either, but it caused them to scatter and gave her time to turn and run herself. She had no idea where her strength was coming from now. It was mind over matter. The matter being her ever-weakening limbs. Her legs felt like jelly, the pain in her right arm so intense she could barely keep hold of the Glock. Eventually, she hit the sand. Sam had begun to paddle out just as she'd told him. Paolo and Ari were at the top of the steps now, but to her surprise, they had not followed her down them. She heard a gunshot. Were they being chased? She knew she had only seconds to get into the water before they followed her onto the beach to find better cover.

EWAN COULD SEE the men legging it across the sloping lawn towards the steps down to the sea. A good way ahead of them were Pinkie and the boy, who was in the lead, carrying a surfboard. Ewan broke cover and gave chase. For a second, he lost sight of Pinkie and the boy as they began the descent down the steps. He held on to the hope if the men wanted to use her and the boy as a shield, they needed them alive. His ankle was killing him as his heart pounded with the effort of narrowing the gap to get them in range. He'd have to shoot soon if only to give her time to get away. Once they had her and Sam, they'd have the upper hand, and he couldn't trust Matt and his team not to fuck it up and get the pair of them killed. He could see her again now as he got closer. The two men had reached the top of the steps. She was crouching, firing at them, he guessed, to protect the boy. They crouched too, ready to fight back. They hadn't seen him yet. The first shot had to count. He had no cover and if the Albanian was worth the price of his tattoos and got a shot in, he was likely to hit. He stood still, took his stance and aimed. The bullet hit the Albanian in the neck on the right side. Reaching up with his left hand as if he'd been stung by a wasp to where the blood was spurting, the man slowly turned to look for the source of his injury. Bemused, it took him a second or two to zoom in on Ewan, who had dropped and lay flat on the ground, his arms shielding his head. The hulk lifted his gun, swayed, then toppled backwards, pulling the trigger as he fell, the bullet whizzing past Ewan's left ear and burying itself in the turf.

Ewan watched with horror as Paolo bent to retrieve the gun and raced away down the steps. Ewan jumped to his feet and ran after him leaping over the body of the Albanian and clearing the first three steps. The boy was already in the water, paddling hard out to sea. Pinkie was zig-zagging her way across the sand towards the water, trying to make herself as difficult a target as possible. Paolo was on her heels. Why didn't she turn and fire? The boy ... she was afraid he'd fire back and hit the boy. She was waiting for him to paddle out of range. She ran into the sea. Paolo followed.

———

AS SHE ENTERED THE WATER, Pinkie felt her heart leap again. She prayed the men shooting were Matt's men, and she stayed conscious long enough to tell them she'd been poisoned.

The truth was she was scared, and it was not the useful kind. This paralysing terror left her cowering in the water before an unpredictable enemy whose breath on her neck made her freeze. Her hair dripping down her back, a dull ache creeping through every bone in her body; she was finished. Looking back to shore, she could make out a third man on the steps and Paolo on the beach heading towards her. The was no sign of Ari, but Paolo had a gun. She dared not swim out further for fear of collapse. She had to stay as still as possible. She watched him wading out; the gun held high pointing right at her. Was she in range? She didn't think so, but her thoughts were beginning to muddle, and her vision was blurred. She took the biggest breath she could and dipped under the surface.

She didn't see where the first bullet came from that hit the water a short distance away but she felt the second as it struck her shoulder with a thud. From the stabbing pain, she guessed the brachial plexus. She was bleeding out; she knew that much. It must have nicked an artery. The sudden numbness down her right side confirmed it.

She was shivering uncontrollably now, her teeth chattering in her ears as she tried to shout to Sam. 'Keep paddling … don't stop … don't …'

Her knees buckled as a wave toppled her from behind.

The urge to give into the freefall out of consciousness in the hope of disconnecting from her broken body was overwhelming. Her left arm hung limp and useless as she felt with her other hand for the rocks beneath, managing to push herself back up onto her feet only to stagger a few steps before falling face down into the water. She knew she didn't have long. She closed her eyes. The shivering had stopped. The water felt warm, and she imagined she was back in Cornwall, on Porthtowan beach with the rest of the Water Babes. She could hear them laughing, calling her name.

Should she pray; was this the time to confess her sins, would she get absolution, or would the door be slammed in her face with a resounding 'too late' ringing in her ears? She read somewhere never to expect too much from life; that the journey was its own reward; was that it, the secret to it all. Take it while you can?

She heard another loud shot and felt herself drift away into oblivion.

EWAN HAMMERED across the sand after them, his heart in his throat as he watched the young man lift his gun and fire. The first shot hit the water with a thud. Pinkie ducked beneath the waves re-emerging a metre or so to the left. Paolo turned to fire again. Ewan lifted his gun and fired, hitting Paolo in the shoulder just as the young man pulled the trigger. Paolo dropped the gun, turned and, clutching his arm, began to drag himself through the water, taking a parallel route back to the beach, desperate now unarmed, to get away. Ewan waded in. Pinkie had gone under and hadn't come back up. Where the hell was she? Paolo hadn't hit her, had he?

A helicopter circled above him and he could see a rib heading towards Sam to lift him off the bodyboard. There was blood in the water. He slid his gun into its holster, trying to remember where Pinkie was the last time he saw her go down. He waded out further and dived under, his lungs bursting as he swam around in circles trying to find her. He came up for air and dived again.

Please, please, God...

He spotted her. Jesus Christ, she was unconscious, blood gushing like ink from a wound in her shoulder. He grabbed her and began pulling her through the water to the shore.

He was exhausted, ears ringing.

'Don't you die on me, don't you fucking dare.' He couldn't tell if the bullet had exited or not. Was there an internal bleed? Was that why she wasn't coming around?

He pulled her up onto the sand and, kneeling, put his head to her chest. He couldn't hear a bloody thing through the din of the helicopter landing above the beach on Joyce's lawn. He lifted both arms above his head and, fisting his hands together, brought them down with a thud onto her chest and listened again. He felt her neck for a pulse. Faint, very faint like the flutter of a bird. He took off his t-shirt to stem the bleeding, pressing hard.

Four men, two medics and two in full riot gear, were racing down the steps. Two headed up the beach towards Paolo, the medics, towards him and Pinkie.

'What's the damage?'

'I don't know. I can't make it out. She's been shot, the pulse is weak and she's out of it.'

They moved in and he stood back, pacing around them,

hands clasped on top of his head, trying to keep a lid on the swell of emotion threatening to topple him.

The one examining her turned to the other.

'Fetch a stretcher and radio the hospital. Tell them to clear the pad. We'll be there in thirty minutes. She needs surgery,' he said, slipping an oxygen mask over Pinkie's face.

'Is she gonna be alright?' asked Ewan, his face laddered with fear.

'You did your best.'

Ewan slumped onto the sand, head in his hands and wept.

Chapter Forty-One

PINKIE PEELED OPEN HER EYELIDS, letting the light slowly banish the darkness to the far corners of the room. Where the hell was she?

She wasn't in pain as such but felt stiff, and her throat was dry. For a split second, engulfed by claustrophobia and panic, she thought she was still constrained; still being held by Angelina and Paolo, but no, she remembered she'd escaped to the beach with Sam. Blinking away the fog stopping her brain from sparking, she grappled for the last thing she remembered.

She was in the water with Sam. She'd been hit and lost sight of him. She'd watched him paddle away on his bodyboard but had they caught up with him after she passed out? Was he safe?

She moved to reach up to her shoulder, to the spot where the bullet had entered, only to find she was restricted by the IV line fastened with strips of tape to the back of her hand. Hospital bed rails penned her in, and above a drip bag fed her fluid or drugs; she wasn't sure which. She certainly felt disorientated enough for it to be drugs.

She took a deep breath, trying to fill what felt like shredded lungs. Her head cleared a little, and slowly things began to come back to her. Sam was okay. Someone had told her that, she was sure of it. Who ... Matt?

She remembered being brought here, but not in the back of an ambulance. It had been noisy, so noisy she couldn't hear a thing, just the steady, *whop whop whop* of helicopter blades, then a hospital trolly and the pain; a knife-twisting pain, like nothing she had felt before. She remembered the clamour of people in hospital scrubs. Portuguese voices speaking so fast she couldn't understand a word, and another voice shouting just as loudly.

She heard the door swing open and the sound of someone crossing the room. A tanned young face looked down at her.

'Good, you are awake,' he said, unhooking her chart from the bottom of her bed. 'We need to keep you on the analgesics for another couple of days, then we can get you moving around. I can call your friend in if you like, he has been sitting outside all morning waiting for you to wake up.'

'My friend?' Pinkie asked.

Her throat was sandpaper sore, and her voice a scratchy whisper.

'The gentleman who brought you in, Mr Davies.'

Ewan, it was Ewan's voice she heard. It was him who told her Sam was safe and she was going to be okay.

She nodded.

'Not too long, though. You need your rest. Here let me lift you up a little.'

She winced as he lifted her, propping her pillows behind her.

'There, is that okay?'

'Yes, thank you.'

A few minutes later, Ewan walked through the door. He looked dreadful, and for a moment, she wondered whether the grey pallor and red-rimmed eyes were the remnants of a hangover until she saw the tears on his lashes.

'Thank God, you had me worried for a minute there,' he sniffed.

Had she not been feeling as if she'd been run over by a bus, she would have called him out and laughed off his uncharacteristic show of emotion. But she felt sore and vulnerable, and it was comforting to have a friend at her side.

'The doctor said I can be unhooked from this lot soon,' she said, lifting her drip.

'And you're listening to him now, are you?'

'What do you mean?'

'Well, you didn't have much time for his opinion when we got here and he told you you'd had a heart attack.'

'What?'

'You told him you'd been shot ... "what the hell kind of doctor can't spot a gunshot wound?" I think that's the gist of what you told him until he had the good sense to knock you out with the anaesthetic.'

A lump grew in Pinkie's throat.

'Heart attack?'

Ewan pulled up a chair.

'They performed an emergency bypass and fitted an ICD which I'm told is a kind of defibrillator to shock you back to life if your heart ever stops again.'

Pinkie's stomach roiled as she tried to grasp the enormity of what he was saying.

'But I was shot, I know I was. There was blood.'

'A nick to your shoulder, that's all. They sutured it, but it's nothing much. You had a cardiac arrest in the water.'

'But how did you get me here?'

'I can't take the credit. You can thank Matt for that. He called in the helicopter. They performed CPR and got you here. I just came along for the ride. You know me, I'll never turn down the chance of a ride in a Chinook. Like old times.'

She wanted to respond, but couldn't get past the words, *emergency bypass*.

He did the noble thing. He kept talking, filling in the gaps. He did his comic best to distract her from an unpalatable truth, but when he finally left, she lay between the crisp hospital sheets, derelict and irrelevant, imagining cold lumpy soil landing on her coffin lid.

The consultant visited later. Looking like a teenager in a borrowed suit, he reassured her the prognosis was good and slowly but surely, she would be able to return to normal life. *Normal life*, what the hell did she know about normal life? Her life had always been thoroughly abnormal, and that's the way she liked it. He recommended a visit to her GP when she got back to the UK to book an appointment with a cardiologist and arrange some special physiotherapy designed for those like her who had heart conditions.

Ewan visited every day. On day three, he'd told her Ross Trenear had taken Sam back to Cornwall to be reunited with his grandmother, who was his next of kin now his father and grandfather were dead. Matt had decided to keep her name out of it. That way, she wouldn't have to explain to anyone where she'd been when she got home, and the authorities didn't need to suffer the embarrassment of admitting one of their former operators had gone rogue and killed a high court judge.

Ross Trenear had not fared so well. He had strayed from the rule book one time too many. Faced with the ultimatum to keep his mouth shut about Carlisle, leave voluntarily and keep his pension or face dismissal and possible charges of perverting the course of justice, he opted for the former. Pinkie thought it was a great shame and a big mistake. After all, he had been spot on about her. Those who blindly followed the rules had obvious value in a world in need of order, but intuitive mavericks like Trenear, who cared enough to take personal risks, were rare birds these days and getting rarer by the minute. Her own forced retirement, this time for real, would be another feather in the cap for those who sought to wipe them out altogether. She took some solace in knowing she'd achieved what she'd come to Portugal to do and kept her promise. Liz had her grandson back.

She learnt from Ewan that Matt's mission had, on the whole, been a great success. Though Kurti had managed to disappear into thin air, he had captured all of his men alive bar one, who had been one of the three who followed Pinkie onto the beach. He, like Paolo, had been shot by Ewan.

She was grateful her friend had saved her life but was equally relieved he'd managed to do it without killing Margarita's son.

Margarita had sent her a get-well card full of apologies and regret for all she had suffered as a result of her absentmindedly telling Angelina about Sam's planned adventure. She confirmed Lionel had died the day of the raid, peacefully in his sleep.

As she'd hoped, the woman she had come to think of as a friend had been totally ignorant of Kurti's true identity, Paolo's involvement with him and Angelina's lucrative sideline running sex workers for the Mafia Shqiptare. Matt had not believed her at first but had finally been persuaded into accepting it was the truth. In the same way as she could see no wrong in Lionel, sticking by him until the very end, she refused to read the signs or accept the truth about her son. She would pay the price for both. Pinkie knew what a terrible thing it was to lose trust in those you loved.

Ewan walked through the door carrying a droopy bunch of carnations which she guessed he'd bought at the kiosk on the way in. They suited her mood.

'How are you feeling today?'

'Peachy.' She knew she sounded churlish and ungrateful. He'd saved her life after all. 'I'm beginning to get a bit of feeling back in my fingers, but everything's a bit hot and tingly.'

'Well, you can't expect to be feeling one hundred per cent.'

Hot tears welled, and she turned her head into her pillow to hide them.

Ewan reached out and touched her cheek.

'They said the oleander poisoning started the arrhythmia, but they found an underlying problem which it triggered. My heart stopped, actually stopped.' Her voice broke and she began to sob.

'Well, I can tell you mine didn't fare much better. At least you've got a bloody pacemaker to sort yours out if it happens again. Frankly, I'm sick of what you do to mine. My heart stopped that day on the beach, but it also stopped the first day I saw you and several times since. It's all down to you, and I want to know what you're gonna do about it. You've got all these people running around after you, but what about poor broken-hearted me? Here, move over, lend me your bed. I think I need it more than you.'

The large grin across his stupid face drew a tear-choked laugh.

'I never thought you were sentimental.'

'I'm Welsh. Of course I'm sentimental, it's genetic.'

'Have they told you when you'll be coming home?'

'The end of next week.'

'Tell you what, why don't I come back with you? I've got nothing keeping me here or anywhere else for that matter. I can help with the physio.'

Though she was smiling, tears streamed down her cheeks. 'Thank you, Ewan, for being there and for saving my life.'

'Old habits die hard, and don't worry, I'll be calling the favour in.'

Chapter Forty-Two

ROSS SAT on the slipway wall opposite the pub, sipping his coffee, listening to the town drag itself out of bed. Behind him, a van driver jumped out to click back wing mirrors likely to snap off as he squeezed his way along Bethesda Hill to make his deliveries. To his left, the window cleaner's squeaky chamois washed away the previous day's salty cataracts. The smell of saffron as a batch of warm buns arrived from the bakery and the whiff of bacon through the open window of one of the holiday cottages along the Digey made his stomach rumble. God, it was good to be home.

The morning felt crisp, the first bite of Autumn in the air. On the coast, the season was never one of mellow fruitfulness, although there was always plenty of mist. It was the change in the famous St. Ives light that let you know summer was over. Flamingo sky in the morning, rolling rain and afternoon rainbows. The sea inky, and the sand greywhite, less buttery but with more sparkle once the sun lowered its wattage.

None of this had happened yet, but as Ross sat contemplating his life and what the hell he was going to do with it, he could smell the change in the air.

By the time he'd got to speak properly to his DCI, Luke Parish had calmed down a little but not enough for the outcome to change. He could jump or be pushed. The choice was his. He'd decided to jump. At least the landing would be less brutal. After the bowel-clenching drive with the two Portuguese psychos, he'd decided he'd had enough anyway. From Luke's tone, he guessed he felt much the same way about the lot he'd been working with. He'd said he couldn't wait to finish the secondment and get back to Cornwall. It was strange to think that the next time they met it would be as friends rather than as colleagues.

Luke hadn't divulged the ins and outs of the operation, and Ross guessed he probably never would. He did say it was a cross-border mission involving MI5, Europol, the border police and something called CTIUs, which Ross had needed to look up after he put the phone down. He told him he'd been seconded to the counter-terrorist command in London because of their intel about a Cornish connexion with the Mafia Shqiptare. Ross's only comment had been a long exhaled; 'Fu...ck'.

Luke said they'd had Joyce's villa under surveillance for months and that Philippa Floyd was part of the team working undercover for the head honcho in Portugal, to which Ross had thought *double fuck* but had kept his opinion to himself. Luke brought up Jem Fielding's name, and for a second, he'd reeled with the memory of the man who had tried to ruin him and had almost cost him his son's life in the process. Luke had sworn him to secrecy about all of it, but when he'd commented no one would believe him anyway, his boss hadn't argued. He'd avoided a disciplinary, and he'd still get his pension, and it wasn't as if he didn't have a job to go to. He could run the pub with Karenza; take over where her dad had left off. They'd save on staffing costs, and he'd have more time with the family and to surf, of course. The rest of them at the station would envy him. He'd be living the dream. So why wasn't he doing cartwheels at the prospect? He supposed he might feel differently if he'd been fired for being crap at the job, but he wasn't. He'd been right about Philippa Floyd, Luke as near as damn it told him so, and if it hadn't been confirmed before, it had been the moment they'd handed him Liz Hosking's grandson and booked the pair of them on a flight back to good old Blighty.

Liz had been waiting for them at Newquay airport. The woman looked as if she had wound back the clock ten years since the last time he saw her. She had run towards them, arms outstretched to fold the boy into her, her voice as soft as moss with love and gratitude. Their goodbyes had been lost in the wind as they parted in the car park; the boy's smile as wide as the ocean.

He felt a hand on his shoulder and looked up. Karenza sidled down next to him, her legs dangling over the wall, their flip-flopped feet touching. He loved her small delicate feet, tanned with toes painted a summery tangerine. He'd first noticed them when at sixteen she'd sat on this very wall with him after he'd done a shift at her dad's pub. Back then, she wore a tiny silver toe ring. He'd thought it was sweet and sexy, which summed her up at the time. It had been a lethal combination that had floored his eighteen-year-old self. The toe ring was gone, and the sweetness but the sexy was still there in abundance. In her jeans and t-shirt, hair wet from the shower, she was still gorgeous.

'So are you gonna tell me what's really going on, or are you sticking to your story?'

'I told you I've had enough of it. That last stint on Bodmin Moor was the final straw. I thought, what a waste of bloody time. I could be at home helping you in the pub. I don't need this kind of crap.'

'And what about this kind of crap?' She reached into the back pocket of her jeans and placed two ticket stubs, Faro, to Newquay airport on his knee.

He glanced down at them and then at her, but she was staring out to sea, her brows knitted into a frown as if she was following something on the horizon.

'They were in your bag.'

'It's not what it looks like.'

'And what does it look like, Ross?'

'Well, I suppose it looks like I've taken someone to Portugal for the weekend.'

'Wow. All those years of training certainly paid off. Nothing wrong with your detective skills, DI Trenear,' she said, giving him a slow clap for good measure.

She still hadn't met his eye, and the fact she'd not raised her voice worried him. Karenza had a temper; a throw-your-dinner-against-the-wall kind of temper. This level of self-control was unnerving, like standing over a ticking time bomb you knew would detonate at any moment.

'Okay, okay, I wasn't on Bodmin Moor like I told you. I was on an important mission. Special Ops were involved, MI5 and Europol, Albanian gangsters, and this frumpy middle-aged woman who I thought murdered Carlisle and who turned out to be working undercover. So I wasn't with another woman, honestly, you know I wouldn't …'

Then it came, the storm of anger and exasperation, the flash of lightning fracturing the sky and it was deafening.

'Shut up, just shut the hell up,' she screamed, jumping to her feet. I know you weren't with another woman. You wouldn't bloody dare. I know what you were doing, you moron. I found this in your bag too.'

She pulled out a leaflet he had picked up from the hotel lobby, a wave the size of a sky-scraper promoting Nazaré, on the front. She screwed it up and threw it hard at his head. He didn't reach to pick it up from its resting place on the sand. He didn't need to. He'd memorised the contents; the paragraph describing the shelf in the five-kilometre underwater canyon that causes the sixty-foot swell.

'I don't know which of your work-shy surfing buddies cooked up this little stunt, but you can tell all of them from me they can drink elsewhere from now on. And as for you, you've had your holidays, so you can get your sorry ass behind that bar and start pulling pints. I'm taking the day off.'

Chapter Forty-Three

Six months later

THE MOOR HAD BEEN a revelation for Pinkie; great swathes of treeless landscape under a broad rolling sky that changed with the wind. She had worn her waterproofs for her walk this morning, thinking, as she looked out of the window at a leaded sky every bit as grey as the granite tors rising like giant tombstones from the earth hereabouts, it was bound to rain. An hour later, the sky had cleared, leaving only a few uncommitted clouds, and she was sweltering.

She had given up the physio at Derriford after a couple of months and taken up walking instead, venturing out a little further every day. She had promised herself a present when she could manage five miles; a pup, maybe a spaniel or a chocolate lab. Today she had to get back early. She had parcels arriving she needed to sign for.

She slipped off her jacket, tying it around her waist, and headed home, avoiding the spikey gorse, its yellow flowers shining like fairy lights through the tall feathers of rusty bracken.

The gate was open. She'd have to watch that if she got a dog. There were pockets of livestock on the heathland, sheep and wild ponies, and an untrained dog could run amok.

Inside she heeled off her boots and put the kettle on.

She had fallen in love with the converted barn on the edge of Bodmin Moor. The four acres of scrubland and rough pasture that came with it were a challenge but one she could deal with now she had help and time. Lots of time, she hoped. At least Matt had agreed she could stay in Cornwall, albeit the far end of the county.

She stood at the open patio doors, her steaming cup of coffee misting the glass, watching the sun glint on the greenhouse roof. She smiled to herself, pleased with the position of the new model, away from the overhanging branches of sycamores, whose helicopter seeds had been nigh on impossible to fish out of the vents of the one at her old house.

She was looking forward to christening it. The seeds she'd ordered from the gardening catalogue were arriving that morning, according to the text she'd received from the DHL driver. She had to admit she'd gone a bit mad. The catalogue had been waiting for her on the kitchen table.

The technicoloured flowers had enticed and enthralled, and before she'd known it, her list had run to several hundred pounds. Never mind, she thought, justifying the spend, the greenhouse was empty after all, and she'd be starting from scratch, and many of the cuttings were bound to fail; they always did. She'd taken a trip to the garden centre and bought some compost and pots and couldn't wait to feel the warm soil between her fingers again. She'd put the paraffin heater in the greenhouse for a bit of warmth just in case, but looking at the tender blue spring sky, she knew it would be warm enough without it.

She'd sent a couple of packets of seeds to Liz for Sam to plant. Sunflowers, they were always fun, and he was bound to be interested in the way they lifted their lion-mane heads to follow the path of the sun. Her mother had been no gardener but always bought a packet each year for her and Rob. They'd compete against each other to see which of theirs grew the tallest. She had a photo somewhere of them standing by the garage wall next to their specimens.

She'd left it for a couple of weeks to allow him to settle. She'd had a few sleepless nights worrying the loss of his father and grandfather was a couple of tragedies too many for such a young child to bear. She could never visit in person, of course. The boy would recognise her and all the work Matt had done covering her tracks would have been a waste of time. She would miss her old friends. Some more than others. Oddly enough, it was Agnes she missed the most with her reassuring over interest in everything she said or did. She'd put her in charge of selling the house and clearing the contents, and she'd found a buyer, a retired schoolteacher from Brighton who she'd described as dapper.

On her return to the UK, she'd been told she'd had a lucky escape; that if someone had not been there and spotted her in difficulty during a holiday dip in the Algarve, she could have died while gardening or in front of the telly watching *Strictly*. She should count her blessings she'd had this warning, and the surgeon had done a great job fixing her. As long as she was sensible, ate well, exercised and avoided stress, she could plan for titanium-hipped old age like the best of them.

'I've made a coffee. Do you want one?' she shouted.

'I will when you've told me where to plant this bush,' came back the cry from beyond the shrubbery.

'It's a tree, not a bush.'

'Oh, very sorry, m'lady. You'll have me curtseying next or worse still, wearing bloody Crocs. I'm telling you straight, I draw the line at that. The day you buy me a pair of those bloody things, I'm out of here.'

'You pick a spot. Somewhere I can sit with a gin on summer evenings and take in the wonderful view.'

'Me pick a spot? I don't want to get it wrong and you slip something nasty into that coffee,' said Ewan, pulling off his gloves as he walked across the lawn to join her.

She smiled. 'As if. You're far too valuable a commodity. Gardeners are hard to find in this neck of the woods, and anyway, if you're really worried, there's always bottled beer in the fridge.'

'Now you're talking. See, didn't I tell you every cloud has a silver lining?'

'You know, for once I think you could be right.'

'So which view?' he said, putting his arm around her shoulder. 'This place is nothing but views.'

'The one I'm looking at right now,' she smiled, looking up at him. 'It's about as perfect as they come, although a pair of Crocs might just …'

His kiss tasted of the green grass of home, freedom and all the excitement she would ever need.

Next in The Cornish Crime Series

vinci-books.com/Baptismoffire

One fire. Three dead. A lifetime of questions.

Kit Retallick returns to Cornwall, determined to prove his innocence in a fire that killed his family. With the help of a skeptical lawyer and a relentless investigator, he must unravel deadly secrets—before it's too late.

Turn the page for a free preview…

A Baptism Of Fire: Chapter One

THERE IS A REASON WHY, before mobile phones and the cloud, when asked which one precious item they would save from a burning house, people invariably opted for their photographs. It's the same reason they take the photos in the first place because the past is irreplaceable, it defines us from our first steps to our last breaths. The things we remember and the things we'd rather forget. We can try to hold back the years and lose sleep over our bad choices, but we can never rewind time. It is done and dusted. Nevertheless, there are moments when rewriting our past could transform our future.

The young man sitting on the train that November evening was searching for transformation. He had no need for photographs. His past had survived the furnace. All he had to do to remember was look in the mirror. His history was branded upon his skin.

The tannoy crackled to life, and the nasal recording announced, 'Next station, Truro. Change for connections to Penryn and Falmouth.'

The passengers shuffled in their seats, gathering themselves and their belongings. The student slouched next to him who had missed all the scenery, glued to Instagram on her phone, looked up and stood to heave a rucksack, almost as big as her, from the luggage rack behind.

The movement nudged a heavy-set woman across the aisle who had got on at Bodmin and gossiped incessantly ever since, to finally pause for breath.

'Home for Christmas, love?'

The girl shot her a baffled look as if mystified why anyone over thirty thought they had the right to engage her in conversation. 'Yeah?' she replied in a tone that sounded more like *what's it to you?*

The woman, impervious to the insult, smiled before turning to pick up where she'd left off. 'They turn the Christmas tree lights on at five thirty and the parade starts at six. We can get a bit of shopping done first, then treat ourselves to a glass of Prosecco at The William before it begins.'

'Make that a pizza and two glasses. I'm not shopping this evening. I've been caught out before,' replied her friend. 'They reduce everything nearer Christmas,' she added in a whisper as if imparting a close-guarded retail secret.

He'd forgotten about the lantern parade. He should have realised when he'd struggled to book the Airbnb, there was something going on. He remembered taking part when he was a kid, how they'd spent weeks crafting the giant lanterns out of waxed paper stretched over willow and wire frames for the procession. The theme that year had been the world's oceans and he'd been one of four picked from his class to carry the lantern in the shape of a Great White Shark.

They were crossing the viaduct now, its solid arms

wrapped around the little city like a proud mother. He peered through the train window down at the floodlit cathedral, the fairy-lit terraces cowering in its pious shadow. The place had probably altered; it would be strange if it hadn't after all this time, but he'd put money on the people being the same. The past settled close to the surface in communities like this. If you kicked at the dirt, the dust rose, stifling the appetite for change and settling in the lungs of those who stayed.

They'd be drawing into the station soon. Fifteen years was a long time in anyone's book. He'd left a frightened kid with no idea if he'd ever come back or what he'd face if he did. Now, all grown-up, he was prepared for the worst they could throw at him, but he had no illusions, this was no homecoming. The mayor wouldn't be waiting with a brass band.

He heard the sharp intake of breath from the woman across the aisle as he rose to put on his coat. He turned, clocking her embarrassment as he met her eye. He was used to the reaction. The uncomfortable marriage of disgust and pity.

'Don't worry, missus, it's not catching,' he grinned.

The woman's lips puckered in her struggle to find something to throw back at him. He didn't wait. He moved to the front of the carriage, feeling her eyes pinned to his back like a donkey's tail in a children's party game, as the train wheezed to a halt.

It had started to rain. Not enough to soak you, but enough to frizz hair; the fine drizzle caught in the beam of the platform lights turning the world monochrome. He breathed in deeply with the romantic notion it might conjure an olfactory memory or two. It didn't.

Air is air, you bloody idiot, he thought.

Pulling up his collar, he headed for the exit.

Station Hill was steep, and the granite pavers slippery, but at least his bag had wheels, and the pub where he'd booked a room was at the bottom. A quick change after he'd checked in, then something to eat and an early night. He had an appointment the next morning with Eden Gray, the solicitor he hoped would take on his case, and he needed to be fresh for it.

He spotted the pub as he rounded the corner. Decked in Christmas lights, music blaring, it seemed welcoming enough.

The sweaty heat hit him the minute he opened the door.

The place was buzzing, people wrapped up for the weather, vying for seats near the window to avoid going out in the rain to watch the parade. Families out for the evening relegating the regular boozers to the far corners of the room.

Shaking the rain from his collar, he pushed his way to the bar.

A young woman with crimson braids and a silver ring through her septum hollered above the heads of a couple arguing over the menu.

'What can I get you, love?'

'I'll have a pint of Betty Stogs, thanks. I've booked a room,' he shouted back.

'Right you are,' she said, grabbing a glass, 'I'll get the booking up on the screen in a second.'

She delivered his pint and headed for her laptop.

He took a sip, turning to sneak a peek above the rim of the glass at the packed room, checking for faces he might recognise.

'What's the name?' the girl asked.

He turned back to face her. 'Retallick... Kit Retallick.'

'Well, there's a thing you don't see every day,' a voice boomed from behind. 'The return of the prodigal fucking son.'

The shock of being recognised so soon after arriving hit him like a shot between the eyes. That the individual was someone he had been to school with made it all the more disconcerting. He'd always got on well enough with Rob Davey. He wasn't the sharpest tool in the box or a close friend. He'd played football with him, that was about it. What floored him was that Rob's words sounded like a greeting and not a rebuke.

He was no prodigal son. He was at best the proverbial bad penny and, to many, something far worse, but Rob looked genuinely pleased to see him. It could be the drink talking. From his flushed cheeks and rolling gait, he looked as if he might have been there all afternoon.

'We're over there in the corner by the window,' he gestured, 'me, the missus and a couple of boys you don't know. Why don't you bring your pint and come and join us?'

'Mr Retallick, here's your key. Breakfast is in the bar from seven o'clock until ten thirty.'

The temptation to grab the key from the girl and bolt to his room was overwhelming, but if he allowed himself to be knocked back so easily, let the old insecurities and fears take hold again, he might as well pack his bags and leave right now. His probation officer had said not to expect an easy ride, that in all likelihood there would be a backlash from the local community. She'd even suggested he might consider moving elsewhere. He'd told the woman he'd think about it but knew in his heart he wouldn't.

Rob's friends were waving at him from the corner of the room and he thought there was a likelihood that not following might cause more of a hoo-ha than if he went over, said hello, made his excuses and left. He thrust the key into his pocket.

'Look who we got here, boys. This here's Kit. We were at school together back in the day.'

'What day was that then, Rob, the one day a week you bothered to turn up?' teased the man wearing a Nirvana t-shirt to Kit's left.

'Yeah, yeah, very funny,' said Rob, taking his seat. 'I was just telling this bunch of comedians about the parade when we were kids. How it took us months to make them lanterns and how most of us never got picked to carry the damn things. Did you ever get to carry one, Kit? I know I bloody didn't.'

'Nor me,' Kit lied, taking a nervous sip of his beer.

He noticed the fourth wheel, a pockmarked bloke with a snake tattoo on his forearm, staring.

'Do them scars on your face hurt?' he asked.

Kit resisted the urge to lift his hand and touch them the way he had done when the scars were new and they burned like hot knives all the time. 'Not anymore,' he said.

The redhead Rob had called his missus bucked up, her thickly mascaraed lashes quivering like trapped spiders.

'I think they're sexy,' she grinned, looking Kit up and down as if he were a bus timetable.

Rob shuffled in his seat.

'Go on, ask him how he got 'em.'

Kit took another sip of his beer.

'No, I'm not asking, it's personal, something like that. I don't go round asking you how you got that beer gut, do I?' she said, parting her jelly-red lips into a smile for Kit's benefit.

'Well, we all know how he got that. All bought and paid for,' chipped in the Cobain fan.

'I'll give you a clue, I'm a fire starter, I'm a fire starter,' Rob sang, lolling out his tongue, aping the lead singer of The Prodigy.

'Never heard that one before,' said Kit, trying to make light of it, his stomach clenching. 'Then again,' he continued, hoping to lighten the moment, 'originality was never your strong point, was it, Rob?'

Two young kids on the next table were staring, their mother weighing up whether the tension building next to them warranted a move.

Rob's face turned beetroot as his friends began to laugh and Kit realised he had played this completely wrong and should have kept his mouth shut, let Rob have his cheap shot.

'What's it feel like to be back with the family, eh? Oh no, I forgot, you haven't got a family, they're all fucking dead. Is that original enough for you, weirdo?' Rob snarled.

The woman at the next table shot them a disapproving glare.

'That's enough, keep your voice down,' hissed Rob's girlfriend. 'We don't want to get thrown out. Everywhere else will be packed and we've got a good seat here by the window.'

The table fell silent as Rob took an angry gulp of his beer.

Kit finished his in one and stood to leave.

'Well, nice to see you again, Rob,' he said, hands shaking as he picked up his bag and made his way through the crowds to the stairs at the back of the bar leading to his room.

He was glad to be at the rear of the building, away from

the hullabaloo of the parade. He sat on the bed. He could feel the tension building. He needed to calm down.

He inhaled deeply through his nose, then slowly let the air escape through his mouth, in… out, in… out, the way he had been taught by his therapist until he felt that magical click in his head.

A Baptism Of Fire: Chapter Two

EDEN WATCHED spellbound as a schooner in full sail, so tall she could practically reach out and touch it, passed her first-floor office window. There was something magical about the annual candle-lit march to the beat of drums. The way the soft glimmer from the lanterns warmed the darkened streets, licking upturned faces with the velvety candlelight usually reserved for paintings by long-dead Dutch masters.

The city's Festival of Lights took place every November during the run-up to Christmas. It never failed to draw a crowd, and this evening was no exception. It was always fun, but amid the music and revelry, there were often moments of near silence punctuated only by gasps of awe and wonder from those watching, reverent in the knowledge the fantastical effigies would later burn to nothing. Dust to dust, ashes to ashes, a *memento mori* to all.

'Will Daddy be here soon?' quizzed Flora, Eden's seven-year-old niece, face flushed with nervous delight, as she spotted a giant bug with articulated legs spidering through the crowd.

'Of course, he wouldn't want to miss this.'

Flora's dad, Luke Parish, was supposed to be joining them, but it was anyone's guess when he'd turn up. Working as a DCI in the Devon and Cornwall Police had proved incompatible with his increased parental responsibilities. The promotion from DI had supposedly meant more regular hours, but increasingly, Eden found herself on child-minding duty. They had drifted into a cosy routine with more than a whiff of domesticity about it. Every now and again, she worried she was too invested in her niece and her father. Luke could, and probably would, soon find someone special to replace her sister, and he'd want his new partner to play a major role in his daughter's life. Where would that leave her?

Grab your copy…
vinci-books.com/Baptismoffire

A Letter To My Readers

I have always been fascinated by the schizophrenic character of the windswept Cornish peninsula my family has been lucky enough to call home for generations. Occupied by a cast of reluctant bedfellows; city-slick escapees and us locals who carry the remnants of our myth-ridden history etched on our backs like tattoos, it teeters between the bucket and spade domesticity of modern-day tourism and a superstitious past, riddled with Pagan traditions. The resultant clash of cultures and sensibilities causes friction, resentment and drama. My aim, through my writing is to explore what happens when these divergent worlds collide to expose a darker reality at odds with the picture-perfect landscape. Whilst I was lucky to enjoy a fantastically satisfying career as a lawyer I cannot now imagine anything more joyous than being able to sit at my desk and write knowing others might read and connect with my words. Cornwall has captured the hearts and imagination of countless wonderful writers through the decades; their vivid images now woven into its rich tapestry. If I can add one colourful stitch I will be happy.

About the Author

After training as a lawyer, Julie returned to her native Cornwall to establish her own law firm and to raise her three children. After years of building a successful legal practice, it was time for a new adventure, and she decided to write the stories she had formulated in her head over the years about her community and the lives of those who find themselves on the wrong side of the law.